DIRE BEASTS!

"Got something here," the rider on the far left of the patrol line reported. Dragon Leader pressed his mount's flank with his knee to bring it around to check. *What in the . . . ?* Far below he saw a half-dozen creatures that looked like giant wolves attacking a lone man.

Dragon Leader watched as the speck on the ground retreated before the larger, darker specks that split up to come at him from either side. The tiny figure moved back against the central pylon and raised a weapon of some sort above its head. The attackers were now on either side of him, ready for the final killing lunge.

Dragon Leader winged his mount over and signaled the rest of the squadron to follow. In a compact mass a dozen dragons and their riders burst down on the scene below

THE WIZARDRY COMPILED

RICK COOK

THE WIZARDRY COMPILED

Copyright © 1990 by Rick Cook

A Baen Books Original

Baen Publishing Enterprises
260 Fifth Avenue
New York, N.Y. 10001

ISBN: 0-671-69856-7

Cover art by Larry Schwinger

First printing, January 1990

Distributed by
SIMON & SCHUSTER
1230 Avenue of the Americas
New York, N.Y. 10020

Printed in the United States of America

For the Bixen of course
and for the Sunday Morning Breakfast Club
—because they all had a hand in it.

PART I: LOAD TIME

One

POLITICS AND STRANGE BEDFELLOWS

You can always tell a really good idea by the enemies it makes.

—programmers' axiom

Pelus the wizard paused for dramatic effect. ". . . and so, My Lords, we must act quickly," he concluded ringingly.

For the sixth time that morning.

"Not so quickly, not so quickly," old Honorious said testily from the end of the table. He cleared his throat and prepared to restate his position for the eighth time.

The traceried windows along the south wall of the council chamber had been thrown open and the fitful summer breeze rustled the brightly colored tapestries hung along the buff sandstone walls. Outside trellised roses climbed the walls and peeked in the windows, perfuming the air. The stained glass in the window panes threw patches of brilliant color on the walls, the table and the men and women in the chamber.

Sitting at the long wooden table was the Council of the North. Fifteen of the mightiest wizards in the World—and one programmer from Cupertino, California who was bored out of his skull.

William Irving Zumwalt, "Wiz" to his friends, "Spar-

3

row" to most, tried to shut out the bickering and concentrate on the latest improvement to his magic compiler. It wasn't easy, especially since every so often he would be called on to say something and he had to keep at least one ear cocked to the conversation.

The Council had been arguing over the same point for the entire morning. Everyone knew that eventually they would do it, just as everyone knew the idea was good as soon as it had been proposed. But Agricolus had to get his opinions on record, Juvian saw an opportunity to snipe at Pelus and Honorious was constitutionally opposed to anything that looked like action. The result was a three-hour wrangle over nothing much.

For Wiz, who had made a career out of avoiding bureaucracy in all forms, it was sheer torture.

And I thought ANSI standards committee meetings were bad. He tried to shut out the incessant droning and concentrate on the idea he was developing.

A shimmering green shape began to form in the air in front of him. Wiz realized he had been moving his lips and that was enough to start the spell up. The wizards on either side of him glared and he quickly wiped out his unintentional handiwork, flushing under their eyes.

"Come, My Lords," rumbled Bal-Simba from the head of the table. The enormous black wizard was clad in his usual leopard skin and bone necklace. Somehow he had managed to seem interested through the entire morning. "The hour draws nigh. Let us decide." He gestured to a ray of light moving along a design inlaid in light wood in the darker wood top of the table. The spot of light was almost at the end of the design.

That was one merciful feature of the Council meetings. By custom and for arcane magical reasons they lasted no longer than it took the sun to traverse a certain arc in the sky. That meant about four hours.

So Honorious grumbled, Juvian sniped and Agricolus had one more thing he wanted to make clear, but they voted nonetheless and of course they decided to act.

Wiz stood with the others while Bal-Simba led them

through the closing ritual. *Another morning shot to pieces*, he thought as they filed out of the council chamber. He sighed to himself. *It could have been worse. All the Council members could have been present.*

"Wiz."

He turned and saw Moira waiting for him. The red-headed hedge witch was wearing a gown of sea green that matched her eyes and set off her milk-white freckled skin. Its cut showed off her figure as well. Wiz thoroughly approved.

"Darling, have I told you you look lovely?" he said, hugging her.

She gave him a look that made him catch his breath. "Why no, My Lord," she said, with her green eyes wide. "Not for, oh, at least five minutes."

"Too long." Ignoring the Council members who were knotted about talking, he kissed her.

In a vague way he knew he had improved in the two years since he had been kidnapped to this world. A more active life had put muscle on his slender frame. He had let his dark hair grow shoulder length in the local fashion. Tight breeches and puffy-sleeved shirts had replaced jeans and short-sleeved white shirts. Overall he now looked more like a romantic's idea of a pirate than a pencil-necked computer geek.

But Moira had been beautiful the first day he saw her and she had only gotten more beautiful. Well, he admitted, maybe that was subjective. They had been married for less than a year and brides were always beautiful. Then he looked at her again. Nope, she was definitely more beautiful.

"I wanted to see you and perhaps have lunch with you."

"Is something wrong?"

She shook her head. "Nothing, I just wanted to be with you."

"I wish I could darling, but I hadn't planned on having lunch. I've got a special tutoring session sched-

uled and I'm trying to get the module for the spell
compiler done by the end of the week."

Moira sighed. "Of course. I understand."

"I'm glad to see you though."

"Probably the only chance I'll get," she muttered.

"What?"

"Nothing, my love. Nothing."

"Look, I'll try to get home early tonight, okay?"

"I'll have dinner waiting."

Wiz sighed. "No, you better go ahead and eat. You
know how this works."

"I know," she said softly.

The man in the blue wizard's robe looked around
carefully before stepping into the clearing. A lesser man
might have shivered, but he was of the Mighty and he
knew well how to hold his emotions in check.

There was no sign of life or movement in the open
space. The summer grasses lay pristine and untrampled.
Here and there small red and yellow flowers nodded
above them. The trees surrounding the clearing rustled
and sighed as the breeze played through their tops. The
air at ground level was still and smelled of leaves and
sun-warmed grass.

The blue-robed man knew better than to trust ordinary senses. This was the time and the place appointed
for the meeting and his higher senses told him magic of
a lofty order lurked in that glade.

It is for the good of the entire World, he told himself
firmly.

Still, if any of his fellow wizards found out . . .

Little enough chance of that. No one kept watch on
the Mighty and with the Dark League defeated, watch
of all sorts was lax in the North.

Even so, he had taken good care that the others
would not find out. He had travelled the Wizard's Way
only part of the distance to this place and come the final
league on foot. He left the Capital with a plausible story
about a real enough errand near here, an errand he had

accomplished. If no one inquired too closely into these few hours, there was no way they could find out where he had gone or what he had done. If the other had taken similar precautions, they were both safe.

In the center of the clearing he stopped, extended his staff and traced a design in the air. The sigil glowed bright red and then began to fade imperceptibly toward crimson.

"Welcome magician," a voice hissed out behind him. Whirling, he saw the person he had come to meet.

The man was almost as tall as the blue-robed wizard and cadaverously lean. His skull was shaven, but showed black stubble from lack of recent attention. A wizard's staff was clasped firmly in his right hand. But most striking was his clothing.

In contrast to the blue of the first wizard's robe, the other wore the black robe of a wizard of the Dark League.

Wiz Zumwalt plopped down in the carved oak chair, poured a cup of wine from the carafe on the inlaid table and sighed deeply.

Bal-Simba looked up from the corner of the Wizards' Day Room where he was studying a scroll. "I take it it did not go well?" the giant black wizard asked mildly.

"You might say that." Wiz took a pull on the cup. Then he snorted with laughter.

"May I ask what is so funny?"

Wiz shook his head. "I was just thinking. Two years ago today I was being chased through the Wild Wood by trolls, bandits, Dire Beasts and the sorcerers of the Dark League."

"I remember."

"Now here I am, safe in the Capital of the North, the Dark League is in ruins and," he gestured mock grandly, "I'm supposed to be the greatest magician in the whole World."

"Your point, Sparrow?" Bal-Simba rumbled.

Wiz sighed deeply. "Just that right about now trolls, bandits and evil sorcerers look awfully good."

"I am Seklos," the black-robed one said. "I speak for the Dark League."

"Where is your master?" the northern wizard demanded.

"He is—indisposed," Seklos said. "I serve as his deputy with full authority to act in this matter."

The first one nodded. Since the great battle between the Sparrow and the Dark League, the conclave of sorcerers had been reduced to a pitiful few remnants. Their City of Night on the southern continent lay ruined and deserted and the black-robed ones who had once threatened to engulf the entire North were fugitives everywhere. The leaders of the Dark League, including Toth Set Ra, their chief, had died in the battle and the new leader was much less powerful. There were also disturbing rumors about him. The northern wizard was not surprised he had sent a deputy.

He advanced a step and then stopped. Crouching watchfully next to the wizard was a Shadow Warrior in the tight-fitting black of his kind. A slashing sword hung down his back and his eyes were hard and merciless through the slits in his hood.

"Foolish to bring such to a wizard's meeting," the blue-robed wizard said.

The other shrugged. "It seemed a simple enough precaution."

"We meet under a sign of truce. You need fear nothing from me so long as the sign glows."

Seklos regarded him with amused contempt. "I know the usage. But we did not come here to discuss custom. What is your proposal?"

"My proposal?"

"The sign changes color," the wizard pointed at the glowing character, which was now definitely orange. "Let us not waste time."

He hesitated, thrown off his carefully prepared approach. "Very well. It concerns the Sparrow, this Wiz."

"Ahhh," said Seklos in a way that made the other think that he had known very well what the subject would be.

"You mean you are not—what was that phrase you used?—'living happily ever after'?" Bal-Simba smiled gently. "Few people do, Sparrow."

"Yeah, I know, but I didn't expect it would be anything like what it's turned out to be. I thought I'd be able to finish my magic compiler and teach a few people how to use it. Then I could go on to more advanced magic programs."

Bal-Simba nodded. More than most of this world's wizards, he understood that Wiz's magical power came not from innate talent— Wiz had no talent for magic in the conventional sense. Rather, his abilities rested on his discovery that it was possible to write a magic "language," like the computer languages he had used back in Silicon Valley. Wiz might be spectacularly untalented as a magician, but where computers were concerned he was about as talented as they come.

Wiz shook his head. "I never saw myself sitting in meetings or in a classroom, trying to pound programming into a bunch of apprentices."

"Power makes its own demands, Sparrow," Bal-Simba said gently, laying the scroll aside. "Your new magic makes you powerful indeed."

"You know this Sparrow," the northern wizard hissed. "You know his power. He broke you utterly in a single day."

"And you are cast down from your former high estate in the North," the black robe retorted. "Do you wish our aid in restoring you? A trifle chancy, I fear. As you say, we are not so great as we once were."

"I desire no such thing," the blue robe said with dignity.

"Oh, the presidency of the Council then? To replace Bal-Simba?"

"I desire what we of the north have always sought. Balance, the preservation of the World."

"I fear your Sparrow is proving as dangerous to your precious balance as ever he did to our League," Seklos said. "Well, what did you expect when you Summoned someone so powerful?"

"We did not agree to the Summoning," the other said testily. "That was Patrius's idea and he did not share it with the Council. And as for danger," he went on fiercely, "he is a greater danger than you know. With his outlandish magic he upsets the very balance of the World. Mortals attract attention from those who have ignored us ere now. They are likely to act against us, Council and League both."

Seklos nodded, saying nothing.

"There is still time. He can be stopped before matters come to a head, but to do it I must have your magic behind me."

Seklos laughed. "You propose to become an initiate of the Dark League?"

The blue-robed one gestured angrily. "Do not mock me, wizard. And understand this. We are mortal enemies, you and I. Under other circumstances I would crush you as I would kill a poisonous serpent."

Seklos smiled unpleasantly and cocked his head, but he did not interrupt.

"But," the first man went on, "the Sparrow is a threat to every human magic user in the World. For this once and on this one matter I suggest that we have common cause and propose that we act in concert to rid ourselves of this menace."

"You put the matter succinctly," said the black robe. "Let us therefore consider the destruction of this Sparrow."

"No!"

The other cocked an eyebrow. "Does our new alliance flounder so soon?"

"The Sparrow is to be neutralized, not destroyed."

"Why not?"

"Two reasons. First, I forbid it." Seklos smiled again, but the blue robe ignored him. "Second, if you had a modicum of mother wit you would know his death is your destruction. Kill the Sparrow, harm one hair of him, and every wizard in the North will descend upon you. They will grub you out of your burrows and exterminate you all."

"And doubtless in the inquiry your part in the business would be discovered."

"Doubtless," the blue robe agreed, making a brushing motion as if to shoo off an annoying insect. "No, we cannot kill him. But if he were to disappear there would be many to mourn him aloud and few to lament his passing in private."

"And you suggest . . . ?"

"A Great Summoning to send the Sparrow back where he belongs. Him and his alien magics."

"Such a thing would not be easy to do."

"It would take a number of wizards, but it would not be impossible."

"Patrius did it alone."

"I am not as great a magician as Patrius," the northerner said with dignity. "Nor do I wish to end as he did." He remembered how the Dark League had cut the mighty wizard down as he performed unaided the Great Summoning which brought the Sparrow to this world. "This requires more than I can accomplish alone and the others on the Council who feel as I do will not act."

"And you think we will?"

The northerner shrugged. "You have more reason and less to lose. It cannot be pleasant to be reduced to lording it over field mice and birds."

Seklos' eyes glittered and the other knew his shaft had gone home.

"We can do nothing while he remains in the Capital," Seklos said at last. "He must be brought to us."

"He can be maneuvered out of the Capital."

"He must be brought to—a place. It would be best if

it were done while he treads the Wizard's Way. Then it is a matter of a simple spell."

The blue robe shrugged. Any wizard of the Mighty could be counted on to use that magical means for transport for any journey of over a few leagues.

"How long would it take you to be ready? The next full moon is on . . ."

"I did not say I would do it," Seklos cut him off. "I said we would consider it." He nodded toward the sign hanging in the air, now a deep violet fading to black. "The sigil darkens. Our meeting is at an end." He turned and walked toward the opposite edge of the clearing. Wordlessly the Shadow Warrior followed, moving crabwise to keep his enemy always in sight.

Behind them the blue-robed wizard nodded. He knew full well that the remnants of the Dark League would join him in this. What other choice had they?

Two

NAILING JELLY TO A TREE

Everything always takes twice as long and costs four times as much as you planned.
                                        —programmer's axiom

"I dunno," Wiz sighed again and drained his wine cup. "This isn't working out anything like I thought it would." He set the cup down and leaned toward Bel-Simba, elbows on knees.

"Look, I took the seat on the Council because you wanted me to. I'm not a wizard, I've never been a politician and those meetings are torture."

"Your position and power entitle you to a seat."

"Yeah, but I've got important work to do."

It was Bal-Simba's turn to sigh. He did so gustily and the bones of his necklace clattered with the movement of his barrel chest. "Sparrow, listen to a poor fat old wizard for a moment.

"You talk of finishing your spell engine. But that is only half your task. The other half is teaching others to use it and the largest part of that is getting them to accept it."

Wiz toyed with the cup, running his finger along the rim. "I suppose you're right. I never was any good at teaching. I guess I need to try harder."

13

"Perhaps it would be more to the point if you tried to understand how others feel. Your task is difficult. But you make it more so. Your attitude does not make you friends, either on the Council or among the other wizards and that adds to the hostility against your methods. Specifically, you do yourself no good at all when you belittle the Council."

"I don't belittle the Council!"

Bal-Simba arched a brow. "No? But your work is more important."

"Well . . ."

"Sparrow, the Council of the North has stood for centuries as the shield of humans against malevolent magic, both from the Dark League and from the World at large. It is the closest thing to a ruler this land has."

Wiz nodded. "Look, I'd be the last person to deny you and the other wizards have done a heck of a job. But magical programming changes things. As soon as I get the compiler perfected and get to work on the spells, anyone will be able to use magic. There won't be a need for a Council of wizards to guard and protect humans."

Bal-Simba shook his head. "Sparrow, much as I admire your directness I think it leads you astray. But even if what you say is so, we must still get from where we are to where you wish to be. To do that you need the cooperation of all wizards, especially the Mighty and most especially the Council. You do not get someone's cooperation by telling him he is obsolete and his life's work is outworn."

"It would be easier if some of the Mighty would learn to use the compiler. But they're all so *dense*."

"Wizards do not have the reputation for being stupid," Bal-Simba said with deceptive mildness.

Wiz sighed and rubbed his eyes. "You're right. Stupid isn't the word for it. But they don't generalize. You guys learn one thing at a time and you can't seem to work from a bunch of specifics to a general proposition." He shook his head. "And a lot of programming is generalization."

"Nonsense!" came a firm voice from the doorway. Wiz and Bal-Simba turned to the sound and saw a tall, theatrically handsome man in wizard's blue. His silver hair swept over his ears in carefully arranged waves to perfectly set off his aristocratic features and evenly tanned skin.

Bal-Simba nodded. "My Lord Ebrion."

Wiz stiffened, but he also nodded politely. *Dammit, I will not lose my temper.*

"The essence of magic is in the particular," Ebrion said in his beautifully modulated voice as he came into the room. "To control magic we must understand *this* tree or *this* fire, not these 'classes' you keep on about. All trees are not alike, Sparrow, and it is only by deeply perceiving an object that we may control it magically."

Wiz kept quiet. He had enough trouble with Ebrion and his traditionalist friends already. Like all the traditionalists, Ebrion didn't like Wiz. Unlike most of them he made no secret of his dislike beyond a certain cold civility. Worse, he was a theoretician, or the closest thing to a theoretician of magic this world had ever produced. Wiz's success had thrown him into the shade in his own specialty and that made him dislike Wiz all the more.

"Magic is both organic and particular, Sparrow," Ebrion went on as if lecturing an apprentice. "The best magic cannot be built up from bits and pieces like a jackdaw's nest. It must be conceived of whole."

"Wiz's method seemed effective enough against the Dark League," Bal-Simba said quietly.

"Lord, I have never denied that the Sparrow ranks among the Mighty, but sheer talent does not make his theories correct."

He waved a hand dismissingly. "Oh, I will admit the trick of constructing a demon to recite his spells for him is useful—albeit it was not unknown to us before. But his notion of how magic works?" He shook his head.

"The compiler is a lot more than a spell-reciting demon," Wiz interjected.

"So you have told us repeatedly. But at bottom that is all it does, is it not?"

"No, it's a compiler written in a threaded interpreted language that . . ."

Ebrion touched his fingertips to his forehead, as if stricken with a sudden headache. "Please Sparrow, spare us one of your explanations. You have told us this 'compiler' demon recites the spells you create and that much, at least, is comprehensible."

Wiz started to protest and then clamped his jaw. Ebrion wasn't interested in explanations and he wasn't any good at making them.

"Anyway, you're wrong," he said sullenly. "I don't have any talent for magic. Any one of the Mighty can sense that."

"We can all sense that you do not have our kind of talent. But you have shown us that you have enormous magical ability. What you have not shown us is that your system works. To do that you would have to teach others to make magic with it, by your own admission."

"So I'm a lousy teacher," Wiz said, nettled.

"For over a year you have dwelt here and tried to teach this marvelous system of yours. Have any of us mastered it? Has anyone but yourself learned it?"

"Programming takes time to learn. You didn't learn magic overnight, did you?"

"No, but with a few months study I was able to perform certain useful spells. Your pupils work and work and can do little—and that poorly."

"You've got to learn the basics and work up."

"No Sparrow, this 'general theory of magic' of yours is an illusion. You must learn one spell at a time. You must practice every gesture, every word, understand every influence. One spell at a time, Sparrow." He looked down at Wiz and smiled mockingly.

"*That* is how magic is made."

Wiz ground his teeth. He remembered one of the first classes, back when he was still trying to teach wizards in groups. The lesson was to construct a simple apparition spell, the rough equivalent of the "hello world" program in the C computer language.

Of course, the point was no more making a form appear than the point of the C program was to put the words "hello world" on a computer screen. It was to familiarize the magicians with the basic workings of the magic compiler. Slowly and carefully, Wiz led his class through the fundamentals of his program for constructing magic spells. Then he asked each of them to make the spell with the compiler.

With a disdainful flick of his wand, Ebrion had created a shape that was ten times as real as the shadowy blobby forms the other students were struggling to make through the program.

"*That* is how magic is made," he said in a condescending tone as Wiz and the students stared at his result.

"The theory works," Wiz ground out. "Or did I just imagine taking on the Dark League?"

"Once again, I have never denied you were powerful," Ebrion said, as if repeating a simple lesson to a very slow pupil. "You attacked them with the completely alien magic of your world and overwhelmed them with spells they had never seen before. Thus you established your power. Surprise is ever an important weapon, Sparrow. As for the rest of your power, it would be a simple matter to put it to the test."

Ebrion meant a contest of wizards. Superficially it was a fair way of determining who was the better magician. But there were tricks to such contests, just as there are subtleties to any kind of competition. From apprentices to wizards of the Mighty, all magicians practiced against each other for sport. The only experience Wiz had in such a contest was when he had inadvertently gotten into a duel to the death with the second most powerful wizard of the Dark League. Only Bal-Simba's intervention had saved him.

When he saw Wiz would ignore the implied challenge, Ebrion went on. "You have taught us some new tricks and given us some important insights and for that we must thank you. But they do not amount to revolutionizing the practice of magic, nor do they sweep away all we have done here for hundreds of years. Magic is as it ever was, Sparrow."

"Except that the Wild Wood isn't pushing into human lands any more," Wiz snapped. "The Dark League isn't one step from throttling the entire North and the common people have a defense against hostile magic. You and all your *traditions* couldn't do any of that!"

As soon as the words were out of his mouth, Wiz was sorry. Ebrion's head jerked back as if he had been slapped and he blanched under his tan. He turned his back on Wiz and addressed Bal-Simba.

"My Lord, I came merely to tell you that I will be leaving the Capital for Mountainhame on the morn and to inquire if there was some service I could perform there for you."

"No, nothing," Bal-Simba said.

"Then I will take my leave of you, Lord." And with that he bowed and left the room, ignoring Wiz completely.

"That was ill-done, Sparrow," Bal-Simba said as soon as the door had closed behind Ebrion.

"I know, Lord," Wiz said uncomfortably. "Do you think I should go apologize to him?"

Bal-Simba shook his head. "Leave him for now," he rumbled. "Perhaps when he returns you should speak to him."

"He was trying to get under my skin."

Bal-Simba frowned. "Get under . . . ah, I see what

you mean. So he was, but you let him and that gave him the advantage of the encounter. You must learn to control yourself better."

"I'll try, Lord," Wiz said uncomfortably.

"Let us hope you succeed," Bal-Simba said. "You have students soon, do you not?"

"Yipe! I'm already late."

"Go then, Sparrow. But remember what we have discussed."

Three

STIRRING THE POT

It's never the technical stuff that gets you in trouble. It's the personalities and the politics.

        —programmer's saying

Presumptuous puppy! Ebrion fumed as he made his way down the stairs and out into the main courtyard.

He did not return to his tower or to any of his other usual haunts. Instead he crossed the yard and made for the main gate of the keep. Just inside the gate was a much less plushly appointed day room used by off-duty guardsmen, minor merchants, castle servants, apprentices and others.

The big, low-ceilinged room was several steps down from the yard. Light flooded in through the windows up next to the whitewashed ceiling and reflected down onto the worn plank tables and rough benches and stools.

Heads turned as he came in and then turned back. This was hardly a place for the Mighty, much less a member of the Council, but Ebrion was known for his common touch. Two or three times in every turning of the Moon he could be expected to drop by and exchange a few words with the habitués.

It was a time when apprentices should be at their

studies or serving their masters. Still, Ebrion expected to find the one he sought here and he was not disappointed. Sitting by himself in a corner was a lank man with smoldering brown eyes and bowl-cut brown hair. Arms flat on the table and legs thrust straight out into the aisle, he was scowling into a mug of small beer as if he expected it to rise up and challenge him.

"Well met, Pryddian," Ebrion said pleasantly.

The young man looked up and nodded, but he did not rise as befitted an apprentice in the presence of one of the Mighty.

"My Lord."

Ebrion eased himself down upon the bench and studied the man. Pryddian was the oldest of the Keep's apprentices and now he was an apprentice without a master.

Pryddian seemed oblivious to the scrutiny. He kept his eyes fixed on his mug.

"I would speak with you on a matter of some import," Ebrion said. He made a show of looking around the room and lowered his voice. "What I say must stay between us."

Pryddian looked at him narrowly and nodded. Ebrion did not ask for a binding oath and the apprentice did not offer one.

"I had heard that Juvian released you."

"Arrogant old fool," Pryddian muttered. That earned him a sharp look from the wizard.

"I am sorry, Lord," he said sullenly. "But you know my story. I started my training here in the Capital instead of in some hedge witch's hovel. I am widely acknowledged to have more talent than any of the other apprentices." Ebrion nodded, acknowledging a plain fact and Pryddian took another swallow of beer.

"Yet after two years I am turned off over a trifle. Juvian assured me I would have no trouble finding another master. But no other wizard will take me on and no one will tell me honestly why."

Ebrion nodded sympathetically. That was not the

story Juvian told, but it did not serve his purpose to say so.

"I know. I sought you out because I thought you should know there was more to the matter than a disagreement between you and Juvian." He paused, picking his words.

"Naturally I cannot violate the confidences of my fellow wizards, but I can tell you that today there is more to being a successful apprentice than magical talent and a willingness to work hard. It is also necessary to master the Sparrow's new magic."

Pryddian snorted. He had attended one or two classes and had not done well. Ever since he had made no secret of his contempt for Wiz's methods.

"I know. And between the two of us, I agree." He shrugged and spread his hands. "But who am I? The Sparrow sits on the Council of the North and has Bal-Simba's ear. He can see to it that apprentices either learn the new magic or are no longer apprentices."

"How is this? I thought apprenticeship was a matter between the wizard and pupil alone."

"And so it is," Ebrion assured him. "But a wizard must consider relations with his fellows. You understand these things, surely."

Pryddian nodded. "I suspected there was favor involved, in spite of what everyone says."

"Oh, not *favor*," Ebrion said hurriedly. "We prefer to think of it as maintaining harmonious relations."

"Call it what you will, I am blackballed by the Sparrow."

"Well," the wizard admitted, "it would be—hmm—difficult for any wizard to take you as an apprentice."

"And my ability counts for nothing?"

"Times have changed. It seems the Sparrow's new magic is more important than talent for the old."

"So I am forever barred from becoming a wizard. Unless you . . . ?" He trailed off hopefully.

"The Sparrow knows how I feel about him and his new magic. I would do you little good, I fear."

Pryddian nodded knowingly. "And doubtless it would do you little good to have me."

Ebrion shrugged.

Pryddian finished his beer in a single long pull. "This Sparrow rises above himself," he said darkly.

"Perhaps, but he is of the Mighty." The wizard rose. "In any event, I felt you should know. I cannot speak openly, of course."

"Of course." The would-be apprentice looked up. "I thank you for the information, Lord. And as to this Sparrow, perhaps he needs his feathers plucked." He dropped his eyes to scowl at the now-empty mug as Ebrion left.

Outside the door of the day room, Ebrion allowed himself a smile.

Under any circumstances Pryddian would never have become a wizard. Talent he had, and stubbornness to persist in the face of gentle hints and not-so-gentle discouragement, but he was undisciplined and he had a vindictive streak that ran both broad and deep. If he had started his training in the villages he probably never would have been sent to the Capital. But Ebrion was very glad he was here. His combination of talent, frustration and a viperish tongue made him ideal. *Yes, the wizard thought, he is the perfect choice to bait the Sparrow into some heedless action.*

Four

FENCEPOSTS AND FALLING ROCKS

Those who can't do, teach.
>   —article of faith among students

And vice-versa.
—programmer's addendum to students' article of faith

Malus was waiting impatiently when Wiz arrived, obviously fuming.

To salve wizardly pride, Wiz did most of his teaching of actual wizards in private sessions. Malus was one of his least-favorite pupils. As a person, the pudgy little wizard was nice enough, always merry and joking. But he had particular trouble in grasping concepts and the thought that he was a slow learner made him even more resistant to the new magic.

Malus didn't even let Wiz finish his apology for being late.

"This spell you showed me," he said accusingly. "It does not work."

Wiz sighed inwardly. "Well, let me see your code."

Grudgingly, the plump little sorcerer produced several strips of wood from the sleeve of his robe. Laid in the proper order the characters on them would list out the spell. Putting them on separate pieces of wood was

24

a safety precaution against activating the spell by writing it down.

Wiz arranged the wood strips on the table and frowned briefly at what was written there.

"Oh, you've got a fence post error."

"Fence post?" the wizard asked.

"Yeah. Look, say you've got a hundred feet of fence to put up and you need to put a post every ten feet. How many posts do you need?"

"I am a wizard, not a farmer!" Malus said, drawing himself up to his entire five-foot-four.

"Well, just suppose," Wiz said half-desperately.

Malus thought hard for a minute. "Ten, of course."

"Nope," Wiz said triumphantly. "Eleven. Unless you strung your fence in a circle. Then you only need nine."

"But one hundred taken as tens is ten!"

"Yeah, but if you've got a hundred feet of fence and only ten posts in a straight line, you leave one end of the fence hanging free. And if you put the posts in a closed figure, you only need nine because you can start and end on the same post."

"And how am I to know such things? I told you I am not a farmer."

"Well, just keep it in mind, okay? Boundary conditions are always likely to give you trouble."

"Borders are always unchancy places," Malus agreed.

"Uh, yeah. Let's leave that for a minute. Do you have any other problems?"

"There is this business of names."

For about the fiftieth time, Wiz wished he hadn't been so cavalier in choosing names for the standard routines in his library. To wizards, a thing's name was vitally important and they took the name to be the thing.

"I told you that the names I used aren't necessarily representative."

Malus looked at him like he was crazy. "Very well.

But even granting that, why must the names change haphazardly? That is what I do not understand."

"They don't change at random. They don't really change at all. It's just that an object can be a member of more than one class."

"Classes again!"

"Look at this," Wiz said, dragging out a couple of sheets of parchment and laying them out side by side so all the spell was visible. "Okay, here this variable is called 'elfshot,' right?"

"Why is it named that?"

"It's not named that. That's only what it's called in this routine. Its name is '**dragons__tail**.' "

"Well," demanded the wizard, "if it is '**dragons__tail**,' why do you call it 'elfshot'? And how do you add a '**dragons__tail**' to this, this loop variable?"

"No, no," Wiz said desperately. "It is actually seven at this point in the program and that's what gets added to the loop variable."

"Well, if it's seven then why don't you just say so?" roared the wizard.

"Because it isn't always seven."

The wizard growled in disgust.

"Look, I think I'm getting a headache. Why don't we leave this for right now, okay? Just try working the program through again and we'll go over it in our next session."

The early end to the tutorial with Malus left Wiz with time to spare and a completely ruined temper. He wanted someplace quiet where he could be alone to think. Leaving his workroom door unlocked he left the central keep, threaded his way through two courtyards and climbed a set of stairs to the top of the wall surrounding the entire complex.

The parapet was one of his favorite places. It was usually deserted and the view was spectacular. The Capital perched on a spine of rock where two rivers met. From the north the ridge sloped gently up to drop off precipitously in cliffs hundreds of feet high to the south and along the east and west where the rivers ran.

On the highest part of the ridge stood the great castle of the Council of the North, its towers thrusting skyward above the cliffs. Here the Council and most of the rest of the Mighty had their homes and workshops. Behind the castle and trailing down the spine came the town. In the cliffs below the castle were the caverns that served as aeries for the dragon cavalry. As Wiz stood and watched, a single dragon launched itself from below and climbed out over the valley with a thunder of wings.

The parapet was nearly fifteen feet wide. It sloped gently toward the outer wall so that rainwater and liquid fire thrown by enemies would both drain over the sides and down the cliff. The outer edge was marked by crenellations, waist-high blocks of stone that would protect the defenders from enemy arrows. It always reminded Wiz of the witch's castle in *The Wizard of Oz,* except that this was much grander.

Wiz walked along, guilty about taking the time away from his work and yet happy to be away. The swallows whipped by him as they swooped and dove along the cliff edge to catch the insects borne aloft by the rising current of air.

The day was bright and cloudless and the air soft and warm enough that he appreciated the breeze blowing up from the river. Faintly and in the distance he could hear the sounds of the castle and town. Somewhere a blacksmith was beating iron on an anvil. From this distance it sounded like tiny bells.

There was a place he favored when he wanted to get away, a spot where a bend in the wall and a watch tower combined to shut out all sight and most sound of the Capital. From there he could look out over the green and yellow patchwork of the fields and woods and into the misty blue distance.

He leaned forward, resting his elbows on one of the crenellations. *If only* . . .

He felt the stone shift under his weight but by that time it was too late. The block gave way and he was pitched headlong out over the abyss.

Frantically he lashed out with his arms and miraculously his fingers met stone. His arm was nearly yanked out of its socket as he twisted around and slammed face first into the wall. But his grip held and he was left dangling by one hand against the sheer wall.

The crenellation had taken part of the stone facing with it, leaving the rough inner masonry beneath. Wiz was hanging by his fingertips from the edge of the facing, just below where the stone block had been.

Far below him, between his dangling legs, he saw the dislodged block bouncing and tumbling off the cliff. It hit the water with a splash that looked no bigger than a match head. Wiz sucked in his breath and clinched his eyes tight to ward off the dizziness.

Frantically he scrabbled for a hold for his left hand. First his fingers slipped over the smooth surface of the facing. Then at last they caught on another place where the facing blocks had pulled loose. With both hands secure, Wiz opened his eyes and stared at the stone in front of his nose, breathing heavily.

At last he managed to look up. Bracing his feet against the wall, he levered his way up and snatched another handhold slightly higher up the wall. Then another and another and at last he was able to put his feet on the lip where the facing had pulled away. One more heave and he flopped back on the parapet. Bruised and shaken, he pulled himself back through the space where the crenellation had been.

He moved away from the edge and sank down with his head between his knees, breathing in great shaking gasps. Gradually he got himself back under control and looked around him.

The parapet was deserted. Not even the guards could be seen from this spot and there were no other strollers along the walls. He was completely isolated, but . . .

Was it his imagination or had he seen a figure flit

behind a tower as he pulled himself back onto the parapet?

The rest of the day passed uneventfully. He gave two more private lessons, tried to teach a class of apprentices what the concept of zero was all about and spent nearly half an hour listening to Pelus, who was trying to get him to vote against Juvian at the next Council meeting. The sun had set over the towers of the Capital by the time he left his work room and trudged down the winding stairs to the suite he and Moira shared. Lanterns along the walls cast a warm mellow light on the wide corridors.

Wiz was so tired he barely noticed.

As he came down the hall a young man came toward him. Wiz stepped slightly to the side but instead of moving out of his way the man seemed to step in front of Wiz so he jostled him as they passed.

"Clumsy Sparrow," the young man hissed.

Wiz started to say something, thought better of it, and swept past the sneering young man.

What the hell is his problem? Wiz thought.

He knew the man more-or-less by sight. An apprentice with a vaguely Welsh name. They had never exchanged more than a half a dozen words and now the man was going out of his way to be insulting.

One more thing to worry about. This place was getting to him. He was trying to do a job he wasn't very good at, a lot of the people here seemed to hate him, he couldn't concentrate on the parts he *could* do and even the simplest thing seemed to take forever. He was stretched tauter than a violin string and the fatigue and tension was telling on him.

The door to their apartment was open and he saw Moira sitting in the light of a magical lantern. The light caught her hair and glints of brushed copper played through it. Her mouth was twisted up in a little moue as she bent over the mending in her lap.

Still, Wiz thought, *there are compensations.*

As he came into the room he saw there was someone else there. A painfully thin girl with flyaway brown hair was sitting at Moira's feet working on a piece of embroidery.

Without a word the girl got up and left.

"Hi June," Wiz said to her back as she brushed by.

"What have you been doing?" he said as he came to her.

"Sewing." Moira laughed. "I fear I will never be skilled with a needle."

He leaned over and kissed her. "That's all right. You're good at plenty of other things."

She arched one of her coppery eyebrows. "And how am I to take that, My Lord?"

"As a compliment." He bent down and kissed her again.

"And how has your day been?"

Well, let's see. I insulted one of the most powerful members of the Council, botched a tutoring session and nearly killed myself by falling off the parapet. "Oh, okay," he mumbled.

Moira looked at him sharply. "What did you do to your nose?"

"I ran into a door. How is June?" He asked quickly to change the subject.

Moira gave him an odd look, but she took the bait. "She improves, I think."

Like Moira, June had been found wandering as a child in the Fringe of the Wild Wood. Unlike Moira, no one knew where she came from or who her parents were. She was quiet, as shy and skittish as a woodland animal. She worked as a maid and servant around Wizard's Lodge—when anyone could find her.

Wiz had never heard her speak, although Moira said she occasionally talked.

"Can't you do something to heal her?" Wiz asked.

"Bronwyn, the chief healer, says she is not ill in her mind," Moira said. "That it is merely her way."

"If she's not ill, she's sure peculiar."

"That is odd coming from you, Sparrow," Moira said.

"Hey, I'm alien. I admit it. But she," he jerked his head toward the door, "is about three sigma west of strange."

Moira ignored the comment, something she often did when she didn't understand her husband. "She seems fascinated by your desk," she said.

Wiz looked at the disorderly pile of manuscripts, strips of wood, slates and books on the desk under the window. "Did she touch anything?"

"You know better than that. I would never allow it."

A wizard's working equipment was dangerous. Even Moira would not touch Wiz's desk, though having such a mess in their sitting room pained her.

"Hmm. Do you suppose she has a talent for magic?"

Moira shook her head. "I think it is your guardian that attracts her."

Like any other wizard, Wiz had created a demon to guard his paraphernalia. His took the form of a foot-long scarlet dragon, now curled peacefully asleep atop Wiz's big leather-bound "notebook."

Wiz sat down and reached for the notebook. The dragon demon woke and slithered over to a corner of the desk where it resumed its nap.

For the next quarter hour neither of them said anything. The only sound in the room was the scritching of Wiz's pen and the rustle of fabric as Moira turned the piece in her lap this way and that.

"Oh, I have some news as well," Moira said, putting down her mending.

"That's nice," Wiz said without looking up.

"Bronwyn says she will teach me the rudiments of the healer's art. I am too old for an apprentice, of course. In the village of Blackbrook Bend I often did simple healing and Bronwyn says we can build on that."

Wiz grunted.

"And then I'll sprout wings and grow two extra heads," she said sharply.

Wiz raised his head. "What?"

"You have not heard a word I said, have you?"

Moira threw her mending on the floor and stood up.

"It is bad enough that you are always gone, but when you are here the least you can do is admit that I am alive!"

"I'm sorry, I was just . . ."

"I will *not* be ignored." Moira burst into tears.

Wiz came to her and took her in his arms.

"Oh, darling. I didn't mean to upset you."

"Hold me."

"Moira, I'm sorry I . . ."

"Don't talk, just hold me." She clung to him fiercely as if he were about to be swept away from her.

They made love that night. Afterward they lay in each other's arms without speaking. Wiz didn't fall asleep until long afterward and he didn't think Moira did either.

The next day Wiz stumbled through his classes, groggy from lack of sleep. By the time he got home that evening he was ready to drop, but when Moira suggested they walk out to the drill yard he didn't object.

In the early evenings the Guardsmen held free-form practice on the drill ground. Because there was a gathering of young men there, the young ladies of the castle naturally congregated, to sit in the shade or walk along the colonnaded porch that surrounded the beaten earth of the practice court. And where the young ladies congregated naturally became a gathering place for everyone in the keep. From the highest of the Mighty to the workers in the scullery, it had become the traditional place for an evening stroll.

Wiz and Moira joined the promenade with Moira clinging tightly to his arm. They exchanged small talk with their acquaintances, received respectful bows Wiz's station entitled them to and spent a few minutes talking with Shamus, the Captain of the Guard and a friend of Moira's from her time at the Capital learning to be a hedge witch.

From a window above the practice yard Ebrion watched them pass. It would go hard on the hedge witch when the Sparrow disappeared and looking at them walk arm-in-arm that thought troubled him. With an effort he shook it off. The good of the many was much more important than the feelings of one hedge witch. Besides, there were rumors that the two were not getting along.

She'll get over it quickly enough, he told himself. Then he concentrated on what he knew was about to happen in the courtyard below.

"Look, there's Donal," Moira pointed to a tall dark-haired guardsman who was using a short spear—actually a padded pole—against a man with a sword and shield.

Donal was one of the guardsmen who had accompanied Wiz on his foray into the dungeons beneath the City of Night to rescue Moira. He was skillfully using the length of his weapon to keep his opponent at a distance and flicking the spear out in quick thrusts, searching for a weakness in the man's guard. As they watched he executed a fast double thrust and parry that swept his opponent's sword to the side and finished with a solid thrust to the face.

"Oh, well done!" Moira said, laughing and clapping.

Wiz smiled. In the back of his head a small voice was nagging him about all the work he had to do, but the evening was lovely, the place was pretty, and it was pleasant to walk with a beautiful woman, especially when she was your wife.

As they ambled along, a man stepped out from behind one of the pillars and ran into Wiz, nearly knocking him down.

"Hey, watch it." He saw it was the apprentice who had nearly run into him in the hall the night before.

Pryddian curled his lip. "Clumsy Sparrow. Why not use your magic to fly out of the way?"

Moira gasped. Wiz wanted to smash his sneering

face. Instead he stepped around Pryddian and walked toward the opposite side of the drill field.

"Wiz, you shouldn't let him talk to you like that," Moira hissed once they were out of earshot.

"What should I do? Turn him to stone?"

"Oh, don't be silly," she said angrily. "But at the very least you should put him in his place."

"How?"

Moira considered. Wiz did not have the wizard's manner that came with years of practicing magic. He could not freeze an apprentice with a look the way a real wizard could. Short of using magic on him—a thing unthinkable—there really was nothing he could do.

"I will speak to Bal-Simba about him."

"I wish you wouldn't. It will be all right, really."

Moira pressed her lips together and kept walking.

"Ah, Sparrow, My Lord." They turned and saw Juvian coming toward them, a fussy, balding little man who was always in a hurry.

Wiz nodded respectfully. "My Lord."

"Ah yes," Juvian came panting up. "My Lady, I wonder if you could excuse us for a moment. There is a matter of Council business we must discuss." He took Wiz by the elbow and led him off to the reviewing stand that stood on poles at one side of the field. Wiz threw Moira a helpless look over his shoulder, but he did not try to break the Wizard's hold on his arm.

"He's a lucky man," said a voice behind her.

Moira turned and saw Shamus.

"I doubt he would agree with you at this instant."

"Nonetheless, lucky." He smiled with an infectious warmth Moira remembered from her student days and extended his arm. "While he is occupied would you do me the honor of accompanying me?"

Moira smiled back. "Gladly."

Shamus was a lithe, compact man whose shock of sandy hair was thinning with the approach of middle age. His face was deeply tanned and a little windburned with tiny crinkles of laugh lines at the corners of his

eyes and mouth. Moira had had a minor crush on him
when last she stayed at the Capital, but her studies left
her little time to pursue such things.

"We do not see you out here often enough."

"Wiz's work keeps him busy," Moira said with a trace
more acid than she intended.

"True, but a wife does not have to walk only with her
husband."

"I suppose so," Moira sighed and looked around at
the strolling, chatting people. "It would be pleasant to
be out more."

"It could be pleasant indeed," Shamus said with a
smile. "I would be happy to show you."

Moira understood exactly what he was offering. Such
things were accepted in the Capital and as long as the
affair was carried on discreetly no censure attached to
any of the parties.

Moira glanced over to where Wiz was finishing his conversation with Juvian. *It would serve him right!* she
thought. Then she buried the notion with a guilty start.

"I am sorry, My Lord, but I must decline."

"Ah," said Shamus, looking across the drill yard. "A
very lucky man indeed." He sighed. "You've broken
my heart, you know."

Moira followed his eyes to Wiz standing beneath the
reviewing stand. "I feel it will mend by the time the
next pretty face comes along."

The object of this by-play leaned back against one of
the posts, oblivious to the things being said about him.

In the rings the guardsmen whirled and dodged in
mock combat.

As Wiz put his weight against the post it shifted and
the entire marshal's stand teetered.

"*Look out!*" Moira screamed.

It all seemed to happen in slow motion. The guardsmen
and strollers froze. Wiz looked up, mouth open, to see
the entire mass toppling down on him. He started to
move out of the way, but he was obviously too late.

An armored body hurtled into him, knocking him sideways and slamming him into the earth. Behind them the stand crashed to earth, raising a cloud of dust off the practice field. A few boards fell across the pair, but the guardsman was on top and his armor protected them both.

"Are you all right, Lord?" Wiz opened his eyes and realized that the man on top of him was Donal.

"Fine," he gasped. "I'm fine."

Donal rolled off Wiz and climbed to his feet. Wiz started to rise and fell back, gasping in pain.

"My shoulder. I've done something to my shoulder."

Moira came running across the drill yard, skirts flying. "Are you all right?"

"I've hurt my shoulder."

Moira knelt beside him and ran her fingers lightly over the injured joint. "It is separated." She looked up at Donal. "Help me get his tunic off and I will fix it."

"It would be better if we let the healers handle it."

Moira's green eyes flashed. "Are you saying I cannot heal a shoulder separation?"

Donal met her gaze levelly. "No Lady, only that Bronwyn or one of the others can do it better."

Moira started to snap back, then with a visible effort, she relaxed. "You are right, of course. Send one of your men for her, and quickly."

"Already done, My Lady."

"Oh shit," Wiz muttered, "this hurts."

Moira rested her hand gently on the injured shoulder. "I know, my love. But Bronwyn will be here quickly enough. Try to relax and do not move."

Behind them Shamus was examining the post where it had snapped off. "Rotten wood," he said, wrinkling his nose. He broke a piece off and crumbled it in his fingers. "This needed replacing months ago, and probably all the rest besides."

Arianne knelt by the post, her brown eyes fixed on the break. "Yes," she said and reached up with slender fingers to caress the broken spot. "Yes, they should all be examined most carefully."

Bal-Simba was in his private study when Arianne found him a few hours later.

"You heard that Wiz nearly brought the marshal's stand down on himself on the drill field this afternoon?" she said without preamble.

Bal-Simba grunted. "I heard. Besides all else, our Sparrow is clumsy."

"He is that," she said tonelessly.

Bal-Simba looked up and gave his lieutenant his full attention.

"Meaning?"

"Meaning I examined that post just after the accident. The wood was old and beetle-bored, waiting to fail. So I went back and looked at the place on the parapet where he slipped the other day. It was damp and somewhat slick. There was nothing obviously unusual about either the post or the place on the parapet."

Bal-Simba waited.

"I could find no definite trace of magic about either the post or the damp spot. There seemed to be a hint of—something—about the post, but if it was indeed there it was so faint I could not be sure."

"You obviously think there is more to this than simple accidents," Bal-Simba said. "What?"

Arianne paused, choosing her words carefully. "Lord, I think someone is trying to kill Wiz by magic."

When Bronwyn finally released him, Wiz went looking for Donal. He found him alone in the armory, replacing a strap on his chain mail haubrek by the light of a magic globe.

"I wanted to thank you for this evening," Wiz told him. "You saved my life, I think."

"So clumsily you needed the attention of a healer to put your shoulder right," Donal said wryly.

"I'm alive and that's the important thing. Thank you."

Donal stared down at the new strap. "As you saved mine beneath the City of Night."

"Still . . ."

"Lord, if you wish think of it as payment of a debt." He turned back to the job of threading the strap into place.

"You know, I think about the time we spent at Heart's Ease. You, I, Kenneth and Shiara." His mouth twisted into a half-smile. "Back when there was a clear, simple job to do and all we had to do was do it."

"Yes, Lord," Donal said without looking up from tying the strap into the chain mail.

"Now everything's so complicated and there's so much more to it." He sighed. "What do you do when you're overwhelmed?"

"You do the best you can for as long as you can, Lord."

"And then?"

Donal jerked the strap tight and looked up. "Then, My Lord, you put your back to something and go down fighting."

"I don't think that really applies here," Wiz said.

Donal fixed him with his icy blue eyes. "Lord, I hope you are never in a situation where it does apply."

"Subtle," Bal-Simba said at last. "Subtle indeed. But so subtle it is not sure."

Arianne smiled nervously. "If you mean to make me doubt my suspicions, Lord, you may spare yourself the effort. I do not know if I believe this or not."

"Oh, it is believable," Bal-Simba rumbled. "Overt magic in this place would be too easy to detect—and to trace back to its source. Wiz is known to be clumsy and an accident would be easy to accept. An attack using just the tiniest of magics to set up a mischance could perhaps pass unnoticed. And if the first one did not succeed, the next one might, or the next after that."

"That is my thinking, Lord."

He shook his head. "We have grown lax, Lady. With the Dark League broken we have let down our guard."

"You suspect the Dark League?"

"Who else? They are not all gone, after all, and those who are left would have ample reason for harming our Sparrow."

"There is one other thing, Lord."

"Eh?"

"I did not come by this on my own. Another first suggested the idea to me—before today."

"Who?"

"June, the orphan servant girl. She is convinced Wiz is in danger."

"How is your shoulder?" Moira asked as soon as Wiz came in.

"Fine now." He windmilled the arm. "See?"

"I am glad," she said quietly.

"What's the matter?" he asked, dreading the answer.

Moira bit her lip. "Wiz, we have to talk."

"All right." *I'm losing her*, he thought. *I'm blowing it and I'm going to lose her.*

"I am sorry, I cannot go on like this."

"I know. I've got to stop ignoring you."

"Wiz, you are killing yourself," Moira said desperately. "Your ignoring me, that I could live with—I think. It is in a good cause. But you are burning yourself out trying to do too much."

"I've got to do it. Bal-Simba won't let me off the Council and we've got to have a version of the spell compiler anyone can use."

Moira bit her lip and considered. This wasn't just about her needs. As a hedge witch she had been inculcated with the idea that service to the community came before personal needs. The whole World needed Wiz and what he could do. She pushed her feelings to the back and tried to look at the situation as the helper of one of the Mighty with an important task to perform.

Wiz, lost in his thoughts, missed the shift completely.

"I dunno," he sighed. "Sometimes I think it's getting worse instead of better."

"Worse than you know," the redheaded witch said. "There are some who claim you hide your secrets from us behind a veil of deliberate obscurity. That in this way your power among us grows."

"Oh, bullshit! Look, I'm doing the best I can, all right? But I'm a rotten teacher and these people are so *dense*."

"Some of the wisest and most powerful of our wizards have placed themselves under your tutelage," Moira said sharply. "Are you so superior that they cannot learn the most elementary matters?"

"Of course not! But you people don't think the way we do. I know they're trying but they just don't pick up the concepts."

"I understand that," Moira said more gently. "I remember what it was like when you tried to teach me this new magic. But Wiz, it makes problems for everyone."

"At least the ordinary people seem to appreciate what I'm doing. We've already got a few spells out there that anyone can use. **ddt**, the magic repellent spell, is everywhere and that's solved a lot of problems. But I can't do many more of those until I get the tools built. Meanwhile, I'm trying to teach the system to people who hate it and wasting time sitting in Council meetings listening to endless debates on nothing much."

Moira nodded sympathetically. Wiz was like a blacksmith with a good supply of iron and charcoal but no tools. Given time he could make his own tools, but until he got them made, there was very little else he could do. She wasn't used to thinking of a spell as a thing built up of parts like a wagon, but by analogy she could understand the situation.

"If I could just get the other wizards to see that and take me seriously, I'd be a lot further along. Instead I have Ebrion claiming the spell compiler doesn't work at all!"

"But doesn't **ddt** show Ebrion and the others that your way of magic works?"

"It doesn't penetrate. They see it as a clever hack and claim it's like a non-magician using an enchanted item."

"But you *created* it!"

He shrugged. "So I'm a great magician. Any great magician could come up with something like that, they say. It's all an accident."

"They should have been in the dungeons beneath the City of Night when you broke the Dark League single-handed!"

"They weren't. Most of them didn't find out about the attack until the day it happened and they never had a really clear picture of what was going on. Besides, they claim it only proves my magic was so alien the Dark League didn't know what to expect."

Moira said something very unladylike under her breath.

Wiz made a face. "Look, the truth is they don't see it because they don't want to see it. I can't fight that—at least not until I've got better tools and can teach some more people to use them."

He sighed. "I don't know. I feel as if I'm being nibbled to death by ducks. If I could just put everything else aside and concentrate on writing code I could get this done. But the way it is now," he waved his hand helplessly over the books. "The way it is now I've got so many other things happening I just can't stay with anything long enough to accomplish anything."

"Perhaps you could."

"Yeah, but I've got to have trained helpers. Until I get some people who understand this kind of magic I can't do half the critical stuff."

Suddenly Moira brightened. "I have it!" She turned to Wiz excitedly. "You need help, do you not?"

"Yeah," Wiz sighed, running a hand through his hair. "I need help."

"And there are many in your land who can do what you do?"

"More or less."

"Then the thing to do is to have the Council bring others to your aid. With the Dark League broken they can do a Great Summoning easily enough and . . ."

"*No!*" Wiz snapped around, shaking her arm off his shoulders.

Moira turned white and flinched back as if he had struck her.

"I'm sorry," Wiz said. "I didn't mean to scare you. But no, I'm not going to have that on my conscience."

"Look, what Patrius did to me was a damn dirty trick." He took one of her hands in both of his. "I'll admit it worked out well in the end, but it was still a terrible thing to do. Even with you and all the rest I still get homesick sometimes." He grinned lopsidedly. "There are times I'd trade almost everything for a sausage, pepperoni and mushroom pizza."

He took her in his arms. "Look darling, I know you mean well, but I can't let you do that to someone else. Promise me you won't try to yank someone else through."

Moira blinked back tears. "Very well." She tapped herself on the chest with her fist. "I swear I will not use a Great Summoning to bring someone else here from your world."

"And that you won't influence anyone else to do it either."

She glared at him, but she swore.

"I'll have to ask Bal-Simba to swear that oath tomorrow," he said, releasing her arms.

She stood up straight. "Very well then. What *will* you do?"

"It'll work out," Wiz mumbled. "I'll think of something."

"What? What will you do?"

"Something! Look, leave me alone, will you?" He shook her arm from his shoulder angrily.

Moira stood stiff and straight. "Very well, My Lord." She turned and ran from the room.

Wiz half rose to follow her and then thought better of

it. He sank back to the bench and turned his attention
to the book in front of him.

Let her work it off, he told himself. *She'll come back
when she's calmed down some.* It wasn't a very attractive solution but it was the best he could think of at the
moment.

Moira slammed the door behind her and stormed
down the hall, the cloak she had hastily grabbed slung
over her arm. By the time she reached the stairs she
was crying openly. She paused at the landing to throw
the cloak about her and raise the hood to hide her
tears, then swept out into the main court.

She did not see the figure in the shadows at the foot
of the stairs.

Well, well, Pryddian thought as Moira went past.
Trouble in the Sparrow's nest. He smiled to himself
and continued down the corridor.

Five

SHIARA AGAIN

*Living with a programmer is easy. All you need is
the patience of a saint.*

—programmers' wives' saying

Like the original Heart's Ease, the new one was a
stone tower with an attached hall. The stones of the
tower still bore traces of the fire which had destroyed
the original and the hewn logs of the hall shone white
and new. The freshly raised building exuded the odor
of woods; the faint sweet smell of oak from the floors
and paneling, the resiny tang of pine from the walls and
rafters and the perfume of cedar wafting down from the
shingles that roofed the hall.

Gliding through the hall like a swan, Shiara the Silver absorbed it all. She could not see, but she could
smell and she could touch. What she sensed pleased
her very much.

The warmth streaming in through the diamond-paned
windows told her the day was bright and sunny. Perfect
for sitting outside and enjoying the feel of the summer
breezes.

She smiled. It was somewhat lonely here without
Ugo, her goblin companion killed in the raid that destroyed Heart's Ease. Then Wiz and Moira had gone.

But the Forest Folk took good care of her and Heart's Ease was still well named. It would be pleasant to sit in the sun, feel the breeze and smell the growing things.

Suddenly she stiffened as the presence of magic sent a sharp pain through her.

Either very near and very weak, or not too near and stronger. She considered again. The Forest Folk were careful of her and would not allow magic to approach Heart's Ease without warning her. Further away, then.

She heard the light pit-pat of tiny feet on the floor. "A visitor, Lady," the little creature said. "She is asking for you."

Shiara nodded, stately and graceful. "Make her welcome then. I will receive her here."

As the sound of tiny feet faded into the distance Shiara smiled once more. She had company. Obviously one of the Mighty since she had come on the Wizard's Way. It would be pleasant to talk magic and lore once more. Shiara was no longer of the Mighty. The accident that had deprived her of her sight left her hypersensitive to magic. Living as she did in the deadest Dead Zone in the North, Shiara was spared the pain of magic, but it also meant she was isolated from the World. Still, she enjoyed sitting and talking about what had once been so central to her life. Besides, it was a chance to catch up on the news from the Capital.

"Lady?" came a tremulous voice from the door.

"Moira?" The voice was so strained it was hard to recognize. "Merry met indeed."

"Merry met." Then a pause.

"Lady, I need help and I did not know where else to turn," Moira said miserably.

". . . and there you have it, Lady. I could not stand it, so I went away."

Moira and her hostess sat on a log bench outside the rebuilt keep of Heart's Ease. The night was mild and the moon near full above them. Both had cloaks, but they were only sitting on them rather than wrapping up

in them. The moonlight picked out the glistening tear
streaks down Moira's cheeks.

"Lady, I do not know what to do. There is no living
with him and I'm miserable without him."

Shiara could not see the tears, but she heard them in
Moira's voice.

"Do you love him?" she asked gently.

Moira sniffled. "You know I do, Lady. And I know he
loves me. But that doesn't solve everything."

"It never does," Shiara said with a sigh.

Moira hesitated and Shiara heard her skirt rustle
against her cloak as she turned toward her.

"Lady, did you and Cormac . . ."

Shiara paused at the mention of her dead lover and
quest companion, killed in the same accident that took
her sight and magic. ". . . ever fight?" Shiara finished
the question. "Oh, aye. Often and fiercely. He would
stamp and bellow and bang his fist and I would scream
like a fishwife and throw things. Crockery mostly." She
smiled at the memory.

"That is not part of the legends, is it? Still, it is true.
I think a necessary part of loving someone—loving them
enough to share your life with them—is being able to
have it out with them when needs be."

She put her hand on Moira's shoulder. "You are
strong willed, both of you, and neither is easy. I would
be surprised if you did not fight."

"But it doesn't seem to settle anything," Moira said
despairingly. "We argue and nothing gets any better."

"Now that is another matter," Shiara said.

Shiara turned her sightless eyes to her guest. "I do
not know that I am the person to advise you. I had little
experience in such matters."

"You and Cormac were as famous for your love as for
your deeds." She saw the look that crossed Shiara's
face. "I'm sorry, Lady, I did not mean to pain you."

"Little enough pain in remembering the times you
were happy, child." She shook herself.

"Since you want my advice," she went on practically, "the first thing I suggest is that you start with yourself."

"I have done all I can, Lady."

"Forgive me, that is not quite what I meant. From what you say, it sounds as if you have submerged yourself in the Sparrow and his work. You have told me much of him and his problems, but near nothing about you and what you do. It seems that as Wiz has risen in the World you have come down."

"It is no small thing to be the wife of a member of the Council of the North and the mightiest wizard in the land," Moira said.

"Aye, but that is reflected glory. What do you do yourself?" Shiara asked gently.

Moira stiffened.

"It is no small thing to be hedge witch of a village and have everyone look up to you," Shiara went on. "You are someone in your own right and you do important work. At the Capital you have no such work and your place is less clear, is it not?"

"There is something in that," she admitted grudgingly.

"One of the reasons Cormac and I were so in love was that we both had important work. Neither of us was identified by what the other did."

Moira considered that. "So you are saying I should change?"

"It is easier and more certain to change yourself than to change another person."

"And Wiz?"

"He must change too, in his own way." Shiara frowned. "This may not work. You cannot do all the changing, nor will he change simply because you nag at him. You must both strive, and hard, to succeed."

"I will try, Lady. I think he will also. But he is so weighted down with his work it will be difficult."

"It sounds as if the Sparrow is trying to take all the weight of the world upon his shoulders," Shiara said. "Like a certain hedge witch I once knew."

Moira blushed.

"But Lady, there are none in the World who can help him and he has forbidden us to Summon another from his world."

"Then you must give him the help he needs," Shiara told her.

"But how, Lady? I have no talent at all for this new magic."

"You are resourceful. You will find a way, I think. But that is not the worst of it, is it?"

"No," Moira sighed. "He gets lost in his work and it is as if his soul were stolen away. His body is there, but Wiz is gone."

"Then finally, you will have to train him to stop ignoring you. You must make him take time away from his work to spend with you."

"But how do I do that?"

"Seduction is one way," Shiara said judiciously. "More commonly, you simply must tell him when you feel slighted."

Moira sniffed. "I would think that anyone would recognize the signs."

Shiara sighed. "Anyone but a man."

Wiz sleepwalked through the whole day. He couldn't concentrate, he couldn't work and he knew his teaching was worse than usual. Even Malus noticed and approached him diffidently to ask what was wrong.

Bal-Simba hinted delicately that he was available if Wiz wanted to talk, but Wiz wasn't in the mood. He liked the giant black wizard as much as he respected him, but for the first time since coming to the Capital it was borne on him that he really had no close friends here. He thought about Jerry Andrews, his old cubicle mate, and some of the other people he had known in Silicon Valley and missed them for the first time in months.

He broke off in mid-afternoon and raced back to the apartment, his mind full of all the things he wanted to say to Moira. But there was no one there when he arrived.

Wiz sat down heavily at his desk and tried to work. After shuffling things around for half an hour or so, he gave up even the pretense.

Then he moped about the apartment, trying to think and take his mind off things at the same time. With no stereo, television or movies, it was hard to kill time, he discovered. There weren't even any books to read except a couple of grimores he had borrowed from the wizard's library.

And they don't have much of a plot, he thought sourly.

Finally he opened the sideboard and poured himself a large cup of mead from the small cask Moira kept there. Moira preferred the mead of the villages to the wines of the Capital and she liked to have a cup after supper. Wiz hadn't eaten yet, but it looked to be about supper time to him.

Normally he didn't care for mead, finding its sweetness cloying. But tonight it wasn't half bad. He had a second cup and that wasn't bad at all. The mead didn't exactly make his thinking clearer, but it did seem to narrow down the problem and focus him on the major outlines.

"Priorities," he said, hoisting his third cup to the dragon demon sitting atop his books. "I've got to start setting priorities." He drained the cup in a single long draught and went to the cask to refill it again.

"Moira's priority one," he said waving the cup in the general direction of the demon. "I've gotta get Moira back." He slopped a little mead from the cup and giggled. "Screw the wizards, scroo'm all. Moira's what's important."

He poured half the contents of the cup down his throat in a single swallow.

"Then the compiler. Never mind the Council. They're not important anyway. I finish the compiler and where's the Council, hey? Poof. All gone. Don't need them no more."

It took him a while, but sometime early in the morning he finished the cask of mead.

Well, he thought muzzily as he staggered into the bedroom, *it's one way to pass the time.*

The morning was death with birdsong.

Wiz's head was pounding, his eyeballs felt like they had been sandpapered and his mouth felt as if something small and furry had crawled in there and died.

Now I understand why they invented television, he thought as he splashed cold water on his face and neck. *No hangover.*

There was no food in the apartment and the only things to drink were water and a bottle of mead. The thought of the mead nearly made Wiz lose his stomach and the water wasn't very satisfying.

Somewhere in the back of his head, buried under several layers of pain, he remembered that the wizards had a spell that cured hangovers. He needed that more than he needed anything else right now, *except Moira.* Afterwards he could get breakfast in the refectory with the inhabitants of the castle who chose not to cook for themselves.

He groped his way toward the Wizards' Day Room where he expected to find someone who could put him out of his misery.

Naturally the first person he met was Pryddian.

The ex-apprentice took in Wiz's condition in a single glance. "A good day to you, My Lord," he said, much too loudly.

Wiz mumbled a greeting and tried to step by the man.

"What is the matter this morning, Sparrow?" Pryddian boomed, moving in front of him again. "Suffering from an empty nest?"

"Leave me alone, will you?" Wiz mumbled.

Pryddian was almost shouting now. "Poor Sparrow, his magic fails him this morning. All his mighty spells cannot even cure a simple hangover." Again Wiz tried to move around him and again the man blocked his way.

"You need the help of a real wizard, Sparrow. Maybe he could make you a love philtre while he's at it, eh? Something to keep your wife home at nights."

Suddenly it was all too much.

Wiz whirled on his tormentor. Pryddian caught his look and stepped back, hands up as if warding off a blow.

"backslash," he shouted.

The lines of magical force twisted and shimmered.

Wiz froze with his arm extended and his mouth open. Pryddian shrank back, his face white.

Wiz dropped his arms. **"cancel."**

"I'm sorry," he mumbled. "I didn't mean to . . ."

Pryddian gathered himself and beat a hasty retreat.

Wiz became aware that a dozen people were watching him from doors along the corridor. His face burning, he turned and fled.

Wiz had little less than an hour to contemplate the enormity of what he had almost done before Bal-Simba came calling. The giant black wizard was obviously not in a good mood.

"I must ask you this and I compel you to answer me truthfully," he said as soon as he had closed the door. "Did you threaten to use magic on Pryddian?"

"Yes, Lord," Wiz said miserably.

"And he did not threaten you first?"

"Well, he got in my face."

"But he offered you no threat?"

"No, Lord."

Bal-Simba looked as if he would explode.

"Lord, with the problems with the project and Moira gone and then him . . . Lord, I am sorry."

Bal-Simba scowled like a thundercloud. "No doubt you are. But that would not have saved Pryddian if you had followed through with your intent. Magic is much too powerful to be loosed in anger. You above all others should know that."

"Yes, Lord. But he has been riding me for days."

"Is that an excuse?" Bal-Simba asked sharply. "Do you hold power so lightly that you will loose magic on any person who annoys you? If so, which of us are safe from you?"

"No, Lord," Wiz mumbled, "it isn't an excuse."

The huge wizard relaxed slightly. "Pryddian's behavior has not gone unnoticed. He will be dealt with. The question is what to do with you."

He looked at Wiz speculatively until Wiz fidgeted under his gaze.

"It would be best if you were to absent yourself a while," Bal-Simba said finally. "I believe matters can be smoothed over but it will be easier to do if you are not here."

"Yes, Lord," said Wiz miserably.

"In fact, this would accomplish two things," he said absently. "I have received a request from the village of Leafmarsh Meadow. They have asked for one of the Mighty to assist them. That is sufficient reason for you to be gone, I think.

"Also, we have many reports that this new magic of yours is already at work on the Fringe of the Wild Wood."

"That would be **ddt**, the magic protection spell I hacked up," Wiz told him.

"The reports of the hedge witches and other wizards are somewhat confusing. I want to see what is going on through your eyes."

"Yes, Lord. Uh, what about Moira?"

"I am sure she is safe. If she returns while you are gone, I will tell her where you are.

"I will send a journeyman wizard with you. You will leave tomorrow morning. Meanwhile, it would be best if you were to stay out of sight." He looked down at Wiz. "And take something for that hangover."

This close to the Capital, the woods were carefully tended tree lots rather than the raw forest of the Wild

Wood. But the trees still shut out prying eyes and the relative isolation made prying magic easy to sense. That was the important thing.

Ebrion made his way to the middle of the grove. He looked around cautiously, extended his magical senses for any hint of a watcher and then extended his arm, finger pointing south.

As if on cue, a tiny bird flickered through the trees and landed on his outstretched finger. To the eye it was an ordinary wren, speckled brown on brown. A magician would have sensed instantly that it was no ordinary bird, but part of the reason for meeting in the woods was to keep the bird away from other magicians.

The bird cocked its head to one side and regarded the wizard with a beady eye.

The Sparrow has left the Capital, Ebrion thought at the bird. *He is to be gone perhaps four days and then he will return along the Wizard's Way. Be ready for him.*

He paused and then continued.

One thing more. Your attempts to arrange an accident for the Sparrow have been discovered. I told you I would not have him harmed. Persist and our bargain is broken.

The wren took wing and flashed through the trees. The wizard waited until it rose above the treetops and turned straight south. Then he nodded and started back to the Capital.

Six

APPLICATIONS MAGIC

*Applications programming is a race between soft-
ware engineers, who strive to produce idiot-proof
programs, and the Universe which strives to produce bigger idiots.*
> —software engineers' saying

So far the Universe is winning.
> —applications programmers' saying

Wiz's travelling companion was a wizard named
Philomen, a slender young man with an aristocratic
bearing and a reserved manner. Wiz had met him
briefly, but he didn't know him and he couldn't remember seeing him in any of his classes.

As was custom, they did not walk the Wizard's Way
straight into the village. Instead they arrived on a hill
where the road topped the rise to look down at Leafmarsh
Meadow. From here the village looked neat and peaceful, spread out along the road that ran to the Leafmarsh
Brook and crossed to run deeper into the fringe. This
side of the river was a neat pattern of fields and pas-
tureland. The Fringe started on the other side of the
water and there the land was mostly forest, although
Wiz noted a number of fields, obviously freshly hacked
in the ancient woodland.

Towering over the village was a hill of naked gray granite. It seemed to be a single enormous boulder, placed as if a careless giant had dropped it next to the river. Even to Wiz's relatively untrained senses there was something about the huge rock that hinted of magic.

"This will be my first real trip out of the Capital in almost a year," Wiz said in an effort to make conversation as they started down the hill toward the village.

"Indeed?" Philomen said. "You will find much changed, I think."

Wiz didn't have any good answer to that, so they walked along in silence for a bit.

"Do you have any idea why they wanted help from the Council?"

"None, Lord. If they did not tell one of the Mighty, do you think they would tell one barely raised from apprentice?"

"No, I guess not," Wiz said. "Well, we'll know soon enough. That's the hedge witch's cottage there."

The place was on the outskirts of the village, a single-story house of whitewashed wattle and daub with a thatched roof. The whitewash needed renewing and the thatch was turning black in spots. It was surrounded by a rather weedy garden and all enclosed by a ramshackle fence. The cottage wasn't exactly run down, Wiz decided, but it looked very much like the owner had other things on her mind than the condition of her property.

They came up the flagstone pathway to the door and Philomen rapped sharply upon it with his staff.

"Keep your britches on, I'm coming," came a cracked voice from inside. Then the door was flung open in their faces.

"What the . . ." She stopped dead when she saw her visitors in wizard's cloaks with staffs in their hands. She blinked once and her whole manner changed.

"Merry met, Lords," she said, bobbing a curtsey. "I am Alaina, hedge witch of this place."

She was older than Moira, but how much Wiz couldn't

tell because people aged so fast here on the Fringe. Her hair was gray and a greasy wisp had escaped the bun on the back of her head. She was shaped like a sack of potatoes. Her skin was coarse and her teeth, what were left of them, were yellow. From this distance it was obvious she hadn't bathed recently.

On the whole, she didn't look much worse than the average middle-aged peasant woman, but to Wiz the contrast with the hedge witch he knew best was striking.

Well, Wiz thought, *it would be too much to expect all hedge witches to be like Moira.*

"Merry met, Lady," Wiz and Philomen chorused.

"What brings you to Leafmarsh Meadow?"

"We were sent by the Council in answer to your request," Philomen said.

The hedge witch looked blank. "Request? Oh, yes, the request. Well, what can I be thinking of to keep such guests standing in my garden? Come in, Lords, come in and be welcome."

The place was even more run down and messier on the inside, but it managed to be homey at the same time. The cottage was a single large room with a fireplace at one end and an unmade bed in the corner. At the opposite end was a low work table with rows of shelves above it. Dried herbs and other less identifiable things hung from the rafters, giving the place an odor like hay with anise overtones.

"Please excuse the clutter," Alaina said and she moved piles of things off chairs to give them places to sit. "The girl only comes in three days a week and things do pile up in between times.

"Can I offer you refreshment? I have some very good mead. But of course gentlemen such as yourselves from the Capital do not drink mead."

There was an undercurrent of resentment, Wiz realized. As if she didn't want them here.

"Mead would be most satisfactory," Philomen said.

"None for me, thanks," Wiz said and from the way

they both looked at him he realized he had committed some kind of social error in refusing the hospitality.

"I can't drink just now," he said quickly.

Alaina's expression smoothed. "Ah, a vow. I understand those things, of course. You are saving power for a special spell."

"More like doing penance," Wiz said wryly.

Once they were settled into the somewhat dusty chairs and Philomen and Alaina were clutching cups of mead Wiz decided it was time for serious talk. Alaina was keeping up a steady flow of conversation on inconsequential topics, as if she was trying to ward off discussion. Philomen was responding to her with bored civility, but making no move to come to the point.

"Your pardon, Lady," Wiz said, cutting off an anecdote about the profusion of dragon weed this year, "could you tell us about your problem?"

"My problem, ah yes," Alaina said, draining the rest of her mead in a single gulp. "It is nothing, really. Nothing at all." She reached over for the pitcher and refilled her cup.

"I am honored that you have come to us, do not misunderstand me," she waved an admonitory hand. "But it really was not necessary. Not necessary at all to send two such great wizards from the Capital for this."

"I thought you had asked for help," Wiz said.

Alaina made a dismissing motion, as if shooing off an insect. "That was Andrew, the mayor. He wouldn't give me a minute's peace until I sent off to the Council for aid." She smiled at her visitors. "You know how non-magicians are, My Lords, always frightened around magic and such. But I never dreamed they would send someone so soon. And two of you!"

Meaning you expected to have this all wrapped up before the Council took notice, Wiz thought sourly. *Now here we are and you won't get the additional prestige out of this you thought you would*.

"I am sure your skill is up to the task, Lady," Philomen said soothingly. "It just happened we were coming this way on other business so the Council asked that we come to assess the situation. Consider us merely observers."

That seemed to mollify the hedge witch.

"Well," she said. "Well indeed. I was going to wait until the next full moon to lay this creature. But since your lordships are here, I suppose I can do the job tomorrow."

"Very well then," Philomen said. "I presume there is a place we can get dinner and stay the night."

"Oh, there is no inn in the village," Alaina said. "Much too small, you know." She hesitated.

"I would ask you to sleep here, but . . ." She swept out her arm, indicating the clutter and the single bed. "In any event, I am sure you would be much more comfortable staying at the mayor's house. No, I am sure he will insist that you stay with him as soon as he knows you are here."

"I am sure you know best, Lady," Philomen said.

"He is out on the brook gathering reeds for thatching," the hedge witch told them. "I will have someone send for him immediately." She stood up. "Will you excuse me, Lords?" She bobbed a curtsey and went out.

"Political, huh?" Wiz said once he was sure their hostess was out of earshot.

"Such matters usually are, Lord. At least to some extent. I would suggest that we let her lay this creature." He looked at Wiz. "Unless you have reason to do otherwise."

The man's tone made Wiz uncomfortable. "No, none at all," he said, looking down at his boots.

"Might I further suggest, Lord, that we stand ready to aid her should the need arise? Her style does not give me confidence in her abilities."

Wiz and Philomen sat in uncomfortable silence for a few minutes more. Wiz still wasn't sure whether Philomen's coldness grew out of his nature or a dislike for him. A mixture of both, he suspected increasingly.

Alaina came rushing back breathless with the news that mayor Andrew had been summoned from the reed marsh and his wife was preparing to receive them at their house. It would take a few minutes, she told them, but they would receive a proper reception.

Wiz was becoming increasingly uncomfortable with both of them, so he excused himself.

"I want to stretch my legs a bit," he explained.

Philomen nodded. "As you will," and he turned his attention back to Alaina's latest story.

There wasn't much to the village, just a gaggle of houses spread out along a narrow lane. Most of them were timber or wattle and daub, but a few of the larger ones clustered around the place where the lane widened into a village square were made of native stone.

There weren't many people about, or if there were they were keeping out of sight. Once or twice Wiz passed someone in the street who bowed or curtseyed and then moved on quickly. He saw children peering at him from windows and doors, but very few adults.

Either people hereabouts were afraid of strangers or they knew who he was and they were nervous around wizards. Judging from the reactions he got, Wiz suspected the latter.

At the end of the village, where the stream made a looping bend, there was a grove of poplars on a bank overlooking a water meadow. As Wiz approached he smelled smoke and the smell drew him on toward the trees.

Maybe there will be someone here to talk to, he thought.

There was a wagon, hardly more than a cart, and an ox grazing in the meadow nearby. A man in rough brown breeches and a coarse linen shirt was busy building up a small campfire. He was burly with a greying beard and a seamed, weatherbeaten face. He looked up and smiled a gap-toothed smile as Wiz approached.

"Well met, My Lord."

"Uh, hi. Just passing through, are you?"

"Aye, My Lord," the man chuckled. "Passing through on my way to a better life. I am called Einrich."

"Wiz Zumwalt. Pleased to meet you. But why are you camped out here? I thought the villagers put travellers up where there are no inns."

The man shrugged. "I know no one here and I have no claim to guest right. Doubtless a place could be made for me, but the weather is fair. The people are willing to let me pasture my ox in their meadow and gather wood for my fire. That is sufficient.

"Besides," he added, "they have seen many like me recently. Better to save their hospitality for those who are travelling with their wives and children."

Wiz looked around and realized there were three or four other campfire rings under the trees. No one was using them now, but most of them looked as if they hadn't been long out of use.

"Where is everyone going?"

Einrich grinned, showing the place where his front teeth had been. "Why for land, young Lord. They go into the Wild Wood for land."

"You too?"

Einrich nodded. "I tarry here for a day or so to rest and feed up my ox. Then I am also on my way east for new land."

"All by yourself?"

"My sons and their families stay behind on the old farm to gather in the harvest." He grinned. "They can spare a dotard such as me and this way we can get an early start on our new farm."

Looking at Einrich's powerful frame, Wiz would not have called him a dotard. Old perhaps, by the standards of the peasantry, but he looked like he could still work Wiz into the ground.

"How far are you going?"

"As deep into the Wild Wood as I can. That way when my sons follow we will all be able to claim as much land as my sons and my sons' sons will ever need."

"Aren't you worried about magic?"

"No more!" Einrich said triumphantly. "With the new spell I can defeat any magic in the Wild Wood. Trolls, even elves, I can destroy them all."

Wiz frowned. **ddt**, his magic-protection spell, wouldn't destroy anything. It would only ward off magic and tend to drive magical influences away.

Wiz opened his mouth to say something, but Einrich interrupted him. "Oh, it is a grand time to be alive!" His eyes shone like a child's at Christmas. "Truly grand and I thank Fortune that I lived to see this day. No longer must mortals cower at the threat of magic. Now we can walk free beneath the sun!"

"Wonderful," Wiz said uncomfortably.

"Will you join me for dinner, Lord? Plain fare, I fear, but plenty of it."

"No thanks. I think I am expected back at the village for dinner."

Wiz walked slowly back toward the village square, scowling and scuffing his boot toe in the dust of the road. This was what he had fought for, wasn't it? That people like Einrich could live their lives without having to fear magic constantly. Most of the Fringe and part of the Wild Wood had been human at one time, before the pressures of magic had driven the people back. Wasn't it just that they were reclaiming their own?

Then why do I feel so damn uncomfortable with Einrich and what he's doing?

The mayor met Wiz partway back to the village square. He was a stout, balding man with a face red from exertion. He was wearing a red velvet tunic trimmed with black martin fur obviously thrown hastily over his everyday clothes. He had washed the muck off, but the odor of the reed marsh still clung to him.

Mayor Andrew turned out to be almost as garrulous as Alaina. This time it suited Wiz because it meant that aside from complimenting the mayor on the village and making agreeable noises, he did not have to talk.

Dinner that evening was a formal affair. All the important people of the village turned out in their holiday best to honor their visitors. The villagers' manners were strained as they tried to follow what they thought was polite custom in the Capital. It reminded Wiz of a dinner he had attended once where the principals of an American software company were doing their best to entertain and avoid offending a group of powerful Japanese computer executives. That one turned into a rousing success after both sides discovered they shared a strong taste for single-malt scotch consumed in large quantities. For a moment Wiz considered trying to conjure up a bottle of Glenlivit, but he realized it would take more than booze to help this party.

"What is this thing that threatens you anyway?" Wiz asked Andrew during a particularly strained pause in the conversation as the mountainous platter of boiled beef was being removed and replaced with an equally mountainous plate of roast pork.

Andrew twisted in his chair and pointed. "That!"

Wiz followed the mayor's finger out the window. Hulking against the night sky was the huge granite hill, its mass and shape cutting off the stars near the horizon.

"The hill?"

"Aye, the hill. We have lived in its shadow too long."

Wiz realized everyone was looking at him and the mayor.

"Is it dangerous?"

"Dangerous enough," the mayor said grimly.

"What does it do?"

"It mazes people. Those who climb it are overcome by its power and stricken dumb. For days or even weeks they wander as if simple."

"Young John fell off it and broke his back," a slat-thin woman halfway down the table put in. "The healers said it was a wonder that he ever walked again."

Wiz toyed with the pork that had been heaped on his plate. "Uh, maybe this is a dumb question, but why don't people just stay off the hill?"

There was stony silence all down the table. Philomen

concentrated on his plate and everyone else glared at Wiz.

"Okay, so it was a dumb question," Wiz muttered.

"The thing is magic and I will not have magic so close to my village," Andrew said fiercely.

"Look, don't worry. I'm sure that we can take care of this thing tomorrow so it will never bother you again."

Somehow the rest of the meal passed off without incident.

Deep in the Wild Wood a wren perched on a finger and trilled out its message. Seklos, now second in command of the Dark League, considered carefully the news the bird had brought.

So, he thought, *our Sparrow leaves its nest. Very well, we will be ready when he seeks to return.* He dismissed the wren with a flick of his finger and turned to his work. In concert with the others of the Dark League, he had a demon to create. A most powerful and special demon.

As he reached for a spell book Seklos wondered idly what that fool in the Capital meant about attempts on the Sparrow's life. The Dark League would make only one such attempt. And when it came it would be crushingly, overwhelmingly successful.

Seven

DEMON DEBUG

The three most dangerous things in the world are a programmer with a soldering iron, a hardware type with a program patch and a user with an idea.
—computer saying

The morning was bright and clear. The day promised to be hot, but by the time Wiz and Philomen emerged from the mayor's house the whole village was astir.

"Oh, this is a great day," Mayor Andrew told them, rubbing his palms together. "A great day indeed."

"I am sure it is," Philomen said soothingly. "We are honored to be here to observe. Now, if you will excuse us, we must consult with your hedge witch before the ceremony."

As the villagers drifted in the direction of the monolith, Wiz, Philomen and Alaina retired to one corner of the meadow for some shop talk.

"Okay," Wiz said, looking over his shoulder at the enormous mass of granite. "Probably the best tool for this job is the Demon Deterrent Trap, **ddt.**"

"Why not **demon_debug**?" asked Alaina.

"What's that?"

"A wonderful cure for magic of all sorts," the slatternly hedge witch told him. "It wipes it right out."

"Where did you get it?"

Alaina gestured vaguely. "It is being passed through the villages. Much better than **ddt**, I assure you."

"Well, let's see it."

Alaina nodded and raised her staff.

"**demon__debug exe!**" she bawled at the top of her cracked voice.

There was a shimmering and shifting in the air in front of them and a squat demon perhaps three feet high and nearly as broad appeared on the grass before them.

Wiz looked the thing over and frowned. "This isn't one of my spells."

"Of course not, My Lord," the hedge witch said. "This is better."

The warty green demon leered up at him, showing saw-like rows of teeth in a cavernous mouth. The thing looked singularly unpleasant, even for a demon.

"How does it work?"

Alaina shrugged. "It is magic, of course. How else does a spell work?"

"No, I mean how does it function? Haven't you listed it out to examine the code?"

"List?" Alaina said, puzzled. "Forgive me, Lord, but how do you make a spell lean? And what good would it do."

Wiz shot her a dirty look. Then he realized she was sincere. She didn't have the faintest idea how a spell worked or how to find out.

He shook his head. "Well, let's see then."

Philomen and the hedge witch hung back to watch the master work.

"**Emac.**"

"Yes, master?" A small brown manikin popped up at his feet. It was perhaps three feet high with a head almost grotesquely large for its body. It wore a green eyeshade on its bald brown head and carried a quill pen stuck behind one flaplike ear.

The Emacs were one of the first classes of demons

Wiz had created when he declared his one-man war on the Dark League. They were translators and recorders of spells in Wiz's magic language, magical clerks.

"**backslash**," Wiz commanded.

"**$**," said the Emac.

"**list demon__debug**," Wiz said.

The Emac pulled the pen from behind his ear and began to scribble furiously on the air in front of him. A mixture of runes, numbers, and mathematical symbols appeared in glowing green fire.

Wiz frowned as he studied the symbols.

"It's based on **ddt**, but it's been changed." He turned to the Emac again.

"**backslash**."

"**$**."

"**dif demon__debug/ddt**."

Again the Emac scribbled and again the lambent characters hung in the air. But one section of spell stood out in violent magenta against the neon green.

Wiz bent forward over the Emac's shoulder to study the magenta section. It represented the changes between the original **ddt** and this new version. He traced his finger along the lines and his lips moved as he worked out what the changes did.

"Jesus H. Christ," he breathed at last. "What a nasty piece of work!" He straightened up and glared at the other two magicians.

"Who's responsible for this?"

"Ah, responsible for what, Lord?" Philomen asked.

"This!" Wiz shouted. "It isn't a defensive spell. It's offensive, a magic killer. You turn this loose on any kind of magical creature and it won't just protect you, it will destroy the thing."

"So much the better," the hedge witch said firmly. "That way it will never come around to bother us again."

"But why kill it?"

Alaina set her jaw firmly and her eyes glittered. "Because it is magic and because it threatens us. Perhaps the Mighty do things differently in the Capital, but we are simple folk out here on the Fringe. We treat harmful magic the way we treat posionous serpents."

Before Wiz could reply Philomen placed a hand on his arm. "Forgive me, My Lord, but perhaps we should discuss this. Will you excuse us, My Lady?"

Alaina curtseyed stiffly and withdrew to the other end of the meadow.

"My Lord, it is unwise to give an order you cannot enforce," Philomen said as soon as the hedge witch was out of earshot. "Were you to forbid this, she could simply wait until we are gone and use **demon__debug** herself."

"This is too much. That thing doesn't hurt anyone permanently. From what they say it doesn't even affect anyone who doesn't climb it."

"Still, it is strong magic and that makes it an unchancy neighbor. The villagers' desire to rid themselves of the thing is understandable."

"Great. But where will it all end? Are these people going to go around destroying anything just because it's magic?"

"If they have the opportunity."

"That's crazy!"

"No, it is understandable. It is the people in the villages, especially along the Fringe, who have suffered the most from magic. To you in your pale tower in the Capital magic may be a thing to be learned and applied. Here it is a thing to be hated and feared. Is it any wonder that as soon as they were given an opportunity to practice magic safely, they should go looking for a weapon?"

"I gave them a defense," Wiz protested. "I didn't expect them to turn it into something so dangerous!"

"You did say you wanted even common folk to learn your new way of magic," Philomen said mildly.

"Yes, but not like this!"

"Are you now complaining because someone took you at your word?"

"I'm complaining because this spell is fucking magical napalm!" Wiz yelled. "I expected people to have more sense than this."

"Sense?" Philomen asked with a trace of malice. "My Lord, forgive me, but when have the folk of the villages ever shown such sense?

"Once it was the Council's job to maintain the balance of the World. But as you have said, the Council is outworn and lives beyond its usefulness. Or did you expect the folk along the Fringe to learn restraint and balance overnight?"

"I never said the Council was useless."

"You never put it in words," Philomen retorted. "But you said it with every act, every gesture, every roll of the eyes or yawn in Council meeting. Oh, your message got through, right enough. Even to the villages on the Fringe of the Wild Wood.

"Then you compound your actions by giving villagers a powerful spell they can use freely and telling everyone who would listen that you do not have to be a wizard to practice magic." Philomen's lip curled in contempt. "No, My Lord, you are getting exactly what you strived for."

Wiz couldn't think of anything to say.

"So come, My Lord, let us attend the laying of this thing. And for the sake of what little order remains in the World, let us put a good face on it." With that he turned and walked back across the meadow to where Alaina was waiting. Wiz hesitated for an instant and then followed.

The entire village was gathered before the stone by the time the three magicians arrived. All of them were wearing their holiday best. The adults were clumped together talking excitedly and the children were running around laughing and shrieking at play.

They parted like a wave for the three magicians. Andrew was standing at the front with a few of the other people from the feast last night.

Alaina looked over the crowd, eyes shining and her coarse face split in a huge smile.

"Well," she said briskly, "shall we begin?"

She motioned with her staff and the villagers fell back, Wiz and Philomen with them. Then she turned to face the rock, struck a dramatic pose and thrust her staff skyward.

"demon_debug BEGONE exe!" she bawled.

At first nothing seemed to happen. Wiz could feel the tension rising in the crowd and knotting up in his stomach. He took a firmer grip on his staff and began to review the spells he might use if this only roused the creature.

Maybe it won't work, he thought to himself, half-afraid and half-hopeful. *Maybe the spell will crash.*

Then the rock moaned.

The sound was so low it sent shivers through Wiz's bones, as if someone was playing the lowest possible note on the biggest bass fiddle in the world. It started low and then built and rose until it threatened to drown out all other sound.

There was something else there besides sound, Wiz realized. Some sort of mental influence, as if . . .

Wiz went white. "That thing's alive," he shouted to Philomen. "It's alive and intelligent!"

"Such things often are in their own way," the wizard agreed, keeping his eyes on the mass before them.

"But you can't kill it, it's intelligent!"

"Can we not? Watch."

Still groaning, the stone reared above them, heaving itself free of the earth and towering above them as if it would slam down on them and crush them like bugs. The villagers gasped and shrank back, but the thing slammed to earth in its own bed. The ground shook so hard Wiz nearly lost his balance. The creature reared again, not so high this time, and pounded to the earth once more. It tried to rear a third time, but could only quiver.

"Stop it!" Wiz yelled. "*Stop it!* Can't you see it can't hurt you?"

" 'Tis magic," Andrew replied. " 'Tis magic and must be burned from the land.

"Too long we trembled under the magical ones. Now let them tremble." His voice rose to a shout over the windy moans of the dying stone. "Let *them* know fear!"

The crowd behind him growled agreement.

The thing thinned, its stony gray turning opalescent and gradually lightening until Wiz could dimly see the outline of the hills through it. Then the creature's body went foggy and he could see that the hills were cloaked in summer's green. The outline blurred and became indistinct and finally, at last, the mist dissipated, leaving nothing but a hole in the ground with tendrils of smoke rising from it.

Wiz stood shocked and numb, oblivious to the cheers of the villagers. Someone was pounding him on the back and shouting in his ear, but he couldn't make out the words.

Alaina left in the midst of an excited knot of villagers, talking and cheering and doing everything but hoisting her on their shoulders in triumph. Some of the others remained behind to gape at the huge pit where the rock creature had stood. Then by ones and twos they began to drift back toward the village square.

"A waste, I calls it," one old gaffer said to his younger companion as they passed by where Wiz stood. "They should have pounded it into gravel 'stead of just making it disappear. We needs gravel for our roads, we does."

Finally only Wiz remained, standing at the edge of the pit and looking down.

He didn't know what the thing was that had died here today. He had never heard of such a creature and it may well have been the only one of its kind. But whatever it was it didn't deserve what had been done to it.

His cheeks were wet and he realized he was crying.

There was a footstep behind him. Wiz didn't turn around.

"Are you coming, My Lord?" Philomen asked. "There will be a feast tonight in honor of slaying the monster."

Wiz turned to face the wizard. "No thanks. Right now I don't think my stomach could stand a feast."

"Our presence is expected."

"Vomiting on your hosts is probably bad form, even in this bunch."

Philomen's face froze and he bowed formally. "As you will, My Lord. I will see you at the mayor's house then."

"Maybe." Wiz strode off toward Leafmarsh Brook and the bridge into the Fringe beyond.

"My Lord, where are you going?"

"Into the Wild Wood," Wiz flung back over his shoulder. "Right now I want some civilized company. Weasels maybe, or snakes."

Eight

SIDE EFFECTS

You can't do just one thing.
—Campbell's Law of everything

Sitting under a flowering bush on a hillside, Wiz
called up an Emac and studied the code for **demon__debug**
again.

It was obvious what had happened, he thought as he
traced the glowing lines. Somewhere out in one of the
villages, some bright person with a knack for magic and
a little knowledge of his programming language had
taken **ddt** apart and found a way to make it more
effective. What he or she had done was related to the
magic-absorbing worms Wiz had invented for his attack
on the City of Night. The new spell, **demon__debug**,
sucked the magical energy right out of its victim. It was
crude, it was dangerous and it was absolutely deadly.

Without one hell of a protection spell there was no
way that anything magical could survive **demon__debug**.
Idly he picked up a water-worn pebble and ran his
thumb across it while he thought about the implications.

This must be what Einrich meant when he said he
could destroy any magic he met in the Wild Wood.
That, and the way Alaina talked, made Wiz pretty sure
the spell was spread far and wide through the Fringe.

72

Wiz flung the stone into the weeds. He had screwed this up more thoroughly than he had ever messed up anything in his life. Before he had just affected himself, and perhaps the lives of a few people around him. Now he had managed to meddle in the lives of an entire world; to meddle destructively.

He wasn't sorry he had invented the magic compiler. He thought of the last time he had come this way. He and Moira had stumbled over the burned ruins of a farm shortly after the trolls had raided it. He had dug the grave in the cabbage patch to bury the remains of the people the trolls hadn't eaten after roasting them in the flames of their own homestead. He still had nightmares about that.

He didn't want to go back to the way things had been. But looking down at the village and the scar where the rock creature had stood for time out of mind, he wasn't at all sure what was replacing it was much better.

He stood up and looked down on the village. The evening breeze bore the faint sounds of drunken revelry up the hill to him. In the center of the village people were piling wood head high for a bonfire. *Ding dong the witch is dead!* Never mind that the "witch" had stood harmlessly for longer than the village had been there. Never mind that the people who killed it behaved like a wolf pack with the blood lust up. The witch was dead so let's have a party. And if it's a good party, maybe we can go out tomorrow and find some more witches to murder.

He couldn't go back there. But he didn't want to go back to the Capital with its packs of wizards and no Moira. All he really wanted was to be alone for a while. Say a couple of centuries.

Well, he decided, there really wasn't any reason to go back. He had come to the village with only his cloak, staff and a pouch containing a few magical necessities. He had his staff and pouch and the weather was warm enough that he doubted he would miss his cloak.

Turning his back on the village, Wiz headed down the other side of the hill, toward the Wild Wood.

He very quickly lost any sense of where he was. He might be wandering in circles for all he knew—or cared. If he wanted to go somewhere he could take the Wizard's Way. What he needed was to be alone and to try to sort out the mess.

Once he stopped to munch handfuls of blackberries plucked from a stand of thorny canes. Another time he stopped to drink from a clear rivulet. Most of the time he just walked.

The evening deepened and the shadows grew denser but Wiz barely noticed. Finally, the second time he almost ran into a tree he sat down to think some more. As he sat the dusk darkened to full night. The last vestiges of light faded from the sky and the moon rose over the treetops. The night insects took up their chorus and the nightblooming plants of the Wild Wood opened their blossoms, adding just a hint of perfume to the earth-and-grass smell of the night. Wiz fell asleep under the tree that night. He dreamed uneasily of Moira.

"You step more spritely this morning," Shiara observed as her guest came into the great hall.

"Thank you, Lady, I feel better." She joined Shiara at the trestle table beneath the diamond-paned window and began to help herself to the breakfast spread out there.

"You found a solution then?"

Moira frowned. "Part of a solution, I think."

She heaped berries into an earthenware bowl and poured cream over them. She took an oat cake from the platter and drizzled honey on it. "Wiz always said that when you could not meet a problem straight forward you should come at it straight backwards."

Shiara nibbled reflectively on an oat cake. "That sounds like the kind of thing the Sparrow would say."

Moira nodded. "Once he told me something about a

mountain that could move but wouldn't and a wizard named Mohammed." She wrinkled her nose. "I never understood that, but it gave me an idea."

Shiara chuckled. "Now that truly sounds like our Sparrow. And from this obstinate mountain and a straightbackwards approach, you have discovered something to help you?"

"To help Wiz. But Lady, I need your advice."

"I know nothing about going straight backwards or moving mountains."

"No, but you do know Bal-Simba. He will have to aid me in this."

The sun was high in the sky before it worked its way under the tree where Wiz lay. Twice he wrinkled his nose and shifted his position to keep the beams out of his eyes, but still he slept on.

Wiz was about to shift for the third time when something ran across his chest.

"Wha . . ." Wiz made a brushing motion with his arm. Something small and manlike hurdled his legs, squealing like a frightened rabbit. Wiz sat upright and shook his head to clear the sleep fog. He heard something else moving through the brush. Something—no, several somethings—large and heavy. He clambered to his feet and faced the noise just as a troll crashed through the undergrowth and into the clearing.

Fortuna!

Behind the first came two more, and then a fourth. All of them were more than eight feet high, hairy, filthy and stinking. They wore skins and rags and carried clubs the size of Wiz's leg.

He threw back his arms and raised his staff. Frantically he sought a spell he could use against four trolls.

The trolls stopped short, bunched in a tight clump.

Wiz braced himself for their charge, but there was no charge. There was fear in their eyes. As one they turned and vanished into the forest.

Wiz let out his breath in a long sigh.

"Okay," he called over his shoulder, keeping his eyes on the place where the trolls had disappeared, "you can come out now."

"Thank you, Lord," said a small voice behind him.

There were five of them, all formed as humans and none of them more than a foot high. One of the women had a child no longer than Wiz's forefinger in her arms.

As soon as they came into the open Wiz knew what they were. Moira called them Little Folk. Wiz always thought of them as brownies.

"Thank you, Lord," the one in the lead said again. "We owe you our lives. I am called Lannach." He turned to his companions. "These are called Fleagh, Laoghaire, Breachean and she is Meoan." At the mention of their names each bowed or curtsied in turn.

"Glad I could help," he said uncomfortably. Then he frowned. "You're a little far from home aren't you? I thought you always lived with humans?"

"No more, Lord," the little man said sadly. "Mortals will not have us."

"We lived in the place mortals call Leafmarsh Meadow," Lannach explained. "We were always the friends of mortals. We helped them as best we could, especially with the animals and the household work."

"We asked little enough," the small creature said. "A bowl of milk now and again. A bit of bread on Midsummer's Day as a sign of respect."

"But now mortals have their own magic and they need us no more."

"Need us no more," the little one crooned. "Need us no more. Need us no more. Need us no more." His mother hushed him and he trailed off into babbling.

"You mean they chased you out?" Wiz asked incredulously. Dangerous magic was one thing, but he'd never heard anyone accuse brownies of anything worse than mischief. People were supposed to be glad for the help brownies provided with the chores.

"Chased us out?" Meoan hissed. "They kill us if they can." The little woman was white and shaking with fury. "Look at us, mortal! We are all that are left of the Little Folk of our village."

"She was handfast to one who is no more," Lannach said. "The father of the child."

"They laid in wait for my Dairmuirgh," she said. "When he came to the stable to groom their horses, they set their demon upon him and made him no more." She was crying openly, the tears trickling down her tiny cheeks, and rocking back and forth. "Ay, they murdered him as he sought to help them."

Back in Silicon Valley Wiz had known a few programmers who refused to work on weapons systems or any other kind of military job. He'd always thought that was a little peculiar. The programmer's job was to deliver software on time, in spec and functional. It was the job of the designers and managers to worry about what would be done with it. Now he was confronted by the results of his work and those people didn't seem peculiar at all.

"Oh shit. Look, I'm really sorry." He stopped. "I'm, well I'm responsible in a way," he confessed miserably. "It was my spell they took and hacked up to make that thing."

"We know," Lannach said. "We also heard what happened when that bitch from the village destroyed the Stone." He placed a tiny hand on Wiz's forearm. "Lord, you cannot be responsible for the uses mortals choose to make of your magic."

That made him feel even worse. "Thanks, Lannach. Where will you go now?"

The brownie shrugged. "We do not know. Unlike dryads and some other creatures, we are not tied to one place. But it was our home." He looked up and his limpid brown eyes gazed into Wiz's. "It is hard to lose the place which has been your home for so long."

"I know," Wiz said miserably, thinking of smoggy sunsets over Silicon Valley.

"We would not leave even now save for the little

one," he nodded to Meoan's baby. "He must be protected."

Wiz understood. Children were rare among the man-like immortals. An infant was a cause for great rejoicing and such children as there were were carefully pro-tected. The adults might be willing to stay and die in a place they loved, but they would not risk the baby.

"Lord," said the little man tentatively, "Lord, could we impose upon you further and travel with you?"

"I'm not really sure where I'm going."

The brownie shrugged. "Neither are we, Lord."

The Wild Wood was still a tangle of ancient forest that abounded with dangerous magic, but Wiz wasn't afraid. His own magic was potent and very frankly he wasn't sure how much he cared.

"Sure," he said, "come on."

They spent the rest of the morning travelling. In spite of their size, the brownies moved quickly and had no trouble keeping up with Wiz. They found berries to eat along the way and once the brownies located a tree bearing small wild plums, just going ripe.

It was shortly after noon when they topped a rise and looked down into the heavily forested valley beyond. Six or eight thin curls of smoke arose from scattered locations on the valley's floor and merged to form a thin haze over the whole valley.

Wiz remembered the last time he had come into the Wild Wood. The forest valleys had been an unbroken sea of green. Mortals were not welcome in the Wild Wood and the few who came were not gently treated.

"I didn't know there were so many people out here," Wiz said, looking down on the scene.

"Mortals spread quickly," Lannach observed.

"Aye," agreed Breachean in a rusty voice. "Give them a few harvests and they'll carpet this valley like flies on meat."

"I don't think we want to go that way," Wiz said. "Let's follow the ridge and skirt that place."

It was harder going along the ridge and they used

game trails rather than the well-trod footpath that led down into the valley, but it was more pleasant for all of them. The trees here were huge and old, unscarred by woodsman's axe. The birds sang and the squirrels dashed about as they had for centuries. Most of the time there was neither sight of a clearing nor smell of woodsmoke to remind them of what was going on in the valley.

Still, it was slower going. It was almost evening when they came down off the ridge and into the next valley.

They made their way down the trail in the deepening twilight, looking for a place to camp.

"What's that?" Wiz asked pointing to a strange glow moving through the woods ahead of them.

"Off the trail," Lannach whispered. "Quickly!"

Wiz took a firmer grip on his staff. "Hide?"

"No, just do not stand in their way."

The light came clearer and brighter through the wood, like sky glow at dawn. Then the first of the procession rounded the bend and Wiz saw the light emanated from figures on horseback.

Elves, he thought, *a trooping of elves.*

They came by ones and twos, riding immaculately groomed horses of chestnut, roan and blood bay. They were tall and fair of skin, as all elven kind, and dressed with the kind of subdued magnificence Wiz had come to associate with elves.

They passed Wiz and the brownies by as if they were not there, looking straight ahead toward a distant goal or talking softly among themselves in their own liquid tongue.

Last of all came the lord and the lady of the hold.

The man wore green and blue satin with an embroidered white undertunic. Instead of a simple filet to hold his long cornsilk hair, he wore a silver coronet. He had a hawk on his wrist, unhooded.

The woman was as fair and near as tall as her lord, with hair the same cornsilk color flowing free of her coronet and down her back to almost touch her saddle.

She wore a long gown of deep, deep purple with a train that flowed over her saddle and her horse's rump.

The woman turned her head to look at Wiz where he stood beside the trail. The combination of beauty and sadness clutched at his heart.

Wiz stood open-mouthed in awe long after the party had disappeared.

"They go East," Lannach said. "Beyond the lands of men."

"I didn't think the elves would be bothered," Wiz said numbly. "They're too powerful."

"Not all the Fair Folk are as powerful as your friend Duke Aelric. Oh, doubtless they could protect their hills and a few other spots most dear to them. But what then? The lands they called their own would be changed utterly by the mortals.

"As all the land changes," he added sadly.

Pryddian came into the room a trifle uncertainly.

"You sent for me, Lord?"

Bal-Simba ignored him for a moment and then looked up from the scroll on his desk.

"I did," the great black wizard said. "We have no further need of you here. You are released from your apprenticeship."

Pryddian started. "What?"

"Your presence here is no longer required," Bal-Simba said blandly. "You may go."

"That is a decision for my master!"

"You have no master, nor will any of the wizards here have you." He turned his attention back to the scroll.

Pryddian stood pale and shaking with rage, his lips pressed into a bloodless line.

"So. Because I am the victim of an attack by magic I am to be punished."

"You are not being punished, you are being released."

"And what of the Sparrow, the one who attacked me? What happens to him?"

The giant wizard regarded Pryddian as if he had just

crawled out from beneath a damp log. "The affairs of the Mighty are none of your concern, boy. You have until the sun's setting to be gone from this place." He turned his attention back to the scroll.

"Ebrion will have something to say of this."

"Ebrion is not here."

Pryddian frowned. "Well, when he comes back then."

Bal-Simba looked up. "If Ebrion or any of the other wizards wish to speak for you they may do so. But until they do you are no longer required here."

"I will wait then."

"You may wait. Outside the walls of the Keep."

"I . . ."

"Do you wish to provoke me now?" Bal-Simba rumbled. "I warn you, you would find me harder sport than the Sparrow and perhaps not as forebearing." He smiled, showing off his pointed teeth.

Pryddian snapped his mouth shut, spun on his heel and stalked from the room.

What would Ebrion have to do with that one? Bal-Simba wondered as he listened to the ex-apprentice slam down the corridor. He made a mental note to ask him when he returned.

The clouds rolled in during the morning, light and fleecy at first, but growing grayer and more threatening as the day wore on. Wiz and his companions trudged onward.

At last, just as the threat of rain became overwhelming, they found a rock shelter, a place beneath an overhanging cliff where the rain could not reach. They were barely inside when the skies opened and the summer rain poured down in torrents.

It was still so warm they did not need a fire and Wiz didn't feel like dashing into the rain without a cloak to gather the wood for one. He and the brownies settled down with their backs to the cliff and watched the rain drape traceries of gray over the forest and the hills beyond.

"Scant comfort," Lannach said as they settled themselves among the rocks.

"At least we're dry," Wiz told the brownie. "The last time I came this way I got soaked in one of these storms." He thought of the trek through the dripping forest and the peasant who had sheltered them that night. The one who had gained a farm in the Wild Wood at the cost of his wife and three children dead and a daughter given as a servant to the elves.

Meoan plopped herself down on one of the rocks and yanked at the ties of her bodice.

"We must be grateful for small comforts," she said bitterly. "Those who are driven from their homes had best take what they can find and be happy with it." She pulled down her bodice and offered a breast no larger than the first joint of Wiz's thumb to her baby.

"I'm sorry for what happened to you," he said tentatively.

The little woman looked up at him. "I know you are, Lord. But sorry does not heal what it hurts." Then she sighed deeply. "And I apologize to you. Since we met you have shown us nothing but kindness. I should not blame you for what those others did."

"We're not all like that, you know. Where I come from we learned the hard way that you've got to protect non-human things, to try to live with them."

"Would that the mortals of this world were so wise," Meoan said.

"Maybe they can be. It's just that they've been oppressed by magic for so long they're afraid of it and they want to exterminate it."

"Whether it hurts them or not," the brownie woman sniffed.

"When you're afraid of something it's hard to make fine distinctions. Humans suffered a lot because they had no protection against magic."

Meoan nodded. "I have heard the mothers lamenting for their children, struck down or stolen away by magic."

She held her infant to her breast. "Life has been hard for mortals."

Wiz looked out at the rain. The sun had broken through at the horizon to paint the bottom of the clouds red and purple with its dying rays. The trees of the forest were tinged a glowing gold above, shading to deeper green out of the light. Already the shadows were beginning to thicken and take on substance.

"It's going to be too dark to travel soon," Wiz said. "It looks like we stay here tonight."

He looked around ruefully. The ground was hard and full of sharp rocks fallen from the ceiling with almost no drifted leaves which could be used to make a bed. There were leaves aplenty out on the slope, but they were soaked.

"Well, it won't be our most comfortable night, that's for certain."

"Unless you would care to share other quarters," said a musical voice behind them. "Welcome, Sparrow."

Nine

MEETING BY MOONLIGHT

Friends come and go, but enemies accumulate.
—Murphy's law #1024

and sometimes the real trick is telling the difference.
—Murphy's law #1024a

Wiz whirled and saw an elf standing in the gloaming at the edge of the overhang.

He was tall and straight as a forest pine. His skin was the color of fresh milk. His white long hair was caught back in a circlet of silver set with pale blue opals. Although the forest was dripping and the rain still fell in a light mist, he was completely dry.

"Duke Aelric?"

The elf duke nodded. "The same." Then he smiled and stepped aside to reveal another elf standing behind him.

"And this is Lisella."

She was nearly as tall as Aelric and her skin as milk-fair. But her hair was black and glossy as a raven's wing where Aelric's was snow white and her eyes were green as emeralds rather than icy blue. Her gown was old rose with a subtle embroidery of deeper red. Her figure was slender and elegant.

Wiz gulped and bowed clumsily.

"I discovered you were in the area and thought you might do us the honor of dining with us this evening," Aelric said. He looked around the rock shelter. "Perhaps you would care to guest the night with me as well."

"Why, uh, yes," Wiz said, managing to tear his eyes away from the elf duke's companion. "Thank you, Lord."

"Well then," Aelric said. "If you would care to accompany us. And your friends, of course."

The brownies had dived for cover as soon as Aelric appeared. Now they poked their heads out from behind rocks or from the crevices where they had gone to earth.

"Come on," Wiz said. "He won't hurt you."

Reluctantly the brownies came out and gathered tight around Wiz. Lannach wasn't clinging to his pant leg, but Wiz got the feeling he wanted to.

"Shall we go?"

Aelric and Lisella strode to the back of the shelter and the elf duke made a gesture to the blank stone. Soundlessly the rock dissolved and there was an oak door, magnificently carved and bound with silver. The door swung open and warm golden light flooded out.

Wiz had no idea where he was in the Wild Wood, but he was pretty sure he was a long way from where he and Moira had entered the elf duke's hold the first time they met.

Time and space run strangely in places the elves make their own, Moira had told him then. He shrugged and followed Aelric and Lisella into the hill with a gaggle of brownies close on his heels.

Once again Wiz sat in Aelric's great dining hall. The magical globes floating above the table cast the same warm light onto the scene. The food was as superb as it had been before and the soft music in the background was as enchanting.

But there were differences. The last time he and

Moira had been fugitives, snatched from the pursuing army of the Dark League by Aelric's whim. Now Moira was somewhere else and Wiz was . . . what?

And beyond that there was Lisella.

In the warm glow of the magic lights she was even more beautiful than she had been beneath the moon. Her presence reminded Wiz that before he met Moira he had been attracted to tall slender brunettes.

From time to time their eyes met across the table. Lisella looked at Wiz with a kind of intent interest that both stirred him and reminded him uncomfortably of the way a cat regards a baby bird it can't decide if it wants to play with or eat immediately.

Although Aelric and Lisella were careful to include Wiz in the conversation, he had the distinct feeling that he was missing most of what was actually being said. They were playing some kind of game, he decided, some elaborate elven game with malice at its heart. Whatever these two were they were definitely not lovers.

Throughout dinner Aelric had kept up an easy conversation on inconsequential topics. Wiz had sensed that his host did not want to discuss serious matters and, still in awe of the elf duke, he had likewise avoided them. Finally, as light-footed servants placed bowls of nuts and decanters of wine on the damask-covered table, Lisella rose.

"Alas, My Lords, the hour grows late." She curtseyed to Aelric. "If you will excuse me?"

Aelric stood up and Wiz followed suit. "Of course, My Lady." He bowed and kissed her extended hand.

Then she turned to Wiz and fixed her green eyes on his. "Perhaps we shall meet again," she said softly and with a rustle of her brocaded gown she was gone.

"Remarkable, is she not?" Duke Aelric said. Wiz realized he was gaping and made a determined effort to shut his mouth. Aelric sat down and Wiz followed suit.

"I thought it would amuse you to meet her." He picked up his wine glass and again Wiz followed his lead.

"Uh, why? I mean aside from the fact that she's beautiful."

Aelric cocked an eyebrow. "My dear boy, she *has* been trying to kill you for months."

Wiz choked, spewing wine across Duke Aelric's fine damask table cloth.

The elf duke dabbed the wine drops from his sleeve. "You mean you did not know? Dear me, and I was about to commend you for your insousiance."

"How . . . I mean why? I mean I've never seen her before."

"That is immaterial, Sparrow. As to the how, she has been arranging little 'accidents' for you for some time. So far you have been lucky enough to avoid them."

Wiz remembered the falling stone and the toppled viewing stand and felt sick. Then he looked closely at the elf duke. "Somehow I don't think it's been entirely luck."

Aelric smiled. "Your escapes were at least as much luck as your accidents were mischance."

Wiz absorbed that in silence. All of a sudden he felt like a piece on someone else's chess board. He didn't like it much.

"Thanks, I think. But why is she trying to kill me?"

"Oh, many reasons, I expect. The technical challenge for one. Penetrating a place so thick with magic as your Capital undetected and laying such subtle traps. That required superb skill, I can assure you."

He smiled reminiscently. "So did countering them. You've provided quite a diverting experience."

"And if I had missed that handhold on the parapet? Or hadn't jumped the right way when the stand collapsed?"

Aelric looked at him levelly. "Then the game would have been over."

Wiz was silent again. "You said there were many reasons Lisella wanted to kill me," he said at last. "What are some of the others?"

Duke Aelric poured more of the ruby wine into a

crystal glass with an elaborately wrought and delicately tinted stem. "Surely you can guess. When last we met, I said I would follow your career with interest, Sparrow." He smiled wryly. "I admit I did not expect it to be quite this interesting."

"I didn't either, Lord."

"It is not often a mortal is sufficiently interesting to hold the attention of one of us. You have become interesting enough to fix the attention of quite a number of the never-dying."

The elf duke looked at his guest speculatively. "You have made yourself much hated, you know."

"Yeah," said Wiz miserably. "It wasn't supposed to work this way. Things kind of got out of hand."

"Not unusual when mortals dabble in magic," Aelric said. "Lisella is a minor difficulty. You would do well to dismiss her from your mind—after taking proper precautions, of course. What you have done has deeper consequences."

"You mean the destruction of magic along the Fringe?"

"I mean the destruction of mortals everywhere," the elf duke said. "You mortals make this new magic and in the process you raise forces against yourselves you do not understand. For the first time in memory there is talk of a grand coalition of magic wielders, a coalition aimed at the mortals."

"That's crazy!"

"That is mortal logic, Sparrow. None of these are mortals and many of them are not logical in any sense."

"But, I mean a war."

"They would not think of it as a war. Rather the extermination of a particularly repulsive class of vermin who have made themselves too obvious."

Wiz stared straight into the depths of the elf duke's eyes. "Do you think you could beat us?"

Aelric shrugged gracefully. "I really do not know." Then he caught and held Wiz's gaze. "But I tell you this, Sparrow. Whoever wins, the outcome is likely to be the utter destruction of the World."

Wiz dropped his eyes. "Yeah. But does it have to happen? I mean, can't we prevent it?"

"It would be difficult at best," Aelric said. "That is not a consequence all of us wish to avoid. There are some who hunger for death and destruction on the widest possible scale. There are some who by their very natures cannot comprehend or appreciate the threat. And there are some who would find the end of the World merely diverting. A new experience, so to speak."

"What can I do?"

Aelric shrugged. "Remove the cause. The magical forces of the world make uneasy allies. If the threat were gone, the coalition would dissolve in an eyeblink."

Wiz thought about that, long and hard. Aelric sipped his wine and said nothing more.

He didn't know what the chances of heading this thing off were, but he didn't think they were very good. Given the feelings of the people of the Fringe about magic, and given the power of the tools he had put in their hands, it wasn't going to be easy to get them to quit wiping out magic wherever they found it. Keeping them from pushing into the Wild Wood in search of land would be harder yet.

And he was going to have to have a hand in finding a solution. Not only because he helped create the problem, but because he was the only one who really understood the new kind of magic that lay at the root of it.

Wiz was even less confident of his ability to solve these problems than he was of his capacity as a politician or a teacher, but dammit! he had to try.

"I'm going back to the Capital," he announced. "Maybe I can undo some of this mess."

"A wise decision," Aelric said. "When do you propose to return?"

"I should go back tonight, but I'm beat and there's not much I could do there. First thing in the morning, then."

The elf duke nodded.

Wiz reached for his wine goblet. Then he froze in horror.

"Wait a minute! If Lisella wanted to kill me, she just had the perfect opportunity to poison me or something!" He stared at his goblet as if it had sprouted posion fangs and tried desperately to remember if Lisella's hands had ever been near it.

Duke Aelric chuckled. "Oh no. Murdering you while you sat together at dinner would be gauche. The fair Lisella is never gauche."

Wiz considered that and decided the elf duke was probably right. But he didn't drink any more wine.

"Oh, one other thing. The Little Folk who came with me. Could you, well, could you take care of them for me?"

Aelric looked startled.

"Are they so important?"

"Not important, no. But I kind of feel responsible for them and I can't take them with me."

The elf duke's brow creased and for a second Wiz was afraid he was angry. Then he relaxed and rubbed his chin.

"I doubt they would be happy within my hold," Aelric said finally. "But I could send them on to Heart's Ease under my protection. I do not think those who dwell there would mind their presence."

"Thank you, Lord. I really appreciate it."

Aelric made a throw-away gesture. "You are most welcome." Then he smiled wryly. "Sparrow, it is always a pleasure to share your company. One never knows what you will do next." He sighed. "Or what one is likely to do under your influence."

Lisella was not in evidence the next morning when Wiz bade Aelric farewell. The elf duke and the brownies accompanied him to a clearing outside one of the elf hill's many doors. It seemed impolite to walk the Wizard's Way from inside the hill—something like parking your motorcycle in your host's living room.

"Good luck, Sparrow," Aelric said as Wiz faced in his chosen direction.

"Merry part, Lord."

Aelric looked at him and Wiz flushed, remembering that the elves did not use the human formula.

"Merry meet again," Aelric said finally.

Wiz raised his staff to begin the spell that would take him home.

"**backslash**."

Ten

THE CITY OF NIGHT

Whenever you use a jump, be sure of your destination address.

—programmer's saying

Something had gone wrong!

Wiz felt as if he had been spun around and tackled by a lineman. He was dizzy, pointing in the wrong direction and everything was wrong. His vision blurred, his head hurt and he was on the verge of throwing up.

As his sight cleared, Wiz saw he was in a low stone room. It was cold and lit by torches, not magic globes.

Ebrion stood before him.

"Merry met, my Lord," Wiz said instinctively. Ebrion looked uncomfortable.

"Merry met, Sparrow," came a cackling voice from behind him. "Merry met indeed."

Wiz turned and saw a bent man in the black robe of a wizard of the Dark League. He hobbled forward, leaning heavily on his staff.

The black-robed one smiled, not at all pleasantly. "Welcome, Sparrow. Welcome to your final resting place."

"Stayed behind?" Bal-Simba demanded. "What do you mean he stayed behind?"

"He departed into the Wild Wood when we had finished," Philomen told him.

"And you let him?"

Philomen hesitated. "We had words earlier that morning. I fear he was not well-disposed toward me. Then it turned out this rock creature was in some way sentient and that disturbed him even more. The Sparrow has an unusually tender regard for magical creatures of all sorts. He seems to feel that even the useless ones should be protected."

"So he went off into the Wild Wood. Alone."

"Lord, I tried to reason with him, but he would not listen. I am sorry, Lord."

"No need for that," Bal-Simba said flipping his hand dismissingly. "Perhaps our Sparrow needs some time by himself. And in any event, the longer he stays away the better for the situation here." He sighed. "I only wish he had gone through the settled lands rather than into the Wild Wood. But, no, you did nothing wrong."

"Thank you, Lord," said Philomen and withdrew with a bow.

Bal-Simba stood at the window looking out over the rooftops of the Capital toward the east as the shadows groped their way toward the horizon. Then he sighed again, shook himself and turned away to his desk.

At least he will be in no danger, Bal-Simba told himself. *As long as he stays away from elves he is certainly more powerful than anything he is likely to meet on this wandering.*

Wiz looked around desperately. The chamber was low but wide and long, with rough stone for the walls and floors and a couple of smoking torches to light it. Standing back in the shadows he saw even more black-robed wizards of the Dark League.

"We are going to send you back where you came from, Sparrow," Ebrion said finally. "Back to where you belong."

"But I don't want to go."

"Then you shall not," the other, black robe, said as he hobbled more fully into the light.

Wiz gasped.

The man's eyes glinted like chips of obsidian in a pink hairless mass of scar tissue. His nose was a slit and his ears shriveled like dried apricots. The hand clutching the staff was reduced to a claw, with only the thumb and forefinger remaining. Like the face, the hand was pink with scars.

"That was not the agreement," Ebrion protested.

"The agreement has changed," the other flung over his shoulder as he closed in on Wiz, thrusting his face so close Wiz could see where his eyebrows had been.

"Look upon me, Sparrow. I am called Dzhir Kar and I am your death." His breath stank in Wiz's face.

"My form does not please you?" he said, looking up at his captive. "A pity, Sparrow. For you caused it. A ceiling fell on me when you attacked the City of Night. There was a fire as well and I lay within the flames, slowly roasting and unable to move."

His face split into a hideous grin. "But I do not hold that against you, Sparrow. Oh no, not at all. For as I lay there and burned I discovered new strength within me. As I struggled to recover, I honed that strength. It made me Master of the Dark League, Sparrow."

He grasped Wiz's chin with a claw-like hand and pulled his face close.

"Look at me, little one! For I am your creation."

Wiz twisted his chin from the other's grasp and flinched away.

"Then look at *my* creation, Sparrow. My creation and your doom."

He gestured and two of the black-robed wizards moved forward into the fitful light. Each of them held a heavy chain and on that chain was a thing that made Wiz catch his breath.

It was long and lean, with a body made for coursing. The legs were a hound's legs, although the three ripping talons on each paw were like no dog that ever lived. The head was narrow with ivory fangs protruding from the heavily muscled jaws. Dzhir Kar made a gesture toward Wiz with his staff and the thing lunged and snapped at Wiz. The sound rang like a rifle shot in the gloomy chamber.

"Do you like my pet?" the black-robed wizard crooned, laying a gnarled hand upon the scaly head. "I made him especially for you, Sparrow."

The demon remained impassive under the caress, its yellow eyes fixed hungrily on Wiz.

"Not nearly as powerful as Toth-Set-Ra's demon, but he has seen you and that is enough."

"He is attuned to your magic, Sparrow. Make magic. Oh yes, please make magic. He will be upon you and your end will be truly wonderful to watch."

Wiz started to form a spell mentally. Instantly the creature's yellow eyes flicked open and its ears pricked forward.

"Go ahead," the wizard was almost dancing in anticipation. "Oh my yes, go ahead. We *want* to see this new Northern magic up close, don't we?"

The man was insane, Wiz realized. Crazy and full of spite and malice at the same time.

"No?" said the wizard in a disappointed tone. "Well, we will have to persuade you then. Flaying alive for a start. With salt rubbed well into the flesh to preserve it as the skin is peeled off. Toth-Set-Ra was right, there is *so* much one can do with a wizard's skin."

"*No!*" Ebrion bellowed.

Dzhir Kar stopped and regarded him as if he were an insect.

"I told you I would not have him harmed! We are to return him to his place only. That was our bargain."

"Bargains are made to be broken," Dzhir Kar said. He gestured to the surrounding wizards. "Take this one away."

"Fools," Ebrion shouted. "You seal your own doom."

"We will see who is doomed when the Council is deprived of its most powerful member," Dzhir Kar retorted. "And when it becomes known that one of the most powerful wizards in the North had a hand in the deed."

As the wizards of the Dark League closed in on him Ebrion stepped back and raised his arms. With a crash and a roar a dozen bolts of lightning struck him where he stood. Wiz flinched from the noise and the light.

So did the two wizards holding him. Instinctively, Wiz twisted in their slackened grips and broke free. Before anyone could react he was across the room and out the door.

"*Get him!*" screamed Dzhir Kar and the others leapt past the still smoldering corpse of Ebrion to comply. But Wiz was halfway down the rough flagged passageway and running for his life.

He turned the corner so fast he slipped and a bolt of lightning exploded on the stone behind him. He scrambled to his feet and ran on as the wizards came clattering out behind him.

He ran on at random, turning this way and that on panicked whim. The place seemed to be a maze of low stone passages with rough flagged floors. Behind him always he heard the sound of pursuit, sometimes close at hand and sometimes further away, but always there.

He ran out into a rotunda where five or six corridors came together and dashed down one to his left. Down another corridor he saw the bobbing gleam of torches.

The corridor was long and straight and Wiz ran down it full tilt. He was going so fast he almost ran straight into the wall ahead. Blind alley! He whirled and pounded back the way he had come, ribs aching and breath burning in his throat.

Again out into the rotunda and down another corridor. No sign of the lights now, but he was sure they were not far behind. Halfway down the corridor there was a place where the wall had collapsed. He slowed to avoid the pile of stones and saw lights before him and behind him, distant but coming his way. Without a thought he darted up the rubble pile and through the hole in the wall.

Suddenly he was outside on a narrow street between two- and three-story buildings of rough black stone. It was night, he realized and the moon was hidden by clouds. There was little enough light, but Wiz didn't slow down. He turned right and pounded down the street, heedless of the stitch in his side.

The empty windows of the upper stories gaped down at him like accusing eyes. Here and there an open doorway yawned like a devouring mouth. He ran without purpose or direction, on and on until a red mist fogged his vision. Finally, chest heaving and staggering with exhaustion, he turned into one of those open doorways in search of a place to hide and catch his breath.

Once through the door he sidled to the right, hugging the wall. After half a dozen steps he stumbled over the bottom landing of a stone staircase. Still gasping for breath, he picked his way up the stairs.

The narrow twisting staircase had no railing and the steps were uneven and slick with wear. Wiz hugged the wall and made as much speed as he dared. At last he came to the top of the tower—or what was now the top. The entire upper section was missing, the walls bulged outward and the stonework disrupted as if someone had set off an explosion inside it. Wiz looked out over the blasted, fire-blackened stone and for the first time he knew where he was.

The harbor with its encircling jetty, the ruined towers and the volcano bulking up behind him told him. The City of Night! The capital and base of the Dark League before their power had been broken.

A gibbous moon cast a sullen, fitful light over the landscape, picking out the tops of the ruined towers and the acres of rooftops below him. Wiz looked out over desolation and shivered.

Puffing and blowing, he sank down to sit on the stair, his back against the ruined wall and his feet dangling over emptiness. He tried to remember what he knew about the geography of this place.

Almost none of it was first-hand. He had been here only once before, when he mounted his great attack to free Moira from the League's dungeons deep beneath the city. He had come along the Wizard's Way and departed in the same fashion. In the hours he had been here he had never seen the surface.

The City of Night was on the Southern Continent, he remembered, separated from his home by the Freshened Sea. It was a bleak, barren land, locked in the grip of eternal winter.

Supposedly the city had been deserted after the Dark League had been defeated. Large parts had been destroyed by the forces unleashed in the final battle. The League wizards who had survived had been hunted from their lairs, their slaves had been freed and returned to their homes and the goblins and most of their other creatures had departed as well.

But the land itself was ruined beyond reclamation by decades of exercise of power with no thought to the consequences. For the people of the North the city was a place of fell reputation where no one but would-be apprentices of the Dark League went willingly. There was nothing to attract anyone to the place and even maintaining a watchpost on the Southern Continent had been considered too difficult and not worth the effort. The City of Night had been left unrestored and uninhabited.

If there was anyone here besides the League wizards they were unlikely to help Wiz.

Wiz ground his teeth in frustration. All he had to do to get help or to go home was to use magic. One single, simple spell and it was done.

Of course before he could ever finish that spell the monster in the dungeon would be on him. He remembered the eagerness and ferocity burning in the thing's evil red eyes and he shuddered. He had no doubt at all the wizard had been telling him the truth.

He listened to the wind whistle through the broken tower and tried to decide what to do next.

A clattering in the street below drew his attention. Peering out through the shattered wall, Wiz saw a dark shape cross a silvery patch of moonlight. Then another and another.

"He came this way." The voice floated up to him from the street nearly a hundred feet below.

"He must be near here," the other wizard called out from the shadows. "Down this way."

Wiz could not see which way he pointed, but several pairs of feet pattered off away from his hiding place.

So they weren't waiting for him to use magic! Those searchers were as dangerous to him as the monster. They knew the city and he did not. How many of them were there? Wiz wracked his brain trying to remember how many wizards had been in the room when he appeared. A dozen? Certainly that. And more besides.

And Ebrion. A traitor to the Council and now dead at the hands of his erstwise allies.

Well, Wiz thought grimly, *you brought this on yourself. If you hadn't been so high-handed with the Council, Ebrion never would have gone to the Dark League.*

Somehow the thought didn't make him feel any better.

The wind gusted and Wiz shivered harder. He didn't remember any part of the city being this cold. Perhaps the Dark League had warmed it by magic when they held it. Now there was slick black ice in patches on the streets and occasional piles and drifts of snow in the corners and sheltered spots.

Wiz shifted position and listened again. Save for the moan of the wind down the deserted streets and about the ruined tower, there was no sound. Slowly and cautiously, he rose and started back down the steps. He couldn't stay here and if he didn't find some kind of shelter soon the wind would do what the Dark League and their pet monster hadn't yet been able to.

The moon cast a pale light on the steep, narrow street below when it was not obscured by scudding clouds. The City of Night was built on the flank of a volcano and the whole town sloped up from the harbor. Wiz hugged the side of the buildings and headed downhill. Not only was it easier walking, it was away from the underground room where he had appeared and where the wizards and his demon waited for him.

At every corner he paused and listened. The streets were narrow and the hard black basalt of the buildings turned them into echo chambers. His own footsteps rang so loudly on the pavement he was certain that any pursurer could track him by sound alone. He hoped that he could pick up a trace of anyone in the area the same way.

At the third cross street he paused an especially long time to catch his breath. Up ahead there was the tiniest scuffling sound, as if something was dragging steathlily along the building ahead of him.

Wiz froze and then dropped back into the shadows. Across the narrow street on the other side of the intersection he saw a stealthy movement in the shadows. At first it was just a flicker here and there, then it looked as if the entire shadow on that side of the street had come to life. Then the shadow took form and substance and Wiz held his breath as he realized what it was.

The huge head was man-high off the ground as the serpent glided along. Its tongue flickered in and out constantly as it tested the air for scent of prey. Even in the moonlight Wiz could see the diamond patterns of its scales.

Then it turned and soundlessly whipped down the side street. Wiz caught his breath, but he stayed in hiding for a long time.

"Alone?" Arianne asked wide-eyed. "Alone into the Wild Wood?"

"So it would seem," Bal-Simba told her. He had spent the last two hours trying to control his unease and finally told his deputy what had happened. "Philomen did not stop him."

"He could not very well forbid him," Arianne pointed out. "Wiz is a member of the Council, Lord."

"Yes, but he knows less of the Wild Wood than a child," Bal-Simba said. "Remember the stories Moira told about the troubles she had with him on their last journey."

"The Dark League is not seeking him now."

"True, else I would have every magician and dragon rider in the realm searching for him. But he has barely been out of the city in the last two years and he still has little understanding of the World's dangers."

They were both silent for a moment.

"Lord," Arianne said finally, "what do you think is troubling Sparrow now?"

"If I had to guess, I would say he is discovering the price of power." Bal-Simba made a face. "I do not think he likes it overmuch."

PART II: LINK TIME

Eleven

A BIT OF BURGLARY

Always secure your files. You never know who's lurking about.

—programmer's saying

Pryddian, once apprentice wizard, closed the door softly and looked around the sitting room. He saw no signs of traps or warning devices anywhere. Once the apartment's door had been breached there seemed to be nothing to protect the contents.

There was no reason why there should be. Ordinary theft was virtually unknown in the Wizards' Keep because it was so easy to find thieves by magic. The wizards' workrooms were carefully protected by multiple spells, but there was no reason to extend that protection to living quarters. After all, no one worked in his or her apartment.

With one very important exception.

Pryddian moved cautiously across the sitting room toward the desk piled high with books and papers. With the hedge witch fled and the Sparrow sent away there should be no one here, but the enormity of what he was doing made Pryddian careful nonetheless.

Well, Pryddian thought, *the Sparrow had it coming*.

This was a way to avenge himself and perhaps profit as well.

As he approached the desk beneath, the red dragon demon reared up from among the clutter and hissed at him. Pryddian stopped and studied the creature carefully. He had expected something like this. Not even the Sparrow would be so careless as to leave his secrets completely unguarded.

However, Pryddian had come prepared, just as he had come armed with an unlocking spell for the door. The fact that it was a thing of the Sparrow's made it all the more delicious.

"**ddt exe!**" he whispered, pointing at the guardian demon.

The little red dragon paused in mid-hiss and scampered off the table. Pryddian watched in satisfaction as it ran whimpering for the bedroom.

Eagerly he bent over the desk and began to riffle through the material piled there. The large leatherbound book in the center of the table seemed most important, so he opened it first. But what was inside was the confused mishmash of the nonsense the Sparrow foisted off upon the wizards. Not a true spell in the lot. He slammed the book in disgust and turned to the piles of parchment, slates and tablets stacked around.

Quickly he sorted them, putting aside everything that was too arcane or too fragmentary to be useful. He was left with a sizable amount of material. Stacking the pile on top of the book, he reached into his cloak and produced a pen, a travelling inkwell and a sheaf of parchment. He dipped his pen into the ink and began to copy as fast as he could write, cursing when he blotted something in haste.

This was what he wanted. Not the inane babblings the Sparrow expounded in his classes, but his spells. His real power. Frantically he copied the crabbed smudged characters, taking care to put alternate lines on different sheets of parchment to prevent activating the spells. He added the marginal notes as he went, even though most of them meant nothing to him. With time perhaps he could puzzle out their meanings.

He was perhaps halfway down the pile when he came to the real prize. A powerful searching spell that would show the user anything that went on in the World. Flipping through the parchments he saw the spell commanded three separate sets of demons.

Pryddian licked his lips and his hand trembled. This must be the spell the Sparrow had used to track the Dark League. Like any magician, he believed that knowledge was power and this was a spell that would give him knowledge of the entire world.

The dragon demon peered around the corner at him and occasionally ventured a half-hiss. That Pryddian ignored. Every so often he glanced over his shoulder at the door, gripped by a mixture of elation and terror. If he was caught the consequences did not bear thinking about, but if he got away with this he would possess the essence of the Sparrow's magic.

Throw him out, would they? They would see who was the better wizard before he was through.

As he bent to copy the sheets he looked out between the drawn curtains and saw Moira coming across the courtyard, still wearing her travelling cloak.

Fortuna! The most powerful spell in the Sparrow's arsenal and he did not have time to copy it. Without thinking he thrust the originals inside his jerkin with the wad of copies. Hastily he gathered up his pen and ink and tried to put everything back where he found it.

Moira paused at the branching of the corridor and summoned up her courage.

Well, she thought, *soonest started soonest done.* She took a deep breath, squared her shoulders and strode off down the hall toward the apartment she shared with Wiz.

As she made her way down the hall, a figure in a hooded cloak hurried by her. She nodded and half-voiced a greeting out of habit, but the hooded one

ignored her. As he twisted to pass her she saw that it
was the apprentice who had insulted Wiz on the drill
ground.

If she had been less distracted, Moira might have
wondered what an apprentice was doing in a wing
reserved for wizards. Or why he was wearing a cloak
with the hood up indoors. But she had more important
things on her mind. She paused outside the door to
their apartment, took a deep breath, wiped a sweaty
palm on her skirt and opened the door.

The room was deserted. The little red dragon raised
its head inquiringly as she came in, but there was no
sign of Wiz.

Just like him! Moira thought. She was all steeled for
what must be said and he wasn't here. She plopped
down in her chair, determined to wait for him to come
back.

Around the corner, Pryddian leaned against the wall,
shaking and cursing inwardly. *She saw me!* He ground
his teeth. *The bitch saw me!* True, she had not seen
him come out of their apartment, but she had seen him
in a hall where he had no business being. Once the
Sparrow returned and missed the searching spell, it
would take no great leap to trace the deed to him.

Even if the Sparrow noticed nothing amiss, it meant
his foray was useless. As soon as he started using the
knowledge he had stolen, the hedge witch would remember his presence and it would be obvious to everyone what he must have done. For all his daring and
cunning, he was blocked before he could even begin.
Pryddian turned his face to the wall and beat his fist
against the stone in frustration.

Then he dropped his hand and gained control of
himself. Perhaps he was not so blocked after all. If
he used the Sparrow's magic anywhere in the North he
would be detected as a thief. But there were other
magics—and other places.

He let out a long, deep breath and straightened up.

It was not the path he would have chosen, but there was a way still open to him.

Bal-Simba looked up at the knock upon his study door. He wasn't surprised to see Moira standing there.

"Merry met, Lady," he said, leaning back in his oversize chair. "Come in."

"Merry met, Lord. Where is Wiz?" The words tumbled out almost as a single sentence.

"I sent him on an errand," Bal-Simba told her. "It seemed expedient."

"I heard something . . . Lord, did he really threaten magic against someone?"

Bal-Simba nodded and Moira closed her eyes in pain. "Lord, we have got to help him. We *must!*"

The giant wizard shook his head. "Neither of us has the skill, Lady. We are mere novices at this new magic and Wiz needs the help of the Mighty of his own world to do what needs to be done."

"Lord," she said formally, "I ask it of you and the Council that you do whatever is within your power to aid Wiz."

Bal-Simba smiled, showing his pointed teeth. "Willingly granted Lady, but what would you of us?"

"I have been thinking about this," Moira said. She stopped, gathering herself. Bal-Simba waited. The candles gave a bayberry tang to the air and the evening breeze made them flicker and the shadows dance on the wall.

"Lord," the redhaired witch said slowly, "we promised we would not Summon anyone hither, did we not?"

Bal-Simba looked at her narrowly. "That we did. A most solemn promise."

"So it was," Moira agreed. "But I do not recall ever promising not to *ask* others to help us."

"Eh?"

"Suppose we did not Summon another to us," she went on. "Suppose instead we used a Great Summoning to *send* someone to Wiz's people to appeal for their aid? Would the Council approve, do you think?"

The black giant's face split in an enormous grin. "Brilliant, Lady!" His laughter pealed off the ceiling. "You will wind up on the Council yet."

Then he sobered. "But it would be a dangerous journey."

"True, but think of what we could do if I brought Wiz back one of the Mighty of his world!"

"If *you* brought back . . . Oh no! No, My Lady! Wiz would have my head if I let you go haring off on such a scheme. And he would be richly entitled to it."

"But Lord . . ." Moira began.

"No! Not you. Someone else, but not you. And that's final!"

Wiz leaned back against the stone wall and shivered. He was so tired he could not keep his eyes open, but the least little movement or sound brought him awake with a start.

He was terribly hungry. His last meal had been at Duke Aelric's—how long ago? More than that, he was cold. Desperately, numbingly, bone-chillingly cold. He exhaled and watched his breath puff white.

It would be so simple to be warm again. But with that *thing* around he dared not use magic of any sort. He had only to begin forming a spell in his head and he could feel the quiver of the demon's anticipation. No matter how careful he was, he would be dead before he could ever complete the first line.

In theory he could write the spell out and then summon a demon to execute the code. But that wouldn't buy him much. In the first place, just the act of putting the spell down might be enough to send the demon arrowing after him. In the second place, even if the demon did finish the spell he wouldn't live to see it. He might come up with something that would finish the demon, but he wouldn't be there to see it.

Besides, he thought, *I've got a war to stop. I've got to get back to the Capital.*

He had been stupid to travel unprotected, he saw now. Moira had told him that wizards kept one or more defense spells primed and ready against sudden danger. He'd laughed and told her he didn't need such precautions. With his new magic he could launch a spell in an instant. He remembered that Moira hadn't looked happy, but she hadn't said anything.

If only he had time to prepare he knew he could take the beast, or at least get beyond its grasp. But he had come unsuspecting and unprotected and now it was too late.

He leaned back and thought of Moira. *At least she's safe*, he told himself as he drifted off into a restless half-sleep.

Twelve

STRANGER IN A STRANGE LAND

Never argue with a redhaired witch. It wastes your breath and only delays the inevitable.
                        —the collected sayings of Wiz Zumwalt

"I still think this is too dangerous," Bal-Simba grumbled for the twentieth time.

"Hush, Lord," Moira placed her hand gently on his massive ebony arm. "It is less dangerous for me than for any other. Who else knows as much about Wiz's world?"

"Will you not at least take a couple of guardsmen? Donal and Kenneth . . ."

"No, Lord. From what Wiz has told me they would only attract notice. And perhaps trouble."

"I suppose so." He sighed and looked around the room. Six other wizards were already at their places and the shadow on the sun dial crept ever closer to noon. "Best you take your place then, Lady. Remember, we will search for your signal every day two day-tenths after sunrise and two day-tenths before sunset. When we sense your signal we will perform the Grand Summoning. Do you have the cord?"

"Yes, Lord," Moira said, touching the pouch at her waist, "and thank you." She stretched up to kiss him on the cheek. "Please, when Wiz returns tell him not to worry." Then she turned and strode to her place in the center of the circle of wizards.

Bal-Simba frowned slightly at that. He did not tell her he had expected Wiz back days ago. The great black wizard was beginning to get worried.

"Merry part, Lady."

Moira dropped him a slight curtsey from her position in the center of the floor. "Merry meet again, Lord."

The chant swelled up in six-part harmony as the wizards sought to bend the forces of the Universe to their will. Moira stood straight-backed at her place in the growing maelstrom of magical energies. As the grayness swirled up about her Bal-Simba thought he saw her lip quiver.

Jerry Andrews rattled off the sequence to start compiling the program. Then he leaned back and the chair creaked. He sucked a lungful of the chill, air-conditioned air and rubbed his eyes. The after image of the screen was burned into his vision.

The fix he had just installed was a fairly elegant piece of work. He would have liked to show it to someone, but he was alone. His new cubicle mate was a day person and they seldom met unless Jerry was going home late while he was coming in early.

Whole damn company's going to hell, he thought sourly. *Next thing you know we'll be doing weekly project reviews with input from marketing.* When that happened Jerry intended to bail out. He was an old hand and he knew the signs.

Besides, he thought, *this place hasn't been the same since Wiz Zumwalt went away.*

Wiz's disappearance had shaken people up plenty. There were lights in the parking lot at ZetaSoft now and security guards patrolled the grounds and the buildings.

It wasn't unknown for a late-working programmer to be robbed or killed in a company parking lot, but it still struck hard when it happened close to home. Especially since they never found the body.

Besides, Wiz had been his friend. If it hadn't been for his taste for truly rotten puns, he would have been the perfect work companion.

Well, he thought, *just link this module in and . . .*

There was a sudden blurring of the world and Jerry Andrews realized he had a girl in his lap.

Since most of Jerry's lap was already taken up by his rather ample stomach, she promptly rolled off and landed on the floor.

She shook her mane of red hair and looked up at him, her green eyes wide. "Oh! Crave pardon, My Lord."

Jerry stared at her, stunned.

Moira rose quickly and clutched at the edge of the desk as the room spun around her. Even with Bal-Simba's improved technique she was still dizzy and weak from the aftereffects of the Summoning.

"Uh, hi," Jerry said for want of anything better to say. Not only was this totally unexpected, but she was gorgeous—if you liked busty redheads. Jerry liked busty anything.

"Greetings, My Lord," Moira said, still clutching the edge of the desk. "I am called Moira."

"I'm Jerry Andrews."

Her eyes widened again. "Oh, well met! Wiz has told me a great deal about you."

"Wiz? Wiz Zumwalt?"

"Yes. He is in trouble and he needs help."

"Wiz is alive?"

"Oh yes, but he is not here. There was a Great Summoning and Wiz . . ." she trailed off. "It is a rather long story, I fear, and perhaps a complicated one."

Jerry nodded. "That sounds like Wiz."

They couldn't stay here, he decided. Moira didn't have a badge and sooner or later the guard would come by. But it was early in the morning and there wasn't any place to sit and talk.

Jerry decided to fall back on his first instinct whenever he had a problem. "Let's get something to eat."

The Capital of the North did not so much end as it trailed off in a dispirited gaggle of buildings, set ever further apart along the high street as the rocky promontory slanted down to the surrounding plain. At the upper end of the town, the Front, the houses and shops of the well-to-do crowded close to the walls of the Wizards' Keep. The further you moved down the spine of rock, the meaner and poorer the town became.

Pryddian was no stranger to the Back of the Capital, but this was an area he had little occasion to visit. Down a twisting side street, so narrow the overhanging houses almost blocked the sun, there was a stable. So small and dark was the entrance Pryddian nearly passed the place before he realized it was what he sought. He kept the hood of his cloak up and looked up and down the street before ducking through the low door.

Inside the place smelt of moldy straw and horses ill-kept. The ex-apprentice wrinkled his nose at the odor and wondered what kind of person would keep a horse in such foul quarters.

"You want something?"

He whirled and saw a man standing beside one of the stalls, leaning on a pitchfork.

"I am looking for something."

The other advanced, still holding the pitchfork. Pryddian saw the man was short and powerfully built, with a permanent squint and lank dark hair. As he came closer Pryddian's nose told him he was as ill-kempt as his stable.

"If it's a horse we got 'em. If not, be on your way."

Pryddian licked his lips. If the rumors were wrong about this place he could be in a lot of trouble. But if they were true . . .

"I wish to meet—some people."

"Well, there's none here but myself. Now be off with you!" The man gestured threateningly with the pitchfork.

Pryddian almost turned and ran. But he was desperate, so he stood his ground.

"I need to reach the Dark League."

The man stopped. "You're an apprentice from the castle."

"Former apprentice. I seek a different master and I bring something with me that will be valued in other quarters."

"The way to the Dark League lies south and over the Freshened Sea, as everyone knows," the man said sullenly.

"No more. The City of Night is in ruins and the old roads are closed."

"That's nothing to me. I have no truck with the likes of those."

"A pity," said Pryddian, fingering his pouch. "I am prepared to pay for information." He reached in and pulled out a silver coin. "I pay well." He turned the coin around in his fingers so it flashed in the dim light.

"Well," said the stableman, lowering the pitchfork. "I don't say I know anything and I don't say I don't. But there are those that say that if you take the road west to the Wild Wood there is a place where you might be met, sometimes."

Pryddian held out the coin to the man's grasp. "Tell me more."

Damn! Jerry muttered as he peered around the corner into the lobby. The guard was at the desk reading a supermarket tabloid.

He pulled his head back and stopped to think. Moira had no business being in the building, of course, and right now Jerry didn't think he was up to inventing a good excuse for her presence. He had hoped the guard would be off making a round, but they did rounds at irregular intervals and in this case it looked like the next interval would come when the guard finished his reading.

"Okay," he whispered, "just stay close to me and

don't say anything." Moira nodded and they both saun-
tered around the corner.

As they came into the lobby the guard glanced up
briefly and went back to his reading. Moira was behind
and to one side of Jerry's bulk and the man obviously
missed her.

Jerry leaned over to sign out on the sheet. The guard
kept his nose buried in the tabloid.

"Good night," he said. The guard mumbled a response without looking up from his magazine. As they
went by, Jerry got a glimpse of the headline.

AMERICANS FALLING DOWN
ON THE JOB, PROF WARNS

Wiz took a deep breath and examined the scene in
front of him carefully, weighing the odds. There was a
faint reptilian stink in the air he didn't like at all, but he
was hungry enough and desperate enough to ignore it.

Most of the buildings in this district were utilitarian;
warehouses, barracks, workshops and the like. This one
was different. It was made of glossy dark marble instead
of rough hewn basalt. The slanting late afternoon sun
picked out the fine carving on the window and door
frames. The courtyard itself was paved in an elaborate
pattern of black and white and dark green blocks, laid
in a way that made the surface appear to swoop and
undulate wildly even though it was perfectly flat. Around
the court was a colonnade and extending off the colonnade at close intervals were open doors like gaping
black mouths. Wiz stood in a niche in the gateway for a
moment and studied the place.

He could edge around the courtyard under the colonnade, but that would expose him to anything that might
be hidden in the deepening shadows or lurking in one
of those rooms. The main entrance was directly across
from the gate and in this case the better part of valor
seemed to be a dash across the center of the court.

Place like this ought to have a lot more in it than a

barracks, he thought as he looked around carefully for the last time. *Then again, maybe not.* A place like this would attract looters.

He was halfway across the courtyard when he had another thought. *A place like this would have been guarded, too.*

Then the ground opened up beneath him.

Jerry and Moira stepped out the door into a world Moira found completely unsettling. The sky was gray but the night was not foggy. She wrinkled her nose. The air stank—an odd pungent reek like nothing she had ever smelled before.

In front of them was a large flat area whose black surface was marked with white lines. Here and there curiously shaped and brightly painted metal boxes or sheds stood on the dark surface. Lights on tall metal poles cast an orangish-pink glare over the scene. In the background she heard a continuous whooshing roar.

All in all, it was an unsettling place, stranger than she had imagined. Yet Wiz had come from here so it must be all right.

"Okay," Jerry told her, "the next question is where do we go to eat."

"My Lord, could we get pizza?"

"Right. Pizza it is. Little Italy's just around the corner. Come on, we'll walk." He set off toward the gate with Moira trailing behind.

The Little Italy was the sort of place that develops both regular clients and an idiosyncratic style over the years.

It was four o'clock on Saturday morning, but Mario, the owner, was behind the counter, baking loaves of bread to be used in the day's sandwiches. Jerry knew that at seven Mario's son would relieve him so the old man could go home and get a few hours sleep. Then he would be back for the lunch rush, take a nap in the afternoon and come back for the dinner crowd.

"Well, what do you want?" Jerry said as they came

up to the counter. Mario stopped shaping loaves of dough and came up to wait on them.

"Pizza," Moira told him.

"Yeah, but what do you want on your pizza? What toppings?"

"Toppings?"

"Those things listed on the board."

Moira frowned. "Lord, I cannot read your language," she confessed.

"Look in the bins then." He pointed at the row of stainless steel containers lining the rear of the counter.

"What are you having?" she asked Jerry.

"I'll have my usual. Sausage, ham, salami, pepperoni, hamburger and extra cheese. Medium, to eat here."

Mario nodded and got to work, swabbing the dough with spicy red tomato sauce redolent with basil and oregano. Next he scooped up handfuls of coarsely grated cheese and sprinkled them lavishly over the pizza. He didn't stop until the cheese hid nearly every trace of the sauce.

"Do you want the same thing?" Jerry asked.

"That is a great deal of meat," Moira said dubiously as the old man piled on the toppings. "I think I would prefer something else." She looked at Jerry. "I can have any of those I want?"

"Or any combination. If you come up with an unusual combination Mario names it after you." He nodded toward the board. "Wiz had one up there for a while. Something with jalapeños and pepperoni."

"I want Wiz's pizza."

Mario shook his head. "Don't got no jalapeños."

The hedge witch's brow furrowed and she went back to frowning at the bins, absently brushing back her coppery hair as it fell forward.

"Made up your mind yet, lady?" Mario asked, setting Jerry's pizza aside.

"What are those?" she asked, pointing to one of the bins.

"Anchovies," Jerry told her. "Highly salted fillets of tiny fish."

"I want some of those on mine," Moira said, looking over the bins. "And onions. Lots of onions. Oh, and is that garlic? Can I have some of that as well?

"And what is that on the end, floating in water?"

"That's feta. Goes on the gyros."

"It looks wonderful. I would have that on my pizza as well."

Jerry and Mario exchanged looks, but the counterman marked the order down.

"By the way lady, what's your name?"

"Why do you wish to know?"

"Because," Mario said, "if you eat that, I'm gonna put it on the menu and name it after you."

Even deathtraps need regular maintenance. This one had not been touched since the City of Night fell and it might have been damaged by the earthquakes touched off by the attack. That, and an instinct to keep his feet together, saved Wiz.

Wiz shook his head and climbed slowly to his feet. He was bruised, stunned and his ankles ached from the shock of landing, but he was alive and basically unhurt. He looked up and saw a strip of daylight disappearing as the trap door swung slowly closed with a creaking of unoiled hinges. The door didn't close all the way and by the dim light coming through the remaining crack, Wiz took stock of his surroundings.

On either side of the pit was a contrivance of rotting wood and rusty iron spikes as long as his arm. Wiz wasn't at all sure what it was supposed to do and he didn't want to think about it too closely. Whatever it was, it wasn't working and that had saved him.

Still, his position was precarious enough. The trap was shaped like a bottle, narrow above where the trap door was and wider down at the bottom. Even if the pit had not been twenty feet deep it would have been impossible to climb back out.

Wiz looked around. He didn't think he was going to

get out of this without help and right now he didn't
have the faintest idea where he could find help.

". . . so you see, My Lord," Moira said, "Wiz needs
help."

They had taken a booth in the back while they waited
for their pizza and Moira filled Jerry in on his cubicle-
mate's adventures and current plight.

Jerry considered. The more he considered, the less
likely the whole thing became. There was no way that
Wiz Zumwalt could ever have landed someone like the
redheaded dish sitting across from him. The rest of her
story didn't sound too plausible either.

Still . . . When a beautiful woman drops into your
lap out of thin air, the event demands some explanation. Hers was no more outrageous than any other
theory Jerry could come up with.

"Okay, I believe you," Jerry said. "But it's not going
to be as simple as you think."

"Pizza's ready," Mario called from the counter.

"Excuse me, I'll get them."

Moira fidgeted until he returned with the two steaming pizzas and paraphernalia. He set them down and
shook a dash of red pepper flakes onto his.

"Want some?"

Moira looked at the shaker and liberally lashed her
pizza with them.

"Careful, those are hot."

The hedge witch frowned and shook some flakes into
her palm and popped a hefty pinch into her mouth.

"So they are," she agreed and added some more to
her pizza.

Jerry sighed and took a bite of his own pizza. A
couple of slices of pepperoni fell off the heaped toppings and onto the table.

"What is that?" Moira asked, pointing and wrinkling
her nose.

"That's pepperoni," Jerry said. "Here," he picked a
slice off his pizza, "taste it."

The hedge witch drew away. "Thank you, no. It smells spoiled. I do not mean to be discourteous, My Lord, but I do not see how you can eat that."

Jerry eyed Moira's anchovy, onion, garlic and feta cheese pizza and said nothing.

They ate in silence for a few minutes, Jerry devouring about half his pie and Moira finishing her first slice.

"My Lord," Moira asked finally, "would you be willing to help us?"

"Oh sure. My deal with ZetaSoft is about through. But it isn't that simple."

He took another enormous bite of pizza and dribbled sausage crumbs and a piece of mushroom back onto his plate.

"If what you say is true you're going to need a lot more than me," Jerry said around the mouthful of pizza. "You're talking about taking a one-man program and turning it into full production software, with documentation, a bullet-proof user interface and probably a suite of programmers' tools as well."

Moira regarded him seriously but uncomprehending.

"Now, I presume there's some sort of deadline on this thing?"

"We need it as quickly as possible."

"Okay, that's do-able, but not with just one more programmer. We've got to have more people. We need a full team."

Moira helped herself to another slice of pizza. "Can we get them?"

Jerry considered. "There are some problems. For one thing it will be expensive."

Moira set down her slice of pizza. From the folds of her skirt, she produced a leather pouch. She opened the drawstring and tipped it up. A ringing cascade of golden coins rained out between the hot pepper flakes, grated parmesan and napkin dispenser. One or two of them rang tinnily against the pizza pans.

Behind the counter, Mario continued with his baking, oblivious to the fortune that had just been poured onto one of his formica tabletops.

Jerry stared and licked his lips, tasting pizza grease. Conservatively this redhaired space cadet had just put about $25,000 on the table—literally.

"Will that be enough?" Moira asked innocently. "I can get more, but it would mean another Summoning."

"Lady, for that kind of money we could buy a couple of software startups, programmers and all!" Jerry said fervently.

Then he stopped and frowned. "But that's only half of it. We'll have to recruit them and that's not going to be easy. You need the people fast, right?"

Moira nodded.

"You also need them good. They're going to have to pick up on a new language and a whole new operating environment and charge right into work. This is not gonna be a job for BASIC bozos or COBOL drones."

Moira nodded vigorously. She didn't know what BASIC or COBOL were, except that Wiz said they caused brain damage in those who used them.

"Now there's another thing. This has to be done secretly, correct?"

"We have no objection to telling those of your world how you aided us. Bal-Simba and the Council would not be so mean as to deny them credit."

"The Council?"

"The Council of the North. The wizards who oversee our land. They would gladly provide testimonial."

Jerry thought about what a letter of recommendation from a council of wizards would look like in his resume file.

"Totally secret," he said firmly. "And we need to find the people in a hurry."

"Is there some guild hall or chantry where we might go to find the people?"

Jerry considered while he polished off another slice.

"Well, the headhunters are out, that's for sure."

"I should hope so! We need these people alive."

"That's not what I meant—although with the kind of candidates headhunters turn up it can be hard to tell if they are alive."

"You make sport of me."

"A little, maybe. But it's going to complicate things." He reached for the last slice of pizza on his plate.

"So what we need," he summed up, "are people who are good enough to do the job, who are available and who can be made to believe you." *And*, he added silently, *who are crazy enough to come along on something this dangerous.* "That's not a common combination."

Jerry's eyes fell on one of the handbills tacked to the bulletin board. Even from this distance he could see the picture of the man in full armor and the woman in a long dress.

"I think," he said slowly, "I know just the place."

Jerry took Moira home with him for the night. "There are no motels close by and I live near enough to walk," he explained as they trudged the deserted streets.

Moira simply nodded, unconcerned by the proprieties.

She was yawning behind her hand by the time they reached his apartment. He offered her his bed but she would not hear of it. So he settled her on the couch in his cluttered living room with a blanket and pillow.

"Tomorrow we'll get an early start," he told her. "The place is about an hour and a half from here and it may take us all day to find the people we need."

"Good night, My Lord," Moira said, drawing the blanket over her.

Jerry left her and headed into the bedroom. *If she's not here in the morning I'm not going to believe any of this!* he vowed to himself.

Thirteen

RECRUITING DRIVE

*If you eat a live toad first thing in the morning,
nothing worse will happen all day long.*
                                        —California saying

To you or the toad.
                        —Niven's restatement of California saying

—well, most of the time, anyway . . .
—programmer's caveat to Niven's restatement of
                                        California saying

Wiz spent a cold, miserable night in the freezing pit.
With the dawn his prospects didn't look any brighter. If
he didn't get out of here he was going to die of hunger
and thirst. Actually, he'd probably die of the cold before he could die of hunger or thirst.

Face it, he told himself as he looked around for the
hundredth time, *the only way this could get worse
would be for the sorcerers to find you.*

Up above there was a scraping, as if something was
clawing at the cover of the pit. With a groaning of
hinges the cover moved aside and a shaft of sunlight
streamed down into the depths.

Wiz looked up and saw a huge scaled head peering

down at him. The dragon cocked its head to one side and ran its forked pink tongue over its ivory fangs.

Okay, Wiz thought, *so I was wrong*.

The dragon was a late adolescent, not yet grown to the point of acquiring true intelligence, but not far short of it. It was obviously one of the mounts for the Dark League's dragon cavalry, gone feral.

That meant the animal had all the ferocity native to dragon kind and not the least fear of man.

Again the forked tongue licked out, tasting the air in the pit. Then its lips curled back revealing even more of ripping fangs and the animal growled.

Wiz shrank back against the wall as the dragon inhaled deeply. Instinctively he crouched and turned his back even though he knew it wouldn't help him.

With a *whoosh* the dragon blasted a gout of flame down into the hole.

It was the shape of the trap that saved him. The dragon aimed his fire at Wiz, but Wiz was back out of sight under the overhang. That meant the full force of the dragon fire struck the rock walls of the neck.

The rock was wet, soaked from the eternal damp and the dragon's fire converted a good portion of the moisture into steam. The overhang protected Wiz, but the dragon got a burst of live steam square in the face.

Dragons are not immune to dragon fire, and still less to steam. The beast snapped its head back and roared a high whistling scream like a tea kettle gone berserk. It jerked back from the pit, whipped around and galloped off, roaring and screaming at the top of its lungs.

Son of a bitch! Wiz thought as the dragon's screams faded into the distance. He drew a deep lungful of moist warm air that stank of sulfur and dragon and looked around the pit in wonder.

I'm alive. Son of a bitch! He was still trapped in the pit and he was still hunted, but he was alive.

Wiz threw back his head and laughed at the wonder of it all.

* * *

"Rise and shine," Jerry said as he came out of the bedroom. "We need to get an early start today."

It was mid-morning, which didn't strike Moira as particularly early, but she didn't comment. She watched fascinated as Jerry pulled a couple of packages out of the refrigerator's freezer compartment and popped them into the microwave oven.

"Breakfast will be ready in a couple of minutes. The bathroom's over there if you need to freshen up." Moira nodded and went through the door. Most of the fixtures were strange to her, but fortunately Wiz had told her enough about his world that she was able to figure things out.

"Hope you like country breakfast," Jerry said. "I wasn't expecting company and it's all I've got."

The microwave beeped and Jerry removed the boxes. Moira opened hers and poked the contents dubiously with her fork. The eggs were tough, the sausage patty was tougher and had an odd metallic taste besides. The biscuit and gravy were steaming hot on the surface and icy in the interior. If this was the "fast food" Wiz had raved about there was something seriously wrong with the man's taste buds.

She looked over at Jerry, who was busy shovelling the contents of his box into his mouth.

Well, I have eaten worse, she thought. Wordlessly she began eating what was in front of her.

Jerry drank coffee with his meal. Moira, who had wanted to taste this beverage Wiz had talked about, took one sip and stuck with water.

The day was bright but overcast. Except for the odd stink in the air, it was very pleasant.

"It will take us about an hour and a half to get there," Jerry said as he unlocked the door of his Toyota. "Depending on traffic, of course."

He held the door open for Moira and then went around and slid behind the wheel. Once in he reached back behind himself and pulled a dark cloth strap diagonally across his body. Then he looked at her.

"Strap in."

Moira looked at him, puzzled.

"Reach behind you and pull the belt out, bring it
across and buckle it over beside the seat. No, you've
got to pull it out smoothly or it won't come all the way."

With much tugging and contortions, Moira got the
lap and shoulder belts fastened.

"It's for your own good," Jerry told the hedge witch.
"It will protect you in case of a crash."

"A crash?" Moira echoed faintly.

"Yeah, a wreck. Oh, but that almost never happens,"
he said, catching sight of her face.

Moira barely had the belt fastened when Jerry started
the car and pulled out in traffic. Moira found herself
speeding along at an incredible clip bare inches from
another car moving in the same direction. She looked
up and saw other vehicles charging toward them, only
to whiz by close enough to touch.

Moira gulped and turned white. Jerry, nonchalant
and oblivious, kept his eyes on the road.

They came to an intersection and Jerry whipped the
car through a right angle turn in the face of oncoming
traffic. To Moira it appeared they had missed the truck
bearing down on them by a hair's breadth. She stared
at the dashboard and tried to ignore the outside world.

There was a tremendous roar in her right ear. Moira
jumped at the sound and looked up involuntarily. To
her right, barely an arm's length away sat a man who
was going faster than they were. His arms were extended to the front and his beard and long hair were
whipped into a wild tangle by the wind. The hedge
witch caught a glimpse of the complicated black-and-
silver contrivance he was sitting on before he flicked
away around another car.

Jerry reached a place where the road narrowed and
climbed gently. Instead of slowing on the hill, he speeded
up. Moira moaned softly and concentrated hard on her

lap. Her hand grasped the door handle until the freckles stood out stark against the white knuckles.

Jerry glanced over at her. "Don't pull on that!" he said sharply. "If the door comes open in traffic we could be in real trouble." Moira jerked her hand off the handle as if it had turned into a snake. She reached forward with both hands to grab the dashboard tightly.

Jerry wasn't a very good driver, but he had been driving the California freeways for almost twenty years. He speeded up smoothly and edged left to merge into the center lane of traffic.

Out the right window Moira saw trees and greenery whizzing by so fast they were a blur. She looked left just in time to see Jerry jerk the wheel and slip the car into a space barely longer than the automobile.

They were sandwiched between two semis—roaring, bellowing monsters that threatened to spread Moira and the car between them like butter on a sandwich. She moaned again and closed her eyes.

"It's not bad today," Jerry said conversationally. "You should see it when the traffic's heavy."

Moira mumbled something and kept her eyes on her lap.

"I beg your pardon?"

"I said I hope I never do see that," Moira said more loudly. But she didn't lift her eyes.

Jerry looked at her sympathetically. He was a white knuckle flier himself. "Okay. If there's anything you need, just let me know."

"My Lord," Moira said fiercely, "the only thing I need is for this trip to be over as soon as possible."

Wiz ran his hand over the surface of the stone one more time. There had to be a way out of this. After all, the Dark League would need to retrieve anyone captured in the pit, wouldn't they?

He over looked at the spike-and-wood contraption in the pit. *Then again, maybe not.* It would be perfectly in character for the Dark League to leave a captive to rot in a place like this. Well, he wouldn't get anywhere brooding on that. He would have to see what he could find.

Wiz put both his palms against the wall and pushed. His left hand met unyielding resistance, but the stone under his right hand seemed to shift. He pushed again. Yes, the stone had moved!

A secret door. Wiz didn't know much about dungeons and mantraps, but that fitted perfectly with his conception of them. There must be a passage behind this wall.

He pushed again. The block shifted a little, but nothing else happened. He pushed the stones around it. Some of them also moved but no door opened. He put his fingers on the edge of the block and tugged hard. The stone moved slightly, but that was all.

He dropped his arms. Either he hadn't found the right stones to push or the door was broken. Either way, it seemed like the best thing to do was force the door rather than rely on the mechanism. For that he needed something to pry with.

He looked at the iron spikes of the trap reflectively. The metal was dark and pitted with rust, but it looked strong. Each spike was about three feet long and perhaps two inches around, crudely forged to a point on one end.

He grabbed the end of a spike and tugged. The spike moved ever so slightly. He dug his heels into the stone floor and wrenched back on the spike with all his strength. The spike moved some more.

Eventually he was able to work the spike free of damp and somewhat rotten wood. It was heavier than he expected and his biceps ached from the pulling, but he ignored that and attacked the loose stone in the wall.

The tool was clumsy and there wasn't much of a joint around the stone, but Wiz set to with a will, heedless of the noise he made. His technique was crude and it took a long time before he was able to pry the block part way out of the wall. With hands trembling from eagerness and fatigue, he jammed the bar into the joint and heaved one final time. The block clattered out onto the floor and Wiz thrust his hand into the opening.

Behind the stone was nothing but dirt and rock.

With a groan he threw the iron bar across the trap and slumped to the floor. It wasn't a doorway at all, just a loose stone in the wall. He looked up at the hole in the ceiling. The only way out of here had to be through that hole. That meant he was trapped unless he could climb the overhanging walls or build a ladder.

There was wood in the spiked device, but not nearly enough to reach the surface, even if it were all combined into a single long pole. Stick the spikes into the wall and climb them like a ladder? Not enough spikes. Besides, how would he get past the overhang?

Magic? With that demon on the loose he'd never live to complete the first spell.

And that was it, some half-rotten wood, a few pieces of iron and a block of stone levered from the wall.

A block of stone? Just one?

Wiz stood up and began to try the wall again. He found another loose stone, and then another and another. Most of the wall seemed to be loose, almost every other block could be pried free.

It was the cold, Wiz realized, the cold and the damp working at the stones. When this place was built the City of Night was kept magically warm. But with the fall of the League the magic had vanished and the stones had been subjected to alternate freezing and thawing. The walls of the trap had not been mortared and the working of the water had shifted the stones. The fact that most of the courtyard was paved in dark stone probably helped warm things up.

He picked up the spike and eyed the wall. This wasn't as elegant as a hidden passage and it was sure going to take a lot longer, but it would work. *Besides,* he thought as he attacked the first stone, *I don't have anything better to do*.

The real problem was going to be to get out enough

of the blocks to do some good without bringing the
whole place down on his head, but he had some ideas
on that and it would be a while before he really had to
worry.

Moira did not look up when they turned off the
freeway and headed up a poorly paved road. She did
not know how long they rocked along before they turned
again onto a dirt road and rattled over a cattle crossing.
The dust tickled her nose and made her cough, but she
still didn't look up.

"Well, here we are," Jerry said. "You can look now."
Moira kept staring at the dashboard, as if she intended
to memorize every wrinkle and crack in the vinyl.

"Come on, end of the line. Are you all right?"

"I think," Moira said judiciously, "that Wiz was far
braver than I ever knew."

She tore her eyes away from the dashboard and looked
around. They were in a small valley. The brown hills
above them were crowned with the gray-green of live
oak trees. There was dust everywhere. The stink was
still in the air, but not as strong here as in the city.

The field before them was crammed with vehicles standing cheek-by-jowl and all covered with a thin film of dust.
A steady stream of people filtered out of the field, stopped
at a table by the path and then headed over a low hill.
Most of them were weighted down with bags, boxes,
bundles and long poles of some light-colored wood.

"What is this place?"

"It's a war. These people come here to pretend to be
living in ancient times. Um, something like your place
but with no magic."

Moira looked around, bemused. "They come here to
pretend to be peasants?"

"Well, ah, not exactly."

"And why would the Mighty of your world wish to
pretend there is no magic?"

"Actually," Jerry explained, "some of them are pretending there is magic."

Moira opened her mouth to ask another question and then thought better of it. This was remarkably similar to conversations she had sometimes with Wiz.

"It gets a little complicated. But we've got a better chance of finding what we need here than anyplace else I can think of."

Moira nodded and followed him across the field toward the table. She wondered what awaited them at the end of that path.

Wiz leaned back against the wall and examined his handiwork. Even with the iron bar and the frost-loosened stones it had been a rough job to pry the blocks loose. His knuckles were scraped, his palms were blistered and his shoulders and arms ached from pulling on the prybar.

He had taken the stones in more-or-less a checkerboard around the walls and piled them in the center of the pit directly under the trap door. Standing on the pile, he could reach up to the narrow neck of the pit. He still had a long way to go before he would have enough blocks to reach the top of the trap.

This is going to take forever, he thought, rubbing his shoulders and looking up. But the sooner he got to it the quicker it would be done. Anyway, it took his mind off how cold and hungry he was.

Sighing, Wiz picked up the bar again and went back to work.

"Morning, My Lord, My Lady," said one of the three large young men sitting at the table. "Site fee's five bucks."

While Jerry peeled off several gray-green paper oblongs, Moira studied him, trying to make sense out of what she was seeing.

He was not a guardsman, of that Moira was sure. He had the body of a man but the face was still that of a child. He was dressed in a simple tunic over the sort of blue trousers Wiz called "jeans." He wore a red leather

belt with a cheap, gaudy sword thrust scabbardless
through it. Like a boy pretending to be a warrior, she
thought, but with more self-importance, as if he expected people to take him seriously.

"Okay," the man said. "Medievals are required on
site. You'll have to stop by the hospitaller and get a
loaner costume." He looked over at Moira in her long
green wool skirt and scoop-neck blouse. "Your friend's
fine."

Jerry was fitted with a slightly-too-small tunic in pur-
plish gray, trimmed with darker purple zig-zags and
tied about the middle with a piece of brown cord. The
color made him look ill, but the woman with the trunk
of clothing had nothing else that would fit someone of
his girth.

As they topped the rise Moira gawked at what was
spread out in the small valley below.

Nestled in among the live oaks and chapparal was an
encampment of hundreds of tents of different shapes,
sizes and colors. What seemed like thousands of people
in clothing of every shade and hue milled about the
valley like ants in an anthill.

In the center of the valley was a cleared space with
perhaps two hundred men whaling away at each other
with wooden weapons. The smack of wood on wood,
the clank and clatter of steel and the shouts echoed off
the hillsides.

For an instant she thought they were actually hurting
each other. Then she saw a warrior who had dropped
like a sack of sand under the blow of a pole-ax roll out of
the fight, stand up and walk off the field. As the fighter
came away from the battle, he took off his helm and
shook out a mane of long blond hair. Moira realized
with a shock it was a woman.

"Excuse me, My Lord, My Lady," came a voice
behind them, "but you're blocking the trail."

As they stepped aside a boy of perhaps fourteen
struggled past them loaded down with several bundles
and a half-dozen pole weapons. When he passed, Moira

saw the heads were padding wrapped with some kind of silvery material.

At the bottom of the hill was a market. There were booths along the trail, and tables with cloths spread over them. The smell of roasting meat rose from the food stands and people milled and jostled through the throng, admiring wares, talking, eating and sometimes buying.

Most of the people seemed to be dressed in rags and patches, although here and there a man or a woman might be more substantially dressed. Everyone and everything was covered with fine brownish dust.

Many of the men and a few of the women were wearing what she recognized as armor, mostly concoctions of padded cloth, leather and light metal that looked as if it would come apart at the first serious blow.

Moira looked around eagerly, but missed the thing she had expected to see.

"Where is the hiring block, My Lord?"

"The what?"

"The hiring block. This is a hiring fair, is it not?"

"No, not exactly. In fact most people come here to forget their jobs."

"Then how are we to find the ones we need?"

"We'll have to ask. I think we need to find a herald first."

A man in a green cloak with crossed trumpets approached them. "Excuse me, My Lord, but did I hear you say you needed a herald?"

"Uh, yeah, I have an announcement I'd like you to make. We're looking to hire a number of programmers and other computer specialists for a rather special job."

"And so you came here?" The herald nodded. "Smart move. I think there are more computer types per square foot at one of these wars than at anything this side of an ACM meeting."

"ACM?" Moira asked.

"Association for Computing Machinery, a professional group," Jerry told her. "Anyway," he said turning back to the herald, "we're looking for systems-level programmers, systems analysts, documentation specialists, people with real-time or process control experience—if we can find them—and compiler writers."

"No machine operators?" the herald asked. "Employment or contract?"

"Contract. Probably three to six months."

"Well, normally they frown on even mentioning computers at these events," the herald said. "King Alfonso is a particular stickler for authenticity so you're not going to get it announced at court. But I don't think there'd be any real objection if I announced it in the merchant's area and the non-medieval camping area."

"Great. Uh, is there any place I can sit and talk to people?"

"You can borrow my pavilion," the herald said. "I want to talk to you about this anyway. I'm looking for a change myself."

The herald's pavilion turned out to be an aluminum-framed camping tent hung with banners and set well off to the side of the encampment.

Moira sat at a folding table under an awning, sipping lemonade from a wooden goblet and watching the knot of people who had gathered in response to the herald's announcement.

They didn't look like the Mighty Moira was used to. There wasn't a full gray beard among them and none of them showed the stately bearing and serene self-control she associated with powerful magicians.

The first one into the tent was a dumpy dark-haired woman in a blue-and-silver gown whose long dagged sleeves nearly trailed in the dust. Far too elaborate for such a place, Moira thought, especially since these people did not have cleaning spells.

Behind her were a tall dark-haired woman with piercing dark eyes and a shorter, sandy haired man with a neat spade beard who seemed to be her husband.

Next to them was a lean man going bald on top with his remaining hair pulled back into a pony tail.

She wondered how Jerry was explaining her world's needs to them.

"You certainly seem qualified, Ms. Connally," Jerry said to the woman sitting across from him. "I can't tell you the nature of the job until you sign the nondisclosure agreement."

"Judith, please," the dark-haired woman in the blue-and-silver brocade gown corrected.

"I can tell you it is a short-term contract, probably about six months. The assignment requires that you live on-site until it is completed. The site is remote and rugged and contact with the outside world is very limited."

"A black site?"

Jerry recognized the reference to an ultra-secret project where the programmers were kept totally isolated.

"Kind of dark gray, actually."

Her eyebrows went up. "SDI, right?"

Jerry smiled, as he had seen so many recruiters do. "I am really not at liberty to say.

"Now," he went on, "I should also warn you that there is an element of physical risk in this."

The other's eyes narrowed. "This is legal, isn't it?"

"Yes," Jerry said, "That is, there is absolutely no law against what we are doing." *At least not in California,* he added mentally. *I think Massachusetts still has a law against practicing witchcraft.*

"Now, tell me a little bit more about your background."

The interviews went quickly. Jerry wasn't interested in playing interviewer games, there was no application to fill out and no one had brought a resume to an SCA war. Besides, Jerry was a programmer himself, not some personnel bozo who only had the vaguest notion of what the job entailed.

And nobody is going to ask me to fill out an EEOC report on this one.

He had just talked to the eighth candidate when the herald, who went by the name of ali Akhan, stuck his head into the tent with a peculiar expression on his face.

"His Majesty, King Alfonso of Seville," the herald announced.

Jerry wasn't up on the etiquette, but he stood up as the king entered.

"Your Majesty."

King Alfonso turned out to be a tall, rather lean man in his mid-twenties with an olive complexion and dark, unruly hair. He was wearing a crown of sheet brass set with agates, dark hose, a black velvet doublet and riding boots. A broadsword hung from his hip on a white belt. His clothes were powdered with the brownish dust from the site.

The king stuck out his hand. "Karl Dershowitz," said the king with a distinctly Texas drawl.

"Jerry Andrews."

"So tell me," said the king, pulling up the stool, "what's this super-secret job you're recruiting for?"

"How did you find out?"

He shrugged. "It's all over camp. Did you know you're with the CIA and you're recruiting programmers who are expert swordsmen to fight their way into Afghanistan so they can tap into the Russians' SDI computer network?"

"It's nothing like that," Jerry said uncomfortably.

"Of course not." The king smiled. "If anyone in this bunch has a choice between a good story and the truth, the good story will win out every time."

"Look, I'm sorry if we're interfering with your event, but we needed some people with special talents in a hurry."

The king waved that off. "What interference? You're off in a corner in someone's pavilion talking to people one at a time. Oh, a couple of people did come to me to complain about the announcement you had the heralds make." He snorted. "Down in Texas we called them piss ants."

"Then why are you here?"

"Because my current contract just ran out and the job sounds interesting—Afghanistan or no. Could you tell me about it?"

The next candidate was as unimpressive as the king—Karl, Jerry corrected himself—had been impressive.

At first he thought the kid had wandered in by mistake. He was slightly plump in the face. A downy blond beard decorated his cheeks. His eyes were brown, dark in contrast to his skin and hair. He was wearing a pair of blue jeans and a satin tunic that had probably once been purple but was now faded and stained to something resembling blue. A cheap hunting knife was clipped to his belt and a wooden goblet hung from a leather thong.

Without waiting for an invitation he sat down. "Thorkil du Libre Dragonwatcher. I understand you're looking for programmers."

Jerry eyed him without enthusiasm. "We are. Are you a programmer?"

"Yeah," he said flushing, "and I'm damn good."

"Do you have a degree?"

"I attended Cal Tech."

"Yes, but do you have a degree?"

The kid fidgeted under Jerry's stare.

"Okay, so maybe I don't, but I'm *good*."

Jerry sighed to himself. Well, if you wanted to find frogs you had to kiss a few toads—or however that saying went.

"We need people with experience."

"I've got experience," he protested. "I've worked in TOS 1.4, AmigaDOS and ProDOS."

Jerry, who didn't consider a computer a computer unless it ran at least BSD Unix, winced. "Those are game machines."

"The Amiga's no game machine," the kid flared. "Neither is the ST. Besides, I've done real-time programming in Forth on a Trash 80 Model I."

That was slightly more interesting. From Moira's confused recitation of what Wiz had done, Jerry knew he had used the Forth language for some of the programming. Besides, anyone who could do anything useful in real time on something as limited as a Model I clearly had talent.

"Okay," he said, making a mark on the clipboard, "I'll let you know later."

Panting, Wiz jammed his pry bar into the joint and leaned on it with all his strength again. The stone shifted more. He dropped the bar, got his fingers on the edge and tugged at the stone. The rock moved slightly and its neighbors shifted with it. Instinctively Wiz jumped backwards, lost his balance and went tumbling down the side of the rock pile. With a crash and a roar a whole section of the neck gave way. Stones cascaded down into the pit and went bouncing in every direction.

Coughing from the dust, Wiz looked up. The side of the neck had slumped in on itself. Half the pit was full of blocks and rubble and the vertical wall had collapsed into a steep incline that led out of the trap and into the courtyard.

Wiz shook his head to clear it. *Well, that works too.* Slowly and carefully, he climbed up the pile of rubble and out of the pit.

"Better than I expected," Jerry told Moira at the end of three hours. "We've got systems programmers, documentation specialists, real-time programmers and people with control and simulation experience here."

"Are they of the Mighty?"

"Well, they're a pretty high-powered bunch, especially considering we had to put together the team at such short notice. That first one, Judith Connally, has done real-time programming on military projects. Mike and Nancy Sutton, the husband and wife team, are a process control programmer and a documentation specialist respectively."

He made a face. "If I know Wiz, we're gonna *need* a documentation specialist. Anyway, we've got some good potential here."

"How will you select them?"

"Well, Moira, it's your show. You've got the ultimate say in who we choose."

"I will be guided by you in this, Lord," Moira said. "I know little of such matters. But there is one I would like included. The young one. Thorkil du Libre Dragonwatcher."

Jerry raised his eyebrows. "That kid? He's not in the same league with most of the rest of the people and I think he's a pirate to boot."

"I thought he said he was a programmer."

"A pirate is a kind of programmer. He steals other people's software."

"Nonetheless, I would have him."

Jerry shrugged. "I think he's going to be more trouble than he's worth, but okay. I'll add him to the list." He made a note on the pad and looked up.

"Why do you want him, anyway?"

"A feeling," Moira said. "Just a feeling."

"A premonition?"

Moira smiled. "In this place? No, I just feel that he has something to offer. I do not know, perhaps he reminds me of Wiz."

Jerry made a face. "Now that you mention it, there is a certain resemblance." He scribbled another note on the list. "Okay, then. That's our team."

"Now what?" Moira asked.

"Now we call them back, explain the terms and give them the contract to sign." He made another face. "This is where it is going to get *real* interesting."

There was food in the black and white palace after all. Wandering what had been the kitchen, Wiz found half a flat round loaf of bread and several strips of dried meat which had fallen behind a counter.

The meat was probably tough before it had been

dried and it was certainly stringy. The bread was heavy
and full of what seemed to be sawdust, but after two
days and a night in the pit Wiz was in no mood to
complain. He wolfed down his find and then curled up
in a corner.

Maybe there is justice in the world after all, he
thought drowsily as he drifted off.

". . . and you receive a signing bonus of two point
three ounces of gold and a rate of pay of two point three
ounces of gold per week for the duration of the contract," Jerry told the selected group of programmers
gathered under the awning.

"Gold?" asked ali Akhan, the herald.

Jerry shrugged. "Simplifies matters for the employer."

"This guy's either a libertarian or a drug smuggler,"
Karl Dershowitz said. Jerry didn't reply.

Moira smiled. "We really are . . ."

". . . not at liberty to say," Nancy Sutton finished for
her. "We know the drill."

"Okay," said Cindy Naismith, a short, slender woman
with close-cropped brown hair. "What about performance penalties?"

"None. We can tell you so little about the project
until you get on-site that it wouldn't be fair. However
there is a bonus if the contract is completed on time to
the client's satisfaction."

He pushed the clipboard out into the middle of the
table. "If you accept the terms, sign this agreement."

Ali Akhan sat down and began to read through the
six-page document. Jerry waited to see what happened
when he got to the non-disclosure clause. The contract
was something they had whipped together out of bits
and pieces of contracts Jerry had in his computer at
home. It was pretty much the standard verbiage—except for the non-disclosure agreement.

". . . if this agreement is breached, employee will
immediately be struck by lightning and hereby agrees
to forfeit his immortal soul . . ." ali Akhan read out. He

looked up angrily. "What kind of shit is this? I mean it's very funny, but who's gonna believe that nonsense?"

Moira smiled sweetly. "Oh, I think we can contrive to convince, My Lord."

"This is weird," he muttered, reaching for a pen. Then he looked up and grinned. "You don't want me to sign in blood do you?"

"Oh no, that will not be necessary," Moira told him seriously.

Ali Akhan gave her a funny look and then signed his name. Taking the contract back, Jerry saw that his real name was Larry Fox.

Several other people looked at them strangely after they finished reading the contract, but none of them refused to sign it—much to Jerry's surprise. Either things were slow in the Valley or these people were even stranger than most computer types.

Considering the milieu . . .

"Fine then," he told the assembled group. "We will meet at the back parking lot of Los Alamitos Mall at seven o'clock Wednesday morning. Have someone drive you or leave your cars at home. Transportation will be provided from the meeting point to our destination.

"Come packed and ready to leave. Oh yeah. Don't have anyone wait for you. Security, you know."

Several people looked at him strangely.

"Gotta be SDI," someone muttered.

"I wish we could leave sooner," Moira said as the newly formed team dispersed.

"I know, but we've got to give people time to get their affairs in order. Three days is really pushing it."

"Oh, I know, but I just wish . . ." She looked up at him. "Besides, I miss Wiz terribly."

Jerry studied her expression. "I'm getting kind of anxious to see him myself."

Wiz stayed at the black and white palace for as long as he dared. But there wasn't any more food to be found in the kitchen or the palace storerooms. Besides, the Dark League's search was working its way down into the waterfront neighborhood. He could hear the wizards calling to each other as they searched the streets and warehouses.

With the search moving to the waterfront, he decided the best thing he could do was to head back to the top of the town. Maybe there would be places up there heated by the volcano.

"Is there aught else to do here?" Moira asked after the last of their new employees had signed and left.

"Well, we could head back tonight, but there are a couple of more people here I'd like to talk to. The king has offered us space in his motorhome. Would you mind spending the night?"

"If we left now we would have to drive back the way we came in darkness?"

"Yes."

"Then let us stay the night," Moira said firmly. She wasn't looking forward to the return trip in daylight and the idea of doing it at night was more than she could stand.

While none of the City of Night was warm, there were definitely some parts that were colder than others. Whether because of the natural microclimate or magic, Wiz didn't know. But this street was especially cold.

Water had trickled down the street and frozen into a layer of glare ice, dark, shiny and unbelievably slick.

Wiz picked his way up the edge of the street carefully. The last thing he needed now was a broken leg.

He was so busy watching his step that he forgot to watch where he was going. He turned the corner and literally collided with a black-robe wizard.

They were both knocked flat, but Wiz recovered quicker. He spun onto his hands and knees and took off like a sprinter around the corner.

The wizard pounded around the corner hot on his heels and shouting at the top of his lungs. "*I have found him. To me! To me! I have found HHHHIIIIIIIIIIM-MMMMMMM . . .*"

Wiz ducked into a doorway and looked back to see the wizard go sliding by, flat on his back with his arms and legs waving in the air like a big black beetle. He almost laughed. Then he thought better of it and took off running as fast as he could.

When he stopped running he was more than a half a mile from the icy street. He sank to his heels with his head between his knees while he gasped in great lungfuls of the frigid air. Gradually his breath came back and he began to study his surroundings.

Behind him was a gate big enough to lead an elephant through. Through it he could see a courtyard with rooms opening onto it.

One place is as good as another, he thought. Keeping a wary eye for traps, he started exploring the building.

Nearly three hours later, Wiz stepped through the last smashed door and wrinkled his nose. The storeroom had been thoroughly ransacked, more than once from the looks of it. Besides, it smelled as if something had been lairing here.

But there was nothing here now and a storeroom seemed like the best place to find food. The buildings around this courtyard had apparently been barracks, with the workrooms, armories and storerooms that supported the soldiers. The armories had been stripped to the walls and the barracks were deserted, but there was a chance there might be something left in the storerooms.

This one didn't look promising, he admitted as he poked among the rubble. There were bolts of cloth that had been pulled off the shelves, torn and trampled. Boxes of iron rivets had been broken open and the rivets scattered across the floor. Bundles of leather thongs, cracked and rotted, hung from pegs on one wall. It didn't seem like the kind of place where food had been kept.

Still, he was here and a quick check of the other buildings showed nothing more promising. The barracks kitchen had been easy to locate, but there was nothing to eat there. What hadn't been carried off had been consumed by rats or larger animals.

The City of Night was more complex than he had ever imagined, Wiz thought vaguely as he poked in the piles of rubbish in the corners and turned over debris on the floor. Somewhere there had to be food storehouses to feed the people who had lived here. But he didn't have the faintest notion where.

Wiz stopped short. There, on the very top shelf was a pottery jar with a familiar shape.

Pickled fish, he realized. There were some districts along the Freshened Sea where salted fish was packed in vinegar with garlic, onions, vegetables and spices and sealed in crocks to age and ferment. To the people of those districts pickled fish was a delicacy. Everyone else made jokes about it, especially about its tendency to produce gas.

Apparently the jokes about pickled fish were universal and whoever used this room had kept a personal cache here rather than listen to them.

With shaking hands he took the jar off the shelf. It was full and the clay seal around the lid was unbroken. Quickly he smashed the lid with a piece of wood from the floor.

The contents were dark brown, definitely past their prime and Wiz had made his share of jokes about pickled fish. But this was the most delicious thing he had ever eaten. Heedless of the promissory rumblings of his stomach, he finished the entire crock.

At 7:00 A.M. the group gathered in the back parking lot of the shopping center.

They were carrying everything from designer luggage to backpacks. One or two of them had laptop computers under their arms. Jerry wondered how well those would work where they were going. A couple more had apparently believed the Afghanistan story enough to bring cases of liquor with them. That, at least, would be useful, he decided.

"Okay, people," he called out. "Moira here, will . . ." he looked around. "Where's Moira?"

"Here, Lord." Moira came trotting up with a large flat box under her arm.

"What's in the box?" Jerry asked her.

"A present." She handed it to him. "Will you hold it for me? Be careful not to tip it." Then she looked up and frowned at the sky.

"The haze will make it hard to tell the time," she said. "That complicates matters. Perhaps it would be best to wait for the afternoon time."

"That's smog and it's not going to clear today," Jerry told her. "If you need to tell the time, use my watch." He stripped it off his meaty wrist and handed it to her.

Moira shook her head. "I must know the time in day-tenths after sunrise," she said. "Not the time by your local system."

"Day-tenths?"

"One tenth of the time between sunrise and sunset."

"Wait a minute," said a small man with the face of an intelligent mouse and a mop of brown hair. He stripped off his own wristwatch, and began punching the tiny buttons beneath the face.

"There you go," he said handing the watch to her. "I haven't set it against the Naval Observatory in a couple of months so it may be a tenth of a second off, but I hope it will do."

Moira studied the madly spinning numbers on the display. They looked something like the numbers Wiz used, but she didn't know them well enough to use them.

She handed the watch to Jerry. "Here, My Lord. Tell me when it is two day-tenths."

"Coming up on it now."

"Hey, guys!"

Thorkil du Libre Dragonwatcher—Danny Gavin, Jerry

reminded himself—came running across the parking lot with a back pack slung over one shoulder and bouncing against his hip.

"You are late," Moira said severely.

"Hey, I'm sorry. I had to hitch, okay?"

Moira opened her mouth to say something else, but Jerry interrupted her.

"Time in thirty seconds."

Moira handed her box to Jerry and gestured them all into a tight group. Then she drew out the golden cord Bal-Simba had given her and laid a circle perhaps fifteen feet in diameter in the dusty surface of the parking lot, muttering as she did so.

"Now," she said, turning to the programmers. "You must all stand close together and above all, stay within the circle. Do not step outside it or break it in any way."

Checking the watch Jerry had given her, she raised her wand and began to chant.

At first no one said anything. Then the astonishment began to wear off and the cracks started.

"Is this where the flying saucer shows up?" someone asked.

"Scotty, beam me up," someone else called out.

Moira ignored them and went on with the chant.

"Next stop Oz," Judith chimed in.

And then the world dissolved.

PART III: COMPILE

Fourteen

EMPLOYEE ORIENTATION

You never find out the whole story until after you've signed the contract.
> *—programmer's saying*

They were crowded together on a smooth flagged floor. Looming over them on a dais at one end of the room was an enormous black man in a leopard skin loincloth and a necklace of bones. To his right was a blonde woman in a long gown.

The sun streamed in through narrow windows in the stone walls and struck shafts of gold through the dusty air.

At the points of the compass stood eight men and women in long blue robes, each holding a silver or ebony wand and each surrounded by glowing runes inscribed on the stone floor. Further back stood grim men in chain mail armed with swords and spears.

The programmers goggled.

Finally a female voice from the back of the group broke the silence. "Toto," she whispered hoarsely. "I don't think we're in Kansas any more."

"Merry met," the black man boomed out. "I am called Bal-Simba. I am speaker for the Council of the North and of the Mighty of this place. We are your employers."

"Did anyone bring a copy of that contract?" someone muttered.

Moira curtseyed. "Merry met, Lord. This one is called Jerry Andrews, of whom Wiz spoke often." She gestured to the rest of the group. "These others are also of the Mighty of their place. Jerry enlisted their aid."

Bal-Simba smiled, showing his teeth filed to points. "Excellent. Excellent. My Lords, Ladies, if you will come with me I will show you to your accommodations." The wizards at the compass points moved out of the way as he descended the dais and the guards stepped back. With a dozen thoroughly bewildered programmers trailing in a clump, the giant wizard left the chantry through the carved oak doors and down the stone steps into the flagged courtyard.

The morning sun made the stone walls glow warmly and cast glints of light off the windows. Banners floated from staffs at tower tops, peacock blue and brilliant green against the sky and clouds. Around them men and women stopped to stare at the newcomers and the newcomers slowed to stare back.

"Look!" one of the group pointed off to the east. A gaggle of six dark shapes stood out against the high white clouds, shapes with far too much neck and tail to be birds.

The entire group stopped dead in the courtyard. The programmers craned their necks and shielded their eyes in an effort to see better.

"Are those . . . ?"

"Jesus, they're dragons!"

"How the hell would you know? You've never seen a dragon."

"I have now."

The dragons came closer, dropping lower and making it easier to pick out the details. Their guides made as if to move on but the programmers stood rooted in place.

"Hey, there are people on them!"

The Californians watched awestruck as the dragons glided around the tallest tower in tight V formation, wingtips almost touching as their riders pulled them into the turn. Then as one, the beasts winged over and fell away toward their eyrie in the cliff beneath the castle.

And then they were gone. The newcomers let out a sigh with a single breath and everyone started across the courtyard again.

The programmer standing next to Bal-Simba, a heavy-set dark-haired woman wearing a faded unicorn T-shirt, touched his arm.

"Thank you," she said.

"For what, My Lady?"

She nodded toward where the flight of dragons had disappeared, her eyes shining. "For that. For letting me see that."

Bal-Simba looked at her closely. To him dragons were simply part of the World, sometimes useful, often dangerous, but nothing extraordinary. He had never stopped to think about what dragons on the wing meant. Now, confronted with her wonder, he saw them in a new light.

"Thank you, My Lady," he said gravely.

Not everyone was impressed with the dragons' performance. One who wasn't at all impressed was the leader of the flight.

"Where were you on that last turn?" he demanded of his wingman as they crossed the cavern that served as roost and aerie for the dragon cavalry.

"There's turbulence on the west side of the tower at this time of day," his wingman explained. "I figured it would be safer to open it up a little."

"Turbulence, nothing! That was sloppy. What did you think you were doing hanging out there?"

Behind them the riders and grooms were leading the dragons to their stalls, the rider at the head, holding the bridle and talking gently to his mount and a groom at each wingtip and two at the tail to see that the dragons did not accidently bump and perhaps begin to fight.

Other teams of grooms hurried about, removing saddles and unfastening harnesses. The armorers removed the quivers of magic arrows from the harness and counted each arrow, carefully checking the numbers against the tally sticks before returning them to the armory.

In spite of the lanterns along the walls the aerie was gloomy after the bright morning. The entrance was a rectangle of squintingly bright white. It was noisy as well. The rock walls magnified sound and the shuffle of beasts, the shouts of the men and the occasional snort or hiss of a dragon reverberated through the chamber.

Both dragon riders ignored the noise and the bustle, intent on their conversation. The other members of the troop avoided them until the chewing out was done.

"Playing it safe, sir."

"Safe my ass! Mister, in combat that kind of safety will get you killed."

The wingman bridled. "Sir, there is no one left to fight."

The Dragon Leader grinned nastily. "Want to bet? Do you think the Council keeps us around because we look pretty?"

The wingman didn't answer.

"Well," the Dragon Leader demanded. "Why do you think we exist?"

"To fight, sir."

"Too right we exist to fight. And how much good do you think you're going to be in a melee if you've trained your mount to open wide on the turns? Mister, in my squadron if you are going to do something, you are going to do it right. We exist to fight, and war or no war, you will by damn be ready to fight. Is that clear?"

"Yes sir," the wingman said woodenly, eyes straight ahead.

"Every maneuver, every patrol, you will treat like the real thing. Remember those checklists they drilled into you in school? Well mister, you will live by those checklists. As long as you're in my squadron you will do *everything* by the checklist. Is that clear?"

"Yes, sir."

"Then see to it. And if you float out like that on a turn again you'll spend the next two weeks on stable duty! Now see to your mount."

The Dragon Leader watched the man go and frowned. With the Dark League crushed there were no enemy dragons to face. It was hard to keep an edge on his men. The kid was good, one of the best of the crop of new riders that had come along since the defeat of the Dark League, but he didn't have the same attitude as the men and women who had fought through the long, bitter years of the League's ascendancy.

He could have made it easy on himself and insisted on an experienced second. But somebody had to work these young ones up and if it wasn't done right they wouldn't be worth having if they had to fight.

Meanwhile his muscles were stiff, his flying leathers soaked with sweat and he stank of dragon and exertion. He turned and walked out of the aerie toward the riders' baths.

At the door the Dragon Leader looked back and sighed. *In some ways it was easier when we were at war.*

". . . and there you have it, My Lords," Bal-Simba said finally. "That is our situation and that it what we need."

Jerry, Karl, Bal-Simba and Moira sat around the table. They had talked the day away and a good part of the night. Moira was hoarse, so Bal-Simba had taken over filling in the background while Jerry and Karl shot questions.

The remains of dinner, bread, fruit and cheese, sat on the sideboard and a glowing globe on a wrought iron stand beside the table gave them light.

The soft evening breeze ruffled through the room and stars spangled the velvety blackness outside. Idly Jerry wondered what time it was. Their watches had stopped working at the moment of transition. After midnight, he decided.

The rest of the programmers were bedded down somewhere but Bal-Simba was eager to get started and Jerry was too keyed up to sleep anyway.

"Well, it's hard to say until we've gone over the work that's already been done," Jerry said. "If the libraries and tool kit are sufficiently developed . . ."

"I think it would be best if we left the technical details until Wiz returns," Moira said. Out of the corner of her eye she saw Bal-Simba shift uneasily. "He is the only one among us who really understands them."

"Anyway, the outlines are clear enough," Jerry said. "As I told Moira back in Cupertino I think this is do-able, especially given the work Wiz has already put into it."

"How soon do you need all this?" Karl asked.

"As soon as possible," Bal-Simba told him. "Perhaps a fortnight at most."

Jerry and Karl looked at each other.

"Well," Karl said, "no matter where you go, some things don't change."

Bal-Simba frowned. "Is there a problem?"

Jerry sighed. This was the point where you usually started lying to the client. But this was a very unusual situation and an even more unusual client. Besides, there was no one on this world to undercut them and steal the contract by overpromising.

"Look," he said, leaning forward to rest his elbows on the table, "the truth is, it will take us months to do this job right."

"But Wiz put together his attack on the Dark League in a matter of days!" Bal-Simba protested.

"Right," Jerry nodded. "What Wiz did was create a set of tools and build some simple programs, uh, spells with them. But there's a big difference between something that an expert hacks together for his own use and a production system."

"You need something anyone can use, right?" Karl asked.

"Any wizard," Bal-Simba amended. "But yes, basically."

"Okay, that means you need a lot more support, error checking and utilities and libraries. And it's all got to be wrapped up in a neat package with no loose ends."

The huge wizard thought about that for a minute. "How long will all this take?"

"We won't know that until after we've examined what's been done already and had a chance to talk to Wiz."

"You can begin the examination tomorrow," Bal-Simba said, rising. "There is no need to wait until Sparrow returns." He turned to Moira. "My Lady, will you escort them to their chambers?"

"If you please, My Lord, there is another matter I wish to discuss with you. I will ring for a servant."

The serving man was yawning when he arrived, but he came quickly and ushered the visitors out of Bal-Simba's study.

"Now," Moira said as the door closed behind them, "where is Wiz?"

"Well, as to that, My Lady . . ."

Her face darkened. "Something has happened to him, has it not?"

"Well . . ."

"*Has it not?*" She tried to shout but her strained vocal cords could only produce a whisper.

"We do not know," Bal-Simba told her. "He went off into the Wild Wood and no one has seen him since."

"Fortuna!" Moira stared. "You let him wander into the Wild Wood alone?" Then she laughed bitterly. "And you were concerned about *my* safety?"

Wiz tiptoed down the corridor, stopping every few feet to listen. Outside the bright daylight promised warmth the sun failed to deliver.

He was desperately hungry, but he was past feeling the pangs. In the last two days he had turned up nothing that looked edible. He wasn't the only scavenger going through the rubble. Rat droppings abounded, as did signs of larger, less identifiable creatures.

He stopped to listen again, pressing himself flat against the wall as he did so. He had learned caution the hard way. Twice more since he left the palace with the trap he had barely avoided blundering into searching wizards of the League. Once he ducked into an open doorway just as two of them came around a corner not ten feet in front of him. Another time one of them caught a glimpse of him from one street over. The wizard made the mistake of calling for help and Wiz scampered away before he could get close.

He was surprised that no one had used magic to locate him. Even with the competing magical remnants in the City of Night it should have been easy for wizards who had stood in his presence to track him down, especially since he dared not leave the city. The land beyond the walls was as frozen and barren as Antarctica. Away from the shelter of these buildings he'd be dead in a day and he was sure the wizards knew it.

Perhaps Dzhir Kar was playing with him, stretching out the agony. Through his exhaustion, Wiz realized he could not win. Sooner or later, he had to use magic or fall to the searching wizards or the danger of this place.

Well, not yet. He was still alive and still free. At this minute finding food and warmth were more important to him than his ultimate fate. Moving as quietly as he could he moved down the corridor to the next door.

This place must have been pleasant once, or as pleasant as any in this benighted city ever had been. The building itself was mostly underground, a gloomy mass of tunnels and small rooms dimly lit by slowly fading magic globes. But this wing was built into the face of a cliff. The rooms on the outside had long narrow windows that looked out over the city. Judging by the shattered, soaked junk that remained they had been richly furnished as well.

But shattered, soaked junk was all that remained. What had once been rich fabric lay in sodden rotting piles. Scattered about were pieces of furniture, all hacked, broken and upended.

He looked at the wood regretfully. There were the makings there for a warming fire—if he could figure out how to light one without bringing the demon down on him and if he didn't mind attracting every wizard in the city.

Aside from that, there was no sign of anything useful. No food, no clothing, nothing. He turned to leave when something caught his eye. He bent and plucked it from the litter.

It was a halberd, its head red with rust and its shaft broken to about three feet long. Looking at the end of the shaft, Wiz could see it had been cut halfway through before it snapped, as if the owner had warded a stroke.

Wiz hefted it dubiously. He knew nothing about halberd fighting and this one was broken, useless for its original purpose. But it could still serve as a tool to pry open chests and boxes. Perhaps with it he would have a better chance of finding food.

Clutching his prize, Wiz crept back out into the corridor.

"Wiz kept notes on how his spell compiler worked," Moira explained to the gaggle of programmers who followed her into her apartment the next morning. "He did most of that here rather than in his workroom. I think it would be best if you removed them yourselves, lest I miss something."

"Thanks," Jerry said as he went over to the desk, "we'll get some boxes and . . ."

Then he saw the dragon sitting on top of the leather-bound book. A small, but very alert and obviously upset dragon. The dragon hissed and Jerry realized he, Karl and Moira were suddenly two paces ahead of everyone else in the group.

"What's that?"

"That is the demon guardian Wiz created to protect his spells, especially the book holding most of his secrets. He called it the dragon book," Moira explained.

Karl looked at Moira, Jerry looked at Karl and the dragon eyed them both.

"That *had* to be deliberate," Karl said finally.

Jerry made a face as if he had bitten into something sour. "Believe me, it was."

"Crave pardon?"

"There's a standard text on writing compilers called the dragon book," Jerry explained. "It's got a picture of a dragon on the cover. A red dragon."

"It was orange on my edition."

"As protection of the contents?" Moira asked.

"More like a warning of what the course is like. It's a real bear."

"Then why not put a bear on the cover?"

"Bears aren't red," Karl put in before Jerry could answer. "They're not orange either."

Moira frowned. "Oh," she said in a small voice.

"Anyway, how do we get rid of him?"

"Easily enough. Wiz taught me the dismissal spell." She stepped to the edge of the desk and spoke to the demon.

"puff at ease exe."

The dragon crawled off the book and retired to the corner of the desk.

"That is a spell in Wiz's magic language," she explained, turning back to the programmers. "The word **exe** is the command to start the spell, **at ease** is the spell and **puff** is the name of this demon."

"Well, it is a *magic* dragon," Karl said. A couple of the programmers groaned and Jerry winced again.

"Okay," Jerry said. "We'll get this stuff out of your way and moved to our office as soon as possible. Uh, do you know where we are going to be?"

"The under-seneschal is waiting to show you to your workrooms," Moira said. "He is in the courtyard, I believe."

"Great. Let's go then." Everyone moved back toward the door, except Danny Gavin who was lounging in a chair.

"Are you coming?" Jerry asked.

"No, I think I'll stay here," Danny said. "Unless you need me?"

Jerry looked at Moira and Moira shrugged.

"Just don't wander off."

Almost as soon as the door was closed Danny was out of his chair and over to the Dragon Book. The guardian demon raised its head when he opened it but made no protest.

Now let's see what this magic stuff is like. Danny scanned the first few pages quickly, picking up the basics of the syntax as he went. Then he flipped further back and looked at a few of the commands.

Shit, this is a piece of cake. He went back and re-read the fist part of the book more carefully, already mentally framing his first spell.

"We had to prepare workspace for you on short notice," the under-seneschal said apologetically as he led the group across another courtyard. "I'm afraid all the towers are taken and Lord Bal-Simba doubted you would prefer caves. So to give you a place where you can all work together, we ah, well, we cleaned out an existing building."

He was a small, fussy man who seemed to bob as he walked and kept rubbing his hands together nervously. He had been given an impossible job on very short notice and he was very much afraid his solution would insult some very important people. As they moved across the courtyard he became more and more nervous.

"We weren't expecting so many of you, you see and we are so terribly crowded here . . ." His voice trailed off as they approached the building.

It was sturdily built of stone below and timber above. As they drew nearer, a distinctive aroma gave a hint of its original purpose and once they stepped through the large double doors there was no doubt at all as to what it was.

"A stable?" Jerry said dubiously.

"Well, ah, a cow barn actually," the man almost cringed as he said it.

"Wonderful," Cindy said, "back in the bullpen."

"Oh wow, man," said one of the group, a graying man with his hair pulled back into a pony tail, "like rustic."

"Hell, I've worked in worse," one of the programmers said as he looked around. "I used to be at Boeing."

The room was good-sized, but as cold as every other place in the City of Night. A mullioned window, its tracery in ruins, let in the sharp outside air. Piles of sodden trash and pieces of broken furniture lay here and there. On one wall stood a tall black cabinet, tilting on a broken leg but its doors still shut.

Wiz came into the room eagerly. Maybe there was something in that closed cabinet he could use.

Cold and hunger dulled his caution and he was half-way across the room before a skittering sound behind him told him he had made a mistake.

Wiz whirled at the sound, but it was too late. There, blocking the only way out, was a giant black rat. It was perhaps five feet long in the body and its shoulder reached to Wiz's waist. Its beady eyes glared at Wiz. It lifted its muzzle to sniff the human, showing long yellow teeth. Wiz stepped back again and the rat sniffed once more, whiskers quivering.

Wiz licked his lips and took a firmer grip on the broken halberd shaft. The rat eyed him hungrily and moved all the way into the room, its naked tail still trailing out into the corridor.

Wiz stepped to one side, hoping the rat would follow and leave him room for a dash to the door. But the rat wasn't fooled. It lowered its head and squealed like a piglet caught in a fence. Then it charged.

In spite of his disinclination to exercise, Wiz had naturally fast reflexes. Moreover, his two years in the World had hardened his muscles and increased his wind. He was far from being the self-described "pencil-necked geek" he had been when he had arrived here, but he was even further from being a warrior.

The monster closed in squealing. Wiz swung wildly

with his rusty axe. The giant rat ducked under the blade and leaped for his throat.

Against a halfway competent swordsman the tactic would have worked. But Wiz wasn't even halfway competent. He had swung blindly and he brought his weapon back equally blindly, backhand along the same path.

The spike on the back of the axe caught the rat just below the ear. Any guardsman on the drill field would have winced at such a puny blow, but the spike concentrated the force on a single spot. Wiz felt a "crunch" as the spike penetrated bone. The rat squealed, jerked convulsively and fell in a twitching heap at Wiz's feet.

Wiz's first instinct was to turn and run. But he checked himself. *Think*, he told himself sternly, *you've got to think.* Running wouldn't solve anything. There was nowhere to run to and running burned calories he could ill-afford to lose. Panic wouldn't get him the food he so desperately needed.

Well, he thought, looking down at the gray-furred corpse, *maybe I can use one problem to solve another.*

Kneeling over the body, he set to work with his halberd.

Wiz emerged from the room a while later wiping his mouth on a bit of more-or-less clean rag.

Rat sashimi, Wiz decided, wasn't half bad—if you used lots of wasabe. He didn't have any wasabe, but it still wasn't half bad.

While the rest of the team broke for lunch, Jerry, Karl and Moira went back to the apartment to start sorting through Wiz's papers.

"A barn!" Moira said angrily. "I cannot believe they would do that to you."

"Hey, it's dry and it looks like it can be made fairly comfortable," Karl said. "Besides, it's already divided up into cubicles."

"Well, I can assure you, My Lords . . ." Moira began as she started to open the door.

There was a low moan and the sound of scuffling from the apartment.

Moira threw open the door.

"Danny!" Jerry yelled.

The young programmer was rocking back and forth, his body slamming first forward almost to the desk and then back so forcefully the chair teetered.

"Something's wrong! He's having a stroke or something."

"Stay away from him!" Moira ordered. "He is caught in a spell."

"Stop it."

"I do not know how. The command should be in the book."

Jerry edged around the still-thrashing Danny and hooked the Dragon Book off the desk. The dragon demon ignored him, watching Danny the way a cat watches a new and particularly interesting toy.

"Damn, no index!"

"Try the table of contents," Karl suggested.

"No table of contents, either!" He paged frantically through the book and muttered something about hackers under his breath.

"Here it is." He read hurriedly. "**reset!**" he commanded.

Danny continued to jerk back and forth.

"Exe, My Lord," Moira said frantically. "You must end with exe."

"Oh, right. **reset exe!**"

Suddenly Danny flopped forward and hit the table with a thump.

Moira and Jerry gently raised him up and leaned him back in the chair.

"Are you okay?" Jerry asked as the teenaged programmer gasped for breath.

" 's alright," he slurred as he lifted his head off his chest. " 'll be alright." Jerry saw he was white and shaking but he was breathing more normally.

"What happened?" Danny mumbled.

Moira pressed a cup of wine into his hands.

"You were entrapped by the spell you created, My

Lord," she told him. "The spell repeated endlessly and you could not get out."

"In other words you were stuck in a DO loop," Jerry explained.

Danny raised the cup in both hands and drained it in a gulp.

"Jesus. I was in there and it started and it just kept going over and over. Like a live wire you can't let go." He lowered the cup and it slipped from his numbed grasp to clatter on the table. "Jesus!"

"Tell us what happened."

"Well, I was flipping through the manual and I figured I'd try it out. So I set up a simple little hack, only when it started it just kept going. I didn't think I'd ever get out."

"That was a dumb-ass stunt," Jerry told him. "You're lucky it wasn't worse."

"How the hell was I supposed to know?" Danny snapped. "I didn't think . . ."

"You sure as hell didn't," Jerry cut him off. "And you'd better start thinking before you do a damn fool thing like that again!"

Danny muttered something but Jerry ignored him.

"Okay," Jerry said. "From now on nobody practices this stuff alone."

Wiz was feeling almost jaunty as he made his way up the street with the broken halberd over his shoulder. He was still cold, but on a day as bright as this he could almost ignore that. Besides, the cold was easier to bear when you weren't hungry all the time.

The halberd made a big difference in Wiz's standard of living. There turned out to be a lot more food left in the City of Night than he had realized. But almost all of what remained was locked behind doors or in cupboards or chests. In the last few days he had gotten very good at using the halberd's axe blade and the heavy spike behind to pry, chop and smash things open. Finding food was still a full-time job, but it wasn't quite the hopeless one it had been.

Today he was well-fed on magically preserved meat and bread so dry and brick-like he had to soak it in water before he could eat it. The meat had an odd taste and the water he soaked the bread in hadn't been very clean, but his stomach was still pleasantly full.

And now this neighborhood looked promising. The street was lined with smaller buildings, two and three stories. A number of small buildings, shops or houses, were more likely to yield food than a few big ones. Best of all, the doors and window shutters on nearly every house on the street were intact. That meant they had not been systematically looted and larger scavengers had been kept out.

The weather added to his mood. There was not a trace of the clouds that usually hung low and gray over the Southern Lands. The only thing in the pale-blue sky was the sun and it was almost at its zenith. There wasn't a lot of warmth in it, but there was a certain amount of cheer.

A motion above the buildings caught his eye. Wiz turned his head just in time to see a black-robed wizard drift lazily over the rooftops. The man's robe fluttered about his ankles and his head moved constantly as he scanned the city.

Wiz shrank back against the wall. But he knew he stood out sharply against the dark volcanic rock of the street and buildings. There wasn't even a shadow to hide in and the wizard was floating in his direction. He was as exposed as an ant on a griddle and he would be fried like one as soon as the wizard spotted him.

Wiz bit his lip and silently cursed the bright sun and the shuttered houses. He looked up and down the street frantically, but there was not an open door or window to be seen.

There was a storm sewer opposite. It didn't look big enough to take him and it was covered with an iron grate, but it was the only chance he had. Wiz dashed across the street and levered up the grate with a quick jerk of his halberd. Then heedless of how deep the hole might be he thrust himself through.

It was perhaps eight feet from the street to the trickle of freezing slime that ran through the bottom of the sewer. The shock and the slippery bottom forced him to his hands and knees before he regained his balance. He looked up just in time to see the wizard float down the street housetop high.

Wiz dared not breathe as the man passed over the grating. The sorcerer looked directly down at his hiding place, but floated on by majestically. Apparently the shadows in the hole hid Wiz from him.

Once the man passed out of Wiz's field of vision, he breathed a sigh of relief. Then he froze again. There was something moving in the tunnel behind him. Something big.

The tunnel was as black as the inside of midnight, but Wiz heard a splash-scrape sound as if something too large to move quietly was trying to do so. He listened more intently. Again the splash-scrape, nearer this time.

Wiz realized he was trapped. He couldn't see the flying wizard, but he could not have gone far. Leaving the shelter of the sewer meant exposing himself to his enemies. On the other hand, whatever he was sharing this tunnel with was getting closer by the second.

For some reason it stuck in his mind that he had found no bodies in the ruins. Not even bones.

He listened again. There was no further sound from the tunnel except the drip, drip of water. The lack of sound reminded him of a cat getting ready to pounce.

With one motion he twisted around and lashed upward with the halberd. The spike caught on the edge of the hole and he swung himself up to grab the coping with his other hand.

Behind him came a furious splashing. He swung his leg up and rolled free of the sewer just as a huge pair of jaws snapped shut where he had been. Wiz had a confused impression of a mouth full of ripping teeth and a single evil eye before he rolled away from the opening.

Gasping, Wiz gained his feet and flattened against the building. There was no sign of the flying wizard and the creature in the sewer showed no sign of coming after him.

Muddy, chilled and thoroughly frightened, Wiz ran off down the street, looking for a place to hide.

"Well," said Jerry Andrews, "what have we got?"

The team was crowded into the Wizard's Day Room, which they were using as a temporary office while the last renovations were completed on the cow barn.

For the last two days the programmers had torn into Wiz's spell compiler and the material he had left behind. By ones and twos they had pored over the Dragon Book, Wiz's notes and conducted small and carefully controlled experiments.

Now Jerry had called a meeting to sum up, compare notes and plan strategy. He had set it for late afternoon, so most of the programmers were awake and functional. They had pushed the tables in the Day Room together to make a long table in the middle of the room and, heedless of tradition, pulled chairs from their accustomed spots up around it.

"Does the phrase 'bloody mess' do anything for you?" a lean woman with short black hair and piercing dark eyes asked from halfway down the table. "This thing is written in something that looks like a bastard version of Forth crossed with LISP and some features from C and Modula 2 thrown in for grins."

"When do we get to meet this guy, anyway?" someone else asked. "I'd like to shake him warmly by the throat."

"There may be a problem with that, My Lord," Moira said from her place next to Jerry. "He went off alone into the Wild Wood and we have not yet found him."

"We're going to need him," Nancy said. "Someone has got to explain this mess. Some of this code is literally crawling with bugs."

"You mean figuratively," Jerry corrected.

"I said literally and I mean literally," she retorted. "I tried to run one routine and I got a swarm of electric blue cockroaches." She made a face. "*Four-inch-long* electric blue cockroaches."

"Actually the basic concept of the system is rather elegant and seems to be surprisingly powerful," Karl said.

Nancy snorted.

"No, really. The basic structure is solid. There are a lot of kludges and some real squinky hacks, but at bottom this thing is very good."

"I'll give you another piece of good news," Jerry told them. "Besides the Dragon Book, Wiz left notes with a lot of systems analysis and design. Apparently he had a pretty good handle on what he needed to do, he just didn't have the time to do it. I think we can use most of what he left us with only a minimal review."

"Okay, so far we've just been nibbling around the edges to get the taste of the thing. Now we've got to get down to serious work."

"There's one issue we've got to settle first," Nancy said. "Catching errors."

"What's the matter, don't you like electric blue cockroaches?" Danny asked.

"Cockroaches I can live with. They glow in the dark and that makes them easy to squash. I'm more concerned about HMC or EOI-type errors."

"HMC and EOI?"

"Halt, Melt and Catch fire or Execute Operator Immediately."

"One thing this system has is a heck of an error trapping system," said Jerry.

"That is because the consequences of a mistake in a spell can be terrible," Moira told him. "Remember, a spell is not a computer which will simply crash if you make an error."

The people up and down the table looked serious, even Danny.

"Desk check your programs, people," Jerry said.

"That's not going to be good enough. There are always bugs, and bugs in this stuff can bite—hard. We need a better system for catching major errors."

"There is one way," Judith said thoughtfully.

"How?"

"Redundancy with voting. We use three different processors—demons—and they have to all agree. If they don't, the spell is aborted."

"Fine, so suppose there's a bug in your algorithm?"

"You use three different algorithms. Then you code each primitive three different ways. Say one demon acts like a RISC processor, another is a CISC processor and the third is something like a stack machine. We split up into three teams and each team designs its own demon without talking to any of the others."

"That just tripled the work," someone said.

"Yeah, but it gives us some margin for error."

"I think we've got to go for the maximum safety," Jerry Andrews said finally. "I don't know about the rest of you, but I have no desire to see what a crash looks like from inside the system."

"My Lord, you seem to have made remarkable progress," Moira said as Jerry showed her through the programmers' new quarters.

The team had settled in quickly. Each programmer got his or her own stall and trestle tables filled the center aisle. The stalls were full of men and women hunched over their trestle table desks or leafing through stacks of material. At the far end of the room Judith and another programmer were sketching a diagram in charcoal on the whitewashed barn wall.

"Once you get used to giving verbal commands to an Emac instead of using a keyboard and reading the result in glowing letters in the air, programming spells isn't all that different from programming computers," Jerry told her. "We'd be a lot further along if Wiz were available, but we're not doing badly."

Moira's brow wrinkled. "I wish he was here too. But we cannot even get a message to him, try as we might." She shook the mood off. "It must be very hard to work with spells without having the magician who made them to guide you."

"It's not as bad as it might be," Jerry told her. "Probably our biggest advantage is that we know all the code was written by one person and I'm very familiar with Wiz's programming style.

"Look, a lot of this business is like playing a guessing game with someone. The more you know about the person and the way that person thinks, the more successful you are likely to be."

He sighed. "Still, it would be nice not to have to guess at all. Besides, Wiz is good. He'd be a real asset."

"We are doing everything we can to locate him," Moira said. "Meanwhile, is there anything else you need?"

"A couple of things. First, is there any way to get cold cuts and sandwich fixings brought in? My people tend to miss meals."

"Certainly. Anything else?"

"Well, you don't have coffee, tea or cola here, so I guess not."

"Wiz used to drink blackmoss tea," Moira told him, "but that is terrible stuff."

"Can we try some?" Jerry asked.

Moira rang for a servant and while they waited for the tea, she and Jerry chatted about the work.

"We call the new operating system 'WIZ-DOS'—that's the Wiz Zumwalt Demon Operating System."

"If this thing has a 640K memory limit, I quit!" someone put in from one of the stalls.

"As far as we know there's no limit at all on memory," Jerry said. "It's just that addressing it is kind of convoluted."

Moira didn't understand the last part, but her experience with Wiz had taught her the best thing to do was to ignore the parts she didn't understand. To do otherwise invited an even more incomprehensible "explanation."

"I'm sure Wiz would be honored to have this named after him," she said.

The tea arrived already brewed. Moira, who had used it when she was standing vigil as part of her training, thought it smelled nasty. Jerry didn't seem to notice. Moira poured out a small amount of the swamp-water-brown brew. Dubiously, she extended the cup. Jerry sniffed it, then sipped. Then he drained the cup and smacked his lips. "Not bad," he said appraisingly. "A little weak, but not bad. Can we arrange to have a big pot of this stuff in the Bull Pen while we're working?"

"Of course, My Lord, I'll have the kitchen send up a pot."

"I mean a big pot," Jerry said. "Say thirty or sixty cups."

Moira, remembering the effect that even a cup of blackmoss tea had on her, stared at him.

"Well, there are more than a dozen of us," he said apologetically.

Moira nodded, wondering if there was enough blackmoss in the castle to supply this crew for even a week.

Fifteen

WAR WARNING

A jump gone awry is one of the hardest bugs to locate.

—programmers' saying

Bal-Simba was walking in the castle garden when his deputy found him.

"Lord," Arianne said strangely. "Someone wishes to speak to you."

"Who?" the black wizard asked, catching her mood.

"Aelric, the elf duke."

Duke Aelric, or rather his image, was waiting for him in the Watcher's room. The Watchers, who kept magical watch on the entire world, shifted uneasily at their communications crystals in the elf's presence.

Bal-Simba studied the apparition as he mounted the dais overlooking the sunken floor where the Watchers worked. The elf duke was wearing a simple tunic of dark-brown velvet that set off his milk-white complexion. His long hair was caught back in a golden filet set with small yellow gems at his temples. His face was serene and untroubled, not that that meant anything. Elves were inhumanly good at hiding their feelings and in any event their emotions were not those of mortals.

Bal-Simba had heard Wiz and Moira's story of their

rescue by Duke Aelric and their dinner with him, but this was the first time Bal-Simba had ever seen him. *Come to that, it is the first time I have ever seen any elf this close*, he thought as he seated himself in his chair.

Duke Aelric seemed not to notice Bal-Simba until he was properly settled to receive his guest.

"I seek the Sparrow, but I am told he is not available," Aelric said.

"He is not here."

"Do you know when he will return?"

Bal-Simba considered the question before answering. "I do not. He is off in the Wild Wood, I believe."

Aelric raised a silver eyebrow. "Indeed? Forgive me if I pry, but when did he leave?"

"Forgive my curiosity, but why do you wish to know?"

"Because he was on business of some urgency when he left my hold to return to your city a fortnight hence," Aelric said.

Bal-Simba frowned mightily. "He was coming straight back?"

Aelric waved a hand. "That was his plan. He left upon the Wizard's Way to return here immediately." He looked sharply at the black Wizard.

"I swear to you he did not arrive here," Bal-Simba told him. He struck his chest. "Upon my life I swear it."

"I believe you, oath or no," the image said.

"I will also tell you that we have been trying to contact him for several days without success. Frankly, we are becoming worried."

Elf and mortal fell silent, contemplating the implications.

"It occurs to me," the elf duke said slowly, "that someone may have transgressed upon my hospitality. I do not appreciate interference with those travelling to and from my abode."

"It occurs to me that Wiz may be in dire danger," Bal-Simba said, a trifle sharply.

"I hope not," Aelric told him. "For all our sakes."

It was Bal-Simba's turn to raise an eyebrow.

"A matter of forestalling a war between humans and other users of magic, I think," Duke Aelric explained.

"War?"

"Did you expect your drive to exterminate magical creatures along the Fringe would go unremarked? Or that your expansion deep into the Wild Wood would pass unnoticed?"

"I think that there is a great deal going on out on the Fringe that I and the Council are unaware of."

Aelric waved a languid hand. "That is as it may be. The Sparrow seemed to feel he could turn this human tide before it came to that." Then he sobered and power seemed to radiate out of him like a nimbus.

"But I tell you this, wizard. If you cannot find your Sparrow—and soon—then you may have lost your only chance to forestall a war which would rend the World asunder."

He nodded gravely. "Merry part."

Bal-Simba's eyes widened at the usage, but he nodded in reply. "Merry meet again." And the elf duke's image was gone.

Bal-Simba heaved a great sigh. "When an elf uses human courtesies you know you are in trouble," he remarked to no one in particular. Then the giant black wizard turned to the gaping Watchers in the pit.

"I want every Watcher we have scanning the World for our Sparrow." He turned to Arianne. "Set up a schedule so we may search day and night." Then to one of the wizards with a communication crystal. "Send the word out to all the villages and habitations at once. Wiz must be found. And order the dragon cavalry out to search as well."

"Lord, do you think he meant what he said about war?" Arianne asked.

"Have you ever known an elf to joke?" Bal-Simba said. "He was concerned enough to come to us. That is more than sufficient proof that something very dangerous is in the air."

* * *

"Jerry, I think you'd better look at this."

Judith was standing at the entrance to Jerry's stall with an odd look on her face.

"We got the voting module working and, well, I think you'd better see the result."

Jerry followed her over to her own stall where Karl was looking bemused at three small demons standing together on the table.

"We know that any spell above a certain level of complexity generates a demon as its physical manifestation," Judith explained. "So we expected this thing would produce demons. But watch what happens when we feed it correct code.

"**emac.**" An Emac popped up on the desk next to the trio of demons.

"**backslash test1 exe.**" Judith said and the Emac gabbled at the demons. The demons stood motionless and then the one on the left hummed.

"Okayyy," it sang in a vibrant base.

"Okayyy," the middle one chimed in a rich baritone.

"Okayyyy," sang the third demon in a fine clear tenor.

"Okaayyyyyy," the three demon voices blended in perfect harmony. Then the sound died away and they fell silent.

For a moment none of the programmers said anything.

"The question is, is that a bug or a feature?" Karl asked.

"I guess that depends on how you feel about music," Jerry said. "Anyway, we don't have time to fix it, so we'll call it a feature."

Judith looked at the demons and shook her head. "I'm glad we didn't build four processors. I'm not sure I could take a barbershop quartet."

"I don't think you'd get a barbershop quartet," Jerry said judiciously. "A gospel group seems more likely."

"Worse."

*   *   *

By nature and training Danny needed a lot of time to himself. It had always been his refuge in times of trouble and his joy in times of special happiness.

The castle was too crowded for him to be really alone. But he had found a place on the rooftops where he could look down on the Bull Pen and the courtyards. From here he was hidden from view by any of the wizard's towers and could see out beyond the Wizards' Lodge, over the tile and slate rooftops of the town and off into the rolling blue distance.

Nearly every morning before he settled down to work, Danny would climb the narrow stairs to the attic and then go up the wooden ladder and out through the trap door that took him to his favorite place on the roof. He was not experienced enough in the ways of this World to know that the scuff-marks on the slates meant someone else came here too.

Today Danny had changed his pattern. It was late afternoon, normally a time when he would be settled in the Bull Pen and hard at work. But today his code had turned to shit and Cindy Naismith got on his case for something he said. So he left and came back up here for a while.

He wouldn't be missed, he knew. Not for some little time. Programmers set their own hours and besides, the rest of the team didn't like him very much.

Well, fuck 'em. That wasn't anything new to Danny.

Besides, he told himself, it wasn't like he was goofing off. He was still thinking about the problem, and he needed to clear his head, didn't he?

There was a soft scrabbling noise on the slate roof behind him.

Danny turned and there was thin brown-haired girl with enormous doe eyes.

"Hi," Danny said, half-resenting the interruption.

The girl moved back up the roof, away from him.

"Don't worry, I won't hurt you." The girl froze.

"You okay?"

No response. If he had moved toward her she would have fled, but he kept his place. She sat down on the roof behind and above him and looked out over the city.

Well, if she didn't want to talk . . . Danny turned back to watch the clouds himself. It wasn't as good as being completely alone, but it wasn't bad either.

Danny had taken to computers as a way to shut out the endless arguments that raged through his home. Later, after the divorce, the computer had become a way out of the loneliness, a friend who never turned its back on you or put you down.

At first he hadn't cared for programming, just racking up scores on video games. He had taken out his frustrations destroying aliens and monsters by the thousands and scoring points by the millions. Then he found out you could gimmick some of the games by editing character files. From that it was one small step to cracking copy protection to get games he couldn't afford to buy and one thing led to another. By the time he was sixteen, Danny was a very competent, if unsystematic, programmer.

He was also very, very lonely.

Now here he was in a world something like the ones those games were based in. Full of monsters and where magic worked. And he was still just as alone and just as cut off as he ever had been. Well, fuck 'em. He'd get by, just like he always had.

Without thinking, he reached into his pocket and pulled out the sandwich he had stashed there—smoked meat and sharp cheese on a long roll.

Danny heard the girl shift on the roof behind him.

"Want some?" She obviously did, but she was afraid to approach him.

"Here." He broke off half the sandwich and held it out to her. She looked at him intently but didn't move. He considered tossing the sandwich up to her, but realized it would probably come apart in the air.

He settled for reaching back and stretching out his hand.

"Come on, I won't hurt you."

Slowly, cautiously, the girl crept down the roof toward him. Finally she was close enough to stretch out and snatch the sandwich from him. Then she scrabbled quickly back up the roof. The entire performance reminded Danny of feeding a particularly shy squirrel.

"What's your name?" he asked.

"June," the girl said around a mouthful of sandwich. "I am June."

"This is just like being at fighter practice."

Karl, Judith and several of the other team members were sitting on a low wall by the drill field watching the guardsmen practice. Under the arches of the colonnade Jerry was sitting on a bench watching girls.

Just then a flight of dragon cavalry swept over the castle.

"Okay," Karl amended, "it's almost like being at fighter practice."

Out on the field Donal was practicing spear work against multiple opponents.

"Tricky move with the spear," Karl said to no one in particular as Donal dodged and spun between two opposing swordsmen.

"Why does he keep the butt low like that?" Judith asked.

"He is trying to keep the point directed at his opponent's eyes," a guardsman who was lounging nearby said. "That makes it hard to judge the length of the spear."

Karl nodded. "And it sets him up to make a quick jab to the face, which will make almost anyone flinch."

The guardsman, a sandy-haired older man, looked closely at Karl. "You sound as if you know something of the art, My Lord."

"I'm a fighter. Well, an SCA fighter," he amended

quickly. "We used to fight with rataan weapons. For sport."

"Would not your magic gain you more than weapons skill in war?"

"We don't use swords and spears in war any more," Karl told him. "No, we do it strictly for fun."

The guardsman's seamed face crinkled into a frown. "A most peculiar sport, if you do not mind my saying so, Lord."

"That's what a lot of people in my world thought," Karl sighed. "By the way, I'm Karl Dershowitz." He extended his hand and the other man clasped it.

"I am called Shamus MacMurragh. I command the guardsmen of the castle."

"Pleased to meet you."

"Tell me," Shamus said, "how does our weapons play compare to your world?"

"Very well. We do some things a lot differently and I think we've spent more time on the theory than you have, but on the whole you compare very well with our methods."

"I am very glad to hear it, My Lord," Shamus said mildly. "Could you perhaps show us how you do these things."

Karl wasn't quite sure, but he suspected he had just been trapped. "Be glad to," he said with a casualness he did not feel.

It took a few minutes to outfit Karl in the padded cloth haubrek, greaves, vambraces and helm the guardsmen used for practice. The shield they brought him was a target somewhat over two feet in diameter. Karl, whose SCA fighting style depended in large part on using the points of a heater shield, felt he was at a disadvantage, but he didn't say anything.

The sword they gave him was wood, not rataan, and a good deal heavier than what Karl was used to. Still, the balance was very good and it moved comfortably as he took practice swings.

"Remember to pull your blows, Lord," Shamus said as they faced off. "I do not want to be injured."

Karl nodded and licked his lips. Shamus moved with a catlike grace that suggested the guardsman wasn't the one who should be worried.

Karl came in in his standard fighting stance, shield in front, sword hilt over his head with the blade forward and down, resting on his shield.

Shamus looked at him quizzically for a moment and then stepped in with two cuts to the head. Karl was strong, but his wrist could not absorb or stop the blows. His blade was knocked casually aside and Shamus' sword rang off his helmet. Karl staggered back and nearly dropped the sword.

Shamus grasped his elbow to help support him. "Are you all right, My Lord?"

"Yeah, fine. Uh, in our system if you hit the other guy's sword, the blow is considered blocked."

"Matters are somewhat different in our world," Shamus said dryly. "But tell me, how can you strike anyone with your sword in that position?"

"You mean down in front of the head like that? Easy. You twist your hips, drive your elbow down and throw the forearm out." He demonstrated. "Like that."

"Interesting, but is it strong enough?"

"Well, I can make someone's helm ring pretty good with it."

"Try it on the pell," Shamus invited.

At the far side of the drill field was a row of head-high posts set in the earth. Each was about six inches thick and the dirt around them was freshly dug.

Karl stepped up to the nearest post, assumed his position and struck, overhead and slanting down and into the post. The blade turned in his hand, so first cut only skimmed the post, scraping along the surface and taking a shaving with it. The second cut drove the sword edge perhaps two inches into the pine.

"Surprisingly strong, My Lord," Shamus commented

as Karl stepped back, massaging his wrist from the shock. Then he stepped up, assumed his guard stance and sheared the post off cleanly with a single mighty swing.

"Such blows win battles," he said, stepping back.

"How did you do that?"

"Years of practice," Shamus said with a smile. "Of course there are one or two small tricks. But mostly an hour or two practice every day for, oh, six or seven years and you would be a creditable swordsman." He laughed and clapped the younger man on the shoulder.

"I think I just made a raging fool of myself," Karl muttered to Judith as he came off the field.

"I think it's called 'hubris,' " Judith told him. "How's your head?"

Karl rubbed his wrist. "It's my arm more than my head and it will heal quicker than my pride." He looked back out at the practicing guardsmen. "You know what the worst of it is? I can't use any of this stuff in our combat back home. Our rules are so unrealistic that the techniques that really work won't work for us."

". . . so anyway, we're working on a user interface. It's going to be really neat when we get it done."

June watched Danny and said nothing.

They sat side by side on the roof, looking out over the Capital to where the late afternoon sun turned puffy clouds into a symphony of pale golds and blush pinks.

They had met up on the roof nearly every day since their first encounter. Sometimes one or both of them brought food and they had an impromptu picnic. Sometimes they just sat and talked. Or rather Danny talked and June listened. June hadn't said a dozen words since that first day, but now they sat together on the slates. Sometimes they held hands.

"You ought to come and see the place sometime. It's really pretty interesting."

June smiled and shook her head.

"Well look, I gotta get down there or they're gonna start asking questions. I'll see you tomorrow, okay?"

Danny started to rise, but June took hold of his arm and pulled him close. She kissed him full on the mouth and before Danny could respond she skittered away over the roof ridge.

Danny sat there for a moment longer, tasting her on his lips and trying to understand what had happened. One thing he was sure of. He liked it.

Even by the standards of the City of Night, this place was strange. The windows about the tower gave good light, else he never would have dared to approach the eerie blue glow issuing through the open doorway.

At this level the tower was divided into two rooms. The one beyond the carved black portal must be by far the larger, but this one was substantial as well. Looking at the layout, Wiz had the odd feeling that this level was larger inside than it was on the outside.

This was obviously a wizard's tower and judging by the effects a very powerful wizard at that. Through the inner door Wiz could see forms writhing in the smoky red dark. It might just be fumes from the ever-burning braziers, but he had no intention of crossing the threshold to find out.

This room must have been an adjunct to the workroom. There were shelves along one wall which had obviously held scrolls. Pegs and hooks on another wall had perhaps held ceremonial robes and other magical apparatus.

But none of that was left. The small room had been thoroughly ransacked. Hangings had been pulled off the walls and lay rotting in a heap on the floor. The shelves were empty and broken. The floor was littered with broken glass, smashed crockery and bits of less savory items that might once have been in pots and jars. In one corner an armoire leaned crazily against the

wall, its doors torn half off their hinges and showing the
scars where someone had hastily chopped them open.

Wiz walked over to the cabinet and looked inside.
The shelves were askew and the drawers were ripped
apart. Like the room itself the armoire had been looted.

On an impulse, he stuck his hand into the cabinet.
He struck the back much sooner than he expected and
jammed his fingers painfully.

That wasn't right, he thought as he flexed the aching
digits. The back was closer than it should be. He put
his hand back in the cabinet and reached around to feel
the back from the outside. Yes, there was definitely a
space there. There was a good eight-inch difference
between the inside and outside back.

A careful examination of the inside back and the sides
showed him nothing. The wood was plain and the grain
straight and simple. He pressed and he twisted, but the
back remained in place.

Well, he thought, hefting his halberd, *there's always
the field engineering approach*.

Three quick blows from the halberd splintered the
thin wood of the back. On the third blow the armoire
gave a despairing "sproing" and the remains of the back
fell toward him. Eagerly Wiz reached inside.

At first he thought the compartment was empty. But
when he thrust his hand into the dark recess, his fingers touched cloth. He lifted the garment off the peg
on the side of the recess and brought it out into the
light.

It wasn't much, just a brown wool travelling cloak,
frayed and slightly moth eaten. The kind of thing a
wizard might wear for a disguise, or because he was too
engrossed in his magic to worry about appearances. *It
doesn't even look very warm*, Wiz thought as he fin-
gered the thin cloth. For the hundredth time Wiz
thought of the fine gray and red cloak with the fur trim
he had left in the village.

Well, anything was better than nothing and that's

what I've got now. He threw the cloak over his shoulders and pulled it tightly about him. He was right, it wasn't very warm. Still it was comforting to have something to wrap around himself.

"I saw Moira today, My Lord," Arianne said as she and Bal-Simba finished the day's business in his study. "She asked if there was any news of Wiz."

"If there was news, she would be the first to know," the giant wizard told his deputy. "No, so far our search has turned up nothing." He frowned. "We know an accident did not befall him in the Wild Wood. If he started out on the Wizard's Way and did not return to the Capital, we may assume some magical agency intervened."

"Human?" Arianne asked.

"Perhaps. Although it appears that Sparrow has an unusual number of non-human enemies as well. Powerful ones." He paused for a second and frowned.

"And Lady . . ."

Arianne bent close at his gesture. "Yes, Lord?"

"Inquire—discreetly—into the activities of our own wizards over the last fourteen days. Especially any who have absented themselves from the Capital."

Arianne looked shocked. "Do you think . . ."

"I think," Bal-Simba said, cutting her off, "that we would be remiss if we did not explore every possibility to get our Sparrow back here as quickly as we can."

Arianne turned away to execute his command. "Oh, and Lady . . ."

Arianne turned back. "Yes, Lord?"

"Find that ex-apprentice, Pryddian, and ask him what he knows about this."

"Pryddian?"

"Just a thought. A direct attack on Wiz in the Capital would be difficult. It would be easier if he were outside our walls. Pryddian was the cause of our Sparrow's journey." He shrugged his mountainous shoulders. "Unlikely, but we have to start somewhere."

* * *

Pryddian was sweating as he came over the last rise before his destination and not just from the noon sun. Before him the road curved to the left around the base of a hill, actually a large limestone outcropping. To the right, away from the road and along the outcropping, was a wild jumble of small trees, laurel bushes and boulders. The former apprentice started down the road, his feet kicking up powdery white dust fine as flour as he walked.

When he reached the place where the road curved away he paused for an instant and scanned the bushes on the roadside. The dusty weeds beside the road showed no sign of disturbance, but there was a path there, leading off the road and in among the undergrowth. Pryddian patted the breast of his tunic for reassurance and then stepped off the road and onto the little-used path.

He breasted his way through the bushes, dodged around trees and boulders and followed the meandering path deeper into the woodland. The thick brush and second-growth trees showed that once this place had been logged. But that had obviously been long ago. Getting felled trees out of such a place would be backbreaking and not worth it so close to the Fringe of the Wild Wood. It had been done once and then the wilderness had been allowed to reclaim this place.

Finally the trail took a sharp turn and a dip and Pryddian stumbled through into an opening. He was against the flank of the hill now, in a little hollow hard against sheer rock face. All around him like grotesque sentries stood boulders twice as high as he was. Directly in front of him was a single table-high stone in the midst of a patch of beaten earth. There were dark splotches on the stone, as if something had been spilled there and allowed to dry.

Pryddian walked hesitatingly into the place. Suddenly an arm like iron clamped across his windpipe and he felt cold steel against his neck.

Instinctively he twisted his head and out of the corner of his eye saw that his captor was clad in the close fitting black of the Dark League's dread Shadow Warriors.

The Shadow Warrior pressed the edge to his throat and Pryddian ceased struggling.

"No move, no sound if you value your life," a voice grated behind him.

Pryddian licked his lips and remained silent.

"Better," the voice said at last. "Now, why are you here?"

"I am called Pryddian. I am . . . URK." The Shadow Warrior's grip tightened on his windpipe.

"I did not ask who you were, but why you had come," his unseen questioner said sharply. "Answer only those questions I ask you, apprentice, or you will wish you had never been born."

"I came seeking the Dark League," Pryddian said when the pressure on his throat relaxed.

"And why should the Dark League be interested in the likes of you?"

"I have talent. I desire to become a wizard and I bring you something." He reached toward his tunic, but the Shadow Warrior drew the blade perhaps a quarter of an inch along his skin. He felt the burning sting of the cut and then the warm wetness of blood trickling down his throat.

Pryddian froze, but the Shadow Warrior, reacting to an unseen signal, slackened his grip and moved the knife away from his throat. Slowly he extended his trembling hand and reached into his tunic. Equally slowly he withdrew his hand, holding a roll of parchment.

"I give you the Sparrow's magic," he said.

"Lord, Moira asked again today about Sparrow," Arianne said.

Bal-Simba turned away from his window to face his deputy.

"Today as every day, eh?" He shook his head. "The answer is still the same. We can find no trace of him, in all the World."

"Is he dead then?" Arianne asked.

Bal-Simba shook his head. "Moira does not think so. I trust her judgment in this."

"Moira was away in his world when he left Aelric's hold," Arianne pointed out.

"Still, I think she would know if he had died."

"Then where could he be?"

"There are many possibilities. He might be in a place where he is shielded by magic. He might have been sent beyond the World. He might be held in a state of undeath.

"One thing I think we can safely venture. He is not where he is voluntarily and wherever he is, he needs any aid we can give him." He returned to his desk and sat down again. "On that subject, have you learned more in the matter you were pursuing?"

"You mean the actions of the Mighty? There is one thing new. Ebrion is missing for near three weeks."

"Ebrion?"

Arianne nodded. "There is more. We cannot be sure, but it appears that he may well be dead."

"Dead? How?"

Arianne shrugged. "We do not know. We are not even certain that he is dead."

Bal-Simba sucked his lip against his sharpened teeth thoughtfully. "Ebrion, eh?"

He twisted in his chair to face her. "This should be explored. Investigate closely."

"But discreetly," Arianne agreed. "I am already doing so, Lord."

Just like all the rest, Wiz thought as he surveyed the room in the failing light. Nothing to eat, just more piles of junk. The wind whistled through the broken windows and he shivered as he pulled the worn brown cloak tighter around himself.

Outside the setting sun poked fitfully through the layer of lead-gray clouds. By now Wiz knew the signs of a storm moving in, perhaps with snow. It was going to be another cold, miserable night. Too cold for foraging.

Since his encounter with the flying wizard, Wiz had stayed out of the open, at least in daylight. Every day, unless the winds were too high, one or more wizards of the Dark League floated over the ruined city looking for a sign of him. Now he tried to move from building to building only at night.

Well, none of that this evening. Storms in the Southern Lands were nothing to take lightly. He needed a place to hole up. And food, of course.

He made one more survey of the room. Broken furniture, bits of smashed crockery and junk, and piles of what had probably once been wall hangings or drapes.

He poked at the largest pile, over against the far wall with his broken halberd. Nothing but cloth.

Then he stopped in mid-poke. Maybe he could use this after all. There was a lot more of it here than normal and it was pretty dry. More than enough to make a nest for a human.

Wiz burrowed into the pile of cloth and rolled himself in the rags. He pulled up the hood of his cloak and drew another layer of cloth over him. The material was none too clean. It had been soaked repeatedly and Wiz was not the first creature to nest in it, but it kept out the chill and as his body heat warmed the cloth, Wiz stopped being cold for the first time since he had arrived. As the wind whistled and howled outside, his breathing steadied and he fell deeply asleep for the first time in days.

Voices woke him the next morning. Human voices in the same room.

Beneath the hood of the cloak he could see two men had entered the chamber—men who wore the black robes of the Dark League.

"He is here," the older one protested, "I can smell him!" He cast about like a hunting dog, his head turning this way and that as if he actually was smelling Wiz out.

"He was here," the other one corrected. "Do you see him in the room? Or do you think he has acquired a cloak of invisibility?"

Wiz dared not breathe.

The balding wizard straightened up. "This is foolishness anyway. Why not use spells to find this Sparrow? I have stood in his presence and I could locate him in minutes, even if Dzhir Kar could not."

The other waved a hand airily. "Oh, but that would not be sporting. Our Dread Master desires to have his amusement with this alien wizard before he dies. Think of it as a little something to pay him back for all that he has cost us." He smacked his lips and his eyes sparkled. "And would it not be delicious to have this one slain by magic, unable to use magic in his own defense? You have to admit, Seklos, it has a certain piquancy to it."

"Piquancy be damned! That—creature is dangerous and should be destroyed immediately. Do you play with a louse before you crack it between your fingers?" He looked narrowly at his companion. "Well, you might. And so might he. But it is still foolishness."

The younger wizard shook his head. "No sporting blood. That's your problem, Seklos, you've got no sporting blood at all."

"What I've got," the older wizard said, "is a cold from tramping all over this pest-bedamned city. If it weren't for that, I could smell him even more sharply. Now come on. Let's see if we can track him down and end this charade."

He strode out through the other door with his companion still trailing behind, smiling tolerantly.

It was several minutes after they left that Wiz could even shiver.

Thank God I don't snore! Wiz thought numbly.

For a long time after they left, Wiz stayed huddled in the rags. His bladder was full to bursting, but he did not abandon his shelter for nearly an hour after the wizards left.

They still should have seen me, he thought as he wiggled out of his cocoon. He had been snuggled into the pile of cloth, but he hadn't been completely hidden. The storm had passed during the night and light in the room has been bright enough. But still the wizards had missed him completely.

He paused and listened at the door. The hall was empty and there was no sign or sound of the wizards who had come so close to him. It was full daylight now so he looked around one more time. The only thing he had missed was a cracked and broken mirror hanging askew on the wall. Most of the glass was missing, but the piece that remained reflected back the empty room.

Only it's not empty! I'm here. He looked closely at the mirror. The mirror fragment showed the room, but there was no sign of Wiz. It was as if he was not there.

A cloak of invisibility! That was why the magicians hadn't seen him. He looked in the mirror again, turning this way and that and admiring his lack of reflection.

He'd heard about cloaks of invisibility, but he had never seen one. What was it Moira called it? A tarncape. That was what he had found. He laughed aloud and spun in a full circle, the cloak standing out from his body from the speed.

Then he froze. *Magic*! Wiz thought, his heart pounding. *I've been using magic!* But the demon hadn't come for him. He hadn't even felt the quiver he felt when he tried to frame a spell.

Wiz slumped into the corner, his back against the cold stone wall, and tried to think. What was it the wizard had said?

Or course! The demon wasn't looking for him, it was looking for the kind of magic he made. He knew that the output of his spell compiler "felt" different from normal magic, probably because each of his large spells was built up on many smaller spells—the "words" in his magic language.

But the tarncape wasn't magic he had made. It was someone else's magic he had found. It didn't register with the demon even when he used it. And that meant that he could use magic after all! Provided it was magic not of his making.

Wiz thought about it, but he didn't see how that helped much. Obviously most of the magical items in the City of Night had been carried off in the chaos that followed the Dark League's defeat. There were undoubtedly some things left, but he didn't know how to use them and magical implements did not come with users manuals. Worse, he wasn't a wizard in the conventional sense. He had no training in the usual forms of magic so he probably wouldn't recognize a magical object unless it bit him on the ankle.

Still, he thought, fingering the cloak, *there ought to be something I can do with this*.

The garden was beautiful this early, Moira thought. The sun painted the towers of the Wizards' Keep golden and made the colors of the pennons leap out against the blue of the sky. The dew still filmed the plants and made diamond sparkles on the grass and the occasional spider web. The air was cool and perfumed with the fragrance of roses.

Moira plucked a yellow one off the bush. Wiz had liked yellow roses on her. He thought they looked good against her red hair and fair skin and he especially liked her to wear them in her hair.

What was it he had told her? Some custom in his World where a woman wore a rose over the left ear to show she was taken and the right ear to show she was available. Or was it the other way around?

Moira smiled at the memory and bit her lip to keep from crying.

A shadow fell over her. She gasped and whirled to see Bal-Simba.

"Oh, Lord, you startled me. Merry met."

"Merry met, Lady."

"Is there any news?"

"None, I am afraid, but it is a related errand that brings me to you. Do you recall the three-demon searching spell Wiz created to seek news of you? I mentioned it to Jerry today and he says they have found no trace of such a spell in Wiz's notes."

Moira frowned. "None? I could have sworn he had something, at least the copies on parchment of the wooden slabs he wrote on at Heart's Ease when he created the spell."

"Jerry says there is nothing in the material he has. Is there anything they missed?"

The hedge witch shook her head.

"Nothing." Then she brightened. "But Lord, what about the searching system Wiz set up to find me? Could we not direct the searching demons to seek out Wiz?"

"We thought of that," Bal-Simba told her. "But it appears that the spell requires constant attention. The small searchers, the ones like wisps of dirty fog, are easily blown about by the wind. The larger ones drift as well, given time. A year's storms have scattered the demons beyond recall."

"And without the spell we cannot recreate the work." Unconsciously she crushed the rose in her grasp.

"Wait a minute! Lord, what about the spell Wiz used to find me in the dungeon?" Moira asked. "The Rapid Reconnaissance Directional Demon?"

Bal-Simba slapped his thigh and the sound rang off the walls. "Of course! It could search the entire World in hours."

A quick survey of the notes in the Bull Pen turned up the spell. With Jerry and several of the other programmers who hadn't yet turned in at their heels, Moira and Bal-Simba went out into the courtyard to put the spell into operation.

"Now then," Bal-Simba said to himself as he flipped between the pages where the spell was written, alternate lines on each page to prevent activating the spell by writing it down. "Hmmm, ah. Yes, very well." He faced into the courtyard, squinted into the morning sun and raised one hand.

"**class drone grep wiz**," he commanded in a ringing voice. There was a soft "pop" and a squat demon appeared in the courtyard. Its cylindrical body was white, its domed top was blue and it supported itself on three stubby legs. "**exe!**" commanded Bal-Simba.

The demon emitted a despairing honk and fell forward on its face. A thin trickle of smoke curled out of its innards.

"Let me see that spell again," Bal-Simba said to Moira.

Three repetitions produced no better results. Once the demon simply froze, once it flashed off never to return and once it ran around in tight little circles emitting little beeps and squawks. At last Jerry listed out the spell to see if he could discover the difficulty.

"I think I see what's wrong," Jerry said finally. "But it's not going to be easy to fix."

"What is the problem?" Bal-Simba asked.

"The problem is that this code wasn't written for anyone else to use."

"You mean this spell is protected by magic?" Moira frowned. Such protections were not unknown on powerful spells.

"Worse," Jerry said glumly. "This code is protected by being write-only."

"Eh?" said Bal-Simba.

"Wiz hacked this thing together to do a specific job, right? From the looks of it he was in a tremendous hurry when he did it."

"I was a prisoner of the Dark League," Moira said in a small voice. "He wrote the spell to find me."

"Okay, he needed it fast. He never expected that

anyone else would use it, he used the quickest, dirtiest methods he could find, he didn't worry about conforming to his language specification and he didn't bother commenting on it at all." Jerry looked at the glowing letters again and shook his head. "I don't think *he* could have understood this stuff a month after he wrote it and I don't have the faintest idea what is going on here."

"This," he said pointing to a single line of half a dozen symbols, "apparently does about four different things. Either that or it's some kind of weird jump instruction." He scowled at the code for a minute. "Anyway, the whole program is like that. I don't see three lines in a row any place in this that I understand."

"We do not need to understand the spell," Bal-Simba rumbled. "We only need to use it this once."

Jerry shook his head. "It's not that simple. What are the commands? What are the options you can use? How is it all supposed to work? You already tried this and it failed. Until we understand it we won't know why it failed."

"How long will it take you to find out?"

Jerry shrugged.

"I don't know. The hardest part of a job like this is always getting your head cranked around to see the other guy's way of doing things. Once you do that, sometimes it just falls right into place." He frowned. "And sometimes not. Anyway, I'll put a couple of people on it. I wouldn't count on being able to use this any time soon, though."

"Hopes raised and dashed before breakfast," Bal-Simba said as they walked back across the courtyard. "I am sorry, My Lady. I thought surely we had found the answer."

Moira clenched her jaw and held her head high. Bal-Simba saw she was crying. "There is still one thing we may try," she said tightly. "I will go to Duke Aelric and plead for his help."

Bal-Simba stopped dead. "What?"

"Elven magic is much more powerful than human. Surely they can find him."

"I was under the impression that Duke Aelric was already looking for Wiz."

"Then we can share what we know."

"Dealing with elves is dangerous," Bal-Simba said neutrally.

Moira flicked a grim little smile. "Madness, you mean. But Aelric seems to have a fondness for Wiz and I think he might listen to me."

"I ought to forbid you to do this."

Moira resumed walking. "Forbid away. But do not expect me to heed you."

The hill managed to be peaceful and foreboding at the same time. The moonlight played down on the wooded knoll, silvering the leaves of the trees and the grassy clearing before them.

But the moon also caught the megalith standing at the base of the hill where woods met grass. Three great stones, two upright and one laid across them like the lintel of a door. Was it only a trick of the moonlight that made the shadows within stir?

Moira licked her lips and pressed them firmly together. In spite of her cloak she was chill and she did not think the warm summer night had much to do with it. She took a firmer grip on her staff and strode boldly into the clearing.

"I wish to speak to Duke Aelric," she said loudly.

There was no response, no movement. The hill lay in the moonlight exactly as it had. Moira thought of repeating her request and decided against it. Elves were a touchy breed and much consumed with politeness. A human thought pushy or demanding would be in dire trouble.

"My Lady."

Moira jumped. Duke Aelric was standing in the moon-

light in front of her. He wore a white doublet and hose
embroidered with silver that glinted in the moonlight
and a hip-length cloak of pale blue.

He regarded her with interest but without the warmth
he had showed the last time they had met. Nor did it
escape her notice that the elf duke had not welcomed
her, merely acknowledged her presence.

She licked her lips. "My Lord, we need your help in
finding Wiz."

Aelric arched a silver brow. "An elf helping mortals?
An odd notion, Lady."

"It has been known to happen."

He gestured languidly. "So it has, when it is sufficiently amusing. I fail to see the amusement here."

That was the end of it then, Moira acknowledged as a
cold lump congealed in her stomach. When Wiz and
Moira had first met Aelric, she had told him that elves
acted for their own reasons and no mortal was ever
likely to untangle them. Standing here in the moonlight
with the elf duke she began to appreciate how true that
was.

Moira took a deep breath and gathered all her courage. "Lord, forgive me for mentioning this, but is it not
true that your honor is involved as well? Wiz *did* disappear while travelling from your hold."

Aelric gave her a look that made her go weak in the
knees. For a horrible instant she thought she had offended the elf.

"My honor is my own concern," he said coldly, "and
not a matter for discussion with mortals. I know who
kidnapped him and at the proper time they will feel the
weight of my displeasure."

"But you will not help us find Wiz."

Again the chilling, haughty gaze. "Child, do you
presume to instruct me?"

"No, Lord."

"Then guard your tongue more carefully." Duke Aelric
softened slightly. "Besides, I cannot find him."

He smiled frostily. "That surprises you? It surprises me as well—and tells me that others besides mortals had a hand in this." He motioned fluidly, as if brushing away a fly. "However that is my concern, not yours."

"But you know who kidnapped him?"

"That too is my concern. Little one, among the ever-living revenge is artifice most carefully constructed and sprung only at the proper moment. These ones have offended me and they shall feel the weight of my displeasure at the proper time."

With a sinking feeling Moria realized that to an elf, "the proper time" could mean years—or centuries.

"Now, if you will excuse me." He sketched a bow and Moira dropped a curtsey. When she looked up she was alone in the clearing.

Dzhir Kar eyed the man in front of him skeptically.

"So you bring us the Sparrow's magic?" he said coldly.

"Yes, Lord," Pryddian said. One of the wizards holding him jabbed him sharply in the kidney with his staff. Pryddian gasped and jerked under the influence of the pain spell.

"Yes, master," he corrected himself. "I stole it from the Sparrow himself."

Pryddian was very much the worse for wear. Once he had been passed on to the Dark League's hidden lair he had been questioned. Since the questioning had been merely "rigorous" rather than "severe" he still had all his body parts and could still function. But his back was bruised and bloody, one eye was swollen shut and he was missing a few teeth. It had taken nearly three days before the wizards who had remained behind were convinced he was worth passing on to their master. His trip south had been expeditious rather than comfortable. Now he waited in the arms of his captors for the misshapen creature before him to decide his fate.

Dzhir Kar considered. It was not unknown for apprentices to decide the Dark League offered them more scope than the Northern wizards—rare, but not unheard of. Still, this was neither the time nor the place to add apprentices, especially ones so recently allied with the North. A quiet dagger between the ribs would have been the normal response to such presumption.

But still, a spell of the Sparrow's . . .

"What is this thing?" he asked, flipping through the parchments.

"It is a searching spell. The Sparrow used it to scan the World. It involves three kinds of demons, you see, and . . ." Pryddian gasped again as the wizard prodded him with the pain spell.

"Confine yourself to answering my questions," Dzhir Kar said.

"A searching spell," Pryddian gasped out. "It can search the whole World in a single day."

Dzhir Kar thought quickly. This just might be the answer to his problem. A host of demons could search the City of Night far better than his wizards could. He had a limited ability to train his demon to ignore specific instances of the Sparrow's magic. If it could be trained to ignore these demons, then the combination of the Sparrow's own magic and his demon could do in a single day what his wizards had been unable to do in a matter of weeks.

He waved his hands and the guards released Pryddian and stood away. The ex-apprentice slumped to the floor, his legs unable to support him.

"Very well," Dzhir Kar said. "It amuses me to use the Sparrow's magic to track him down. If you can produce these demons as you say then I will give you your life. Moreover, if they can find the Sparrow, you will be accepted as a novice by the Dark League.

"If you cannot do these things, I will see to it that you suffer for your presumption." He looked up at the wizards. "Take him away."

He nodded to the guards and they half-carried, half-dragged Pryddian out.

*   *   *

They gave Pryddian a cell just off the main workroom and he set out to duplicate Wiz's searching system. It was not a simple matter for an untutored ex-apprentice to unravel the notes he had stolen. Nor was it easy to cast the spells once he learned them. The Sparrow seemed to delight in alternate choices at every step of the spell and the wrong choices did little or nothing. But Pryddian worked until he dropped. His black-robed jailers saw to that with their pain spells.

It might have amused him to know he was not the only person having trouble with the Sparrow's spells.

"This guy was a real hacker," Mike said, leaning over his wife's shoulder to study their latest task.

Nancy nodded and looked back at the code above her desk. "You don't have to tell me that. Jesus! I've seen better commented programs in BASIC." She took another look at the runes glowing blue before her. "And I've seen clearer comments in the London Times crossword puzzle!" She jabbed her finger at one line. "What the hell is this monstrosity? And why the hell did he name it **corned_beef?**"

"Jerry says the name is probably some kind of rotten pun. What does it do?"

"Basically it takes the value of the characters of a demon's name, multiplies them by a number, adds another number and then divides the result by 65,353. Then it uses that result as a subscript in some kind of an array." She shook her head again. "Why 65,353? Jesus! You know, if this guy doesn't come back we may never understand some of this stuff."

The man sighed. "Well, let's get to it. This is going to take a while." He nodded to Wiz's book of notes on his magic compiler. "Hand me the Dragon Book, will you?"

Ghost-gray and insubstantial, the searching demons began to pour from the ruined tower and blanket the City of Night.

Each demon had very little power. It could only absorb impressions from the world around it and forward them to a larger demon which would catalog them. The final step in the process was a demon formed like a weird crystal construct that perched atop the tower. It did the final sorting and alerted the wizards if it found anything that looked worthwhile.

Wiz had endowed the demons with all the mortal senses, but no magical ones. Of those senses, sight was the most important to an airborne creature. Since Wiz wore his tarncape constantly there was little visible sign of him. Demons by the thousands searched every nook and cranny of the city, but they saw nothing of Wiz.

Dzhir Kar ground his teeth in fury at the news and ordered Pryddian beaten to make him fix the spell. But Pryddian could not repair what he did not understand and in spite of the demons Wiz eluded the Dark League.

Sixteen

TROUBLE IN THE NORTH

You can't unscramble an egg.

—old saying

You can if you're powerful enough.
—the collected sayings of Wiz Zumwalt

Dragon Leader looked back over the flight in satisfaction. They weren't parade-perfect, but their spacing was good. Even his wingman was keeping his proper distance and holding position on the turns.

As he moved in easy rhythm with his mount's wing beats, he surveyed the forest below. The trees were dark green in their late summer foliage and the pattern was broken here and there by the lighter green of a natural meadow or the twisting channel of a brown stream wandering among the trees. This far north there were a lot of streams because the land got a lot of rain.

Today's patrol had had good weather all day, thank goodness, and if he was any judge of weather, tomorrow would be fair as well. Only a few clouds, all of them high enough still to be tinted golden by the setting sun—and scattered enough not to provide shelter for possible ambushers, Dragon Leader thought.

No likelihood of that, of course. There were no more

enemy dragons. This was simply a routine patrol over the northernmost reaches of the human lands—a pleasant summer's excursion for men and dragons alike.

Dragon Leader gave a hand signal and applied gentle knee pressure to his mount's neck. As his dragon swept around to the right the three other dragons in the flight followed, speeding up to hold their relative positions. He noticed that his wingman held almost exactly the right distance and speed.

The kid's shaping up, he thought as the dragons swept over a heavily wooded ridge, so low they startled a flock of brightly colored birds out of one of the taller trees. *He'll have his own squadron yet*.

But that was for the future. Just over the next ridge was the Green River and on a bluff above a wide looping bend sat Whitewood Grove, the northernmost of the settlements and their destination for the night.

It didn't have a full aerie, but there was a covered roosting ground for the dragons and snug quarters with their own bath for the riders. Right about now, Dragon Leader reflected, that sounded pretty good.

Again the dragons swept up over a ridge, buoyed by the upwelling currents of air. Dragon Leader started to signal another wide turn to line up on the village. Then he froze in mid-gesture.

What in the . . .

There was the river and a bluff, but there was no village there. Instead the rise was crowned by a grove of large trees.

Could they be that far off course? Unlikely. Although the people of the World did not use maps as the term is commonly understood—the Law of Similarity made any map a magical instrument—they did have lists of landmarks. Dragon Leader had been checking them automatically and they had hit each landmark in turn. Besides, he had been to Whitewood Grove many times. He recognized the shape of the bluff, the bend in the river and the rapids just downstream. He even saw a snag near shore he recalled from his last visit. Everything was exactly as it should be except the village was missing.

The hairs on the back of his neck prickled and his mouth tasted of metal. Suddenly Dragon Leader was very, very alert.

Without using his communications crystal he signaled his flight to break into pairs. A wave of his arm sent the second pair climbing and circling wide around the area. Then with his wingman following he bored straight in to pass over the place where the village should be.

Splitting his forces like this was bad tactics and Dragon Leader didn't like it at all. But if he hadn't made a stupid mistake, then whatever had caused this was probably more than a match for four dragons. Splitting into pairs increased the chances that someone would get word back to the Council. For the first time since the patrol began, Dragon Leader wished he had an entire squadron of a dozen dragons behind him instead of a single flight of four.

They came in low and fast over the bluff, nearly brushing the tops of the trees. It appeared a perfectly ordinary grove of Whitewood trees. This was definitely the spot, but there was no sign of a village. No buildings, no ruins, not even any footpaths. He signaled his wingman and they swept back over the spot, quartering the site.

The village of Whitewood Grove was simply gone. The wharf was gone from the river and even the path that led from the wharf to the village was missing.

They circled the site while Dragon Leader considered. There was nothing on any checklist that applied to a situation like this. Looking over his shoulder at the place where the village of Whitewood Grove should have been, he made a decision.

"Second element, run for the patrol base," he said into his communications crystal. "Fly all night if you have to and as soon as you are over the ridge start reporting to the Capital. Wingman, stay on perimeter patrol. I am going to land and inspect the site on foot. If

I am not back in the air in one half of a day-tenth, run for the patrol base. Now go!"

To his right and high above he saw the second element break off and scoot for the ridge. He waited until they were across before he turned his dragon inward toward the bluff.

There was barely room to land a dragon on the very tip of the bluff. The air currents off the river made it tricky and his dragon didn't like the place at all. She bridled and growled and tried to break off the approach twice. He had to force her down and once on the ground she would not settle. She kept her wings half-spread and her neck extended high in the classic fighting posture. The way she was breathing told Dragon Leader she was building up for an enormous gout of flames.

Which was fine with Dragon Leader. An aroused dragon is far from the worst thing to have at your back in a tight spot.

Sword in hand, he scanned the trees while keeping close to the dragon's bulk. The grove of Whitewoods looked peaceful and quite unremarkable. The early evening sun tinged their glossy green leaves with gold. A slight breeze gently rustled through the branches. Somewhere a bird sang and close to the grove's edge a red squirrel jumped from branch to branch. The grove exuded the faint, sweet aroma of Whitewood blossoms.

None of which made Dragon Leader or his dragon feel any more secure. The dragon stayed poised for combat and on cat feet Dragon Leader moved into the wood.

The Whitewoods were fully mature, large enough that he could not have put his arms around them at their base. The litter on the forest floor was deep with dead leaves and rotting vegetation. There were ferns and there were may apples and here and there a purple forest orchid. But there was not the least little sign of anything that might possibly have once marked human habitation.

Warily Dragon Leader moved out of the grove, keeping watch over his shoulder as if he expected something to pounce on him at any minute. As quickly as he could he mounted, wheeled his dragon and launched her off the bluff. The dragon dived for the river to gain air speed and Dragon Leader finished securing himself to the saddle on the fly. As his wingman came up to join him and the pair ran south for the patrol base, he realized his jerkin was soaked with sweat.

For the first time since the war with the Dark League ended, Dragon Leader was very, very frightened.

Arianne gasped when Bal-Simba told her of the dragon rider's report.

"Lord, what could have caused this?"

"I have not the slightest idea," Bal-Simba told her. "I have never heard of such a thing."

The blonde witch thought hard for a moment. "How many others know of this?"

"In the Capital? So far just two Watchers, you and I."

"Then if I may suggest Lord, perhaps it would be best if we kept it a secret for now."

Bal-Simba nodded. "The Watchers are already sworn to secrecy. But that does not help us get our people back—if they can be gotten back. Nor will it prevent such things in the future."

"Such an attack must have been provoked by the changes on the Fringe," Arianne said slowly. "Else this would have happened before."

"Once again, my thinking. But what provoked it? And what was provoked?"

"Perhaps the elves could tell us."

Bal-Simba snorted like a bull. "You grasp at straws." Then his expression softened. "Besides, I have climbed all over that notion and can find no way in. The elves will have nothing to do with any mortal except Wiz. And even if they would, I doubt I could convince them of our sincerity."

"Will not your word suffice as president of the Council of the North?" Arianne asked him.

"You know the answer to that, Lady," Bal-Simba rumbled. "I am not the mightiest magician among us, and the Council's power ebbs as people realize they do not stand in constant need of us. Wiz may be the most junior member of the Council, but he is our most powerful magician and our best hope for correcting what is wrong."

Arianne shuddered. "So if we do not find him, we face war."

"We must do more than find him, Lady," Bal-Simba said. "We must find him alive and sound."

Seventeen

EVERYTHING WILD

Magic is real—unless declared integer.
   —from the collected sayings of Wiz Zumwalt

"Okay, deal."

Karl, Judith, Mike and Nancy were seated around the table in the Wizard's Day Room, settling in for a quiet session of bridge. Ignoring the glares of the half-dozen or so wizards present, they had pulled a table from its accustomed place and brought chairs in around it.

Mike opened a fresh pack of cards and dealt the first hand with his wife Nancy as the dummy.

Nancy organized her hand and frowned. Every card she held was a heart. By some weird happenstance, she had drawn the entire suite of hearts!

"Damn, what a time to be dummy!"

Then she looked up and saw the strange expressions on the other players' faces.

"What's wrong?"

Wordlessly, Mike laid down his hand, face up. Karl and Judith followed suit. Mike had gotten every club, Judith had all the diamonds and Karl had all the spades.

"Jesus!" Nancy breathed. "Are you sure you shuffled those cards?"

"You saw me," Karl said. "My lord! I wonder what the odds are on that happening?"

208

"Astronomical," Judith said softly. "Simply astronomical."

They all looked at the cards for a minute.

"Well," Mike said finally. "Let's shuffle again and get down to play."

He raked in the four hands and took great care to shuffle the deck thoroughly. Then he dealt them out again.

Nancy picked up her hand, looked at them, and threw them down. "Shit," she said informatively.

The others followed suit. This time Nancy had gotten all the clubs, Karl had the diamonds, Mike had the hearts and Judith had the spades.

"This isn't working," Karl said finally. "Somehow the magic in this place is interfering with the shuffle." He looked at the four piles of cards on the table and made a face. "Do you still want to play?"

"If we can find something that we can play," Judith said. "I don't think bridge is going to do it."

"How about poker?" Mike asked. "We could play for matches or something."

"I don't really know how to play poker," Judith protested.

"We'll make it easy," Mike told her. "Five-card draw."

This time Karl shuffled the cards and dealt the first hand. Then he picked up his cards and looked at them.

The hand was assorted, but it was a dog. Not even a pair and no card higher than a five. Well, that was okay too. Karl played poker for the long haul and the first hand of the game was a good place to find out how the other players would react to a bluff.

Suddenly the top of his head felt wet.

Karl looked up and saw that a tiny thundercloud, no bigger than his hand, had formed above his head. A miniature bolt of lightning flashed from peak to fluffy gray peak and a fine mist of rain settled on him.

"Let me guess," Nancy said. "You got the low hand."

Karl threw down his cards in disgust. "I don't think this universe is designed for card playing."

"Wait a minute," Mike said. "Let's try something that's more strategy and less pure luck of the draw. You ever played Texas Hold 'em?"

"That's a version of seven-card stud isn't it?" Karl asked.

"I don't know," Judith said. "I've never played stud poker."

"It's easy," Nancy told her. "You deal three cards to each player and four face down in the middle of the table. You try to make the best hand with the cards in your hand and the four on the table. You bet after the deal and then again after each card is turned. I'll help you with the first hand, if you like."

"And," Mike continued, "it's got the advantage that the outcome depends on the cards on the table more than the cards in your hand. That and your betting skill."

They had no chips, and match sticks were not a part of this world, but they appropriated a bowl of unshelled nuts from the sideboard by the port, ignoring the audible sniffs of the wizards.

Again Mike shuffled the cards and dealt.

"Three filberts."

"I'll see your filberts and raise you a brazil nut," Judith said. She looked at the zebra-striped nut in her hand. "At least I think it's a brazil nut."

"What did we say, five pecans to a brazil nut?" asked Nancy, shoving into the pile of squirrel fodder.

"Ace," Mike said, flipping the card. "Place your bets."

They went around the table with everyone betting moderately. Mike reached out and flipped the second card.

"Ace again."

Nancy made a strangled sound.

"What's wrong?" her husband asked.

"Just keep going," Nancy said, staring at the cards.

Again everyone bet and again Mike flipped a card.

"Another ace . . . wait a minute!"

There on the table face up were an ace of clubs and ace of diamonds. The last card was the ace of spades.

"What the hell . . ."

He pulled a card from his hand and threw it face up on the table. An ace of spades.

"That makes seven aces," Nancy said, throwing down her and Judith's hands.

"No, nine," Karl said, adding his cards to the pile.

"Ten," Mike said bitterly, adding another ace from his hand. "Come on guys, let's go watch the sunset or something."

Over in the corner Malus and Honorious watched them leave.

"What do you suppose that was all about?"

"Obviously a divination of some sort." He shook his head. "I do not think they liked the outcome."

"I wonder what it portends?" said Agricolus coming over to join them.

"Nothing good, I warrant you," said Juvian from his seat near the window. "I thought the Sparrow was bad with his strange magics and alien ways. Now we have near a score of them and they are all more fey than the Sparrow ever was."

"And they left the table and chairs out of place," Honorious snapped, ringing a silver bell to summon a servant to put them back. "Encroaching mushrooms. No manners at all."

"It is a plague! A veritable plague," Agricolus said.

Juvian, Malus and Honorious all nodded in glum agreement.

"Worse than that, perhaps," said Petronus, a wizard with thinning hair and a pronounced widow's peak, sitting apart from the others. "How much do we know of what these strangers do?"

"They have explained . . ." Agricolus started.

"Did you understand the explanation?"

"Well . . ."

"Just so. They labor endlessly in the very citadel of the North and foist us off with explanations none can understand. Meanwhile non-mortals everywhere prepare against us."

"Do you think something is amiss?" asked Malus.

"And you do not? We stand on the brink of a war of extermination that is somehow bound up with the Sparrow and we let his cohorts work in our very midst doing things they will not explain." He slapped his hand on his knee with a sharp crack. "If these strangers are so powerful, let them give us clear proof and reasonable explanations. As members of the Council of the North we should demand it of them."

"That would be a task for the president of the Council," Agricolus said.

"And I mean to talk to him about it. Now." He rose and bowed to his fellows. "My Lords." With that he swept out of the room.

"He does have a point," Honorious said, lowering his voice as the servant came into the Day Room and started moving the furniture back. "They should not hide what they are doing from us."

"I am not so sure they are hiding from us," Malus said slowly.

"Do you mean you believe that rubbish, that, that 'spell compiler'?" Honorious snorted. "If so, I have an Elixir of Immortality I wish to discuss with you."

The pudgy little wizard frowned. "I did not believe it when there was just the Sparrow and his wild talk. But now? All these newcomers can work magic, all their magic feels like the Sparrow's."

"They are all from his land," Agricolus pointed out.

"And they all claim that anyone can learn this magic," Malus countered. "Perhaps they are telling the truth."

"If they are telling the truth then why can not any of us grasp the essence of this thing?" Agricolus demanded.

"Perhaps we have not tried hard enough," Malus said. "We can hardly be said to have approached the Sparrow's magic with the same openness we would apply to learning a new spell from one of the Mighty."

Honorious snorted again.

"Well," the little wizard said, "I do not put it forward

as fact, only as speculation." He put both hands on the arms of his chair and levered himself erect. "My Lords, I must return to my own work."

"There may be something in what he says," Agricolus said after a moment.

"Fortuna!" exclaimed Honorious. "Not you too?"

Agricolus shrugged. "I pride myself on having an open mind."

"And I find myself in a world gone mad!" Honorious retorted, ostentatiously picking up the scroll he had laid aside when the conversation began.

"My Lord, I think we have a problem," Moira told Karl when she found him in the Bull Pen the next morning.

"You mean another problem," he said looking up from the stack of wood strips he was pawing through. "What now? Can't you get us more parchment?"

"No, not that—although that will be a problem if your people don't start using slates for simple notes. This is more serious, I think."

"Won't wait until Jerry gets in, eh? Well, lay it on me."

"Some members of the Council have formally petitioned to have your work stopped until they are satisfied that what you do is safe and effective." She made a face. "Forever, in other words."

"But why?"

"Oh, many reasons. Jealousy is one of them. Some of the Council fears any change. But mostly I think because none of them understand what you do."

"But they must have some idea. I thought Wiz had been teaching classes all along."

"Oh, he was. That is part of the problem. Your magic is so complicated and your ways of thinking are so alien none of our wizards were able to learn what Wiz tried to teach them.

"Some of them claim his teaching was a smoke screen, designed to hide the real secret of his magic. But I

know that is not so. He struggled hard to teach us and
none of us could learn."

Jerry tapped a scroll thoughtfully against his cheek.
"Well, programming sure isn't the easiest thing around,
but it's not near that hard."

"For you perhaps. For us even the simplest things
dissolve into confusion."

"Give me an example."

Moira paused and frowned. Very prettily, Karl
thought. For the hundredth time he regretted she was
taken.

"Well, there are these variables that are named one
thing, called another thing and have a value of something else. Wiz must have explained that to me once a
moon and I still don't think I understand it."

"Oh boy, I'm not surprised at that one," Karl told
her. "It's near the trickiest notion in programming and
it's something that confuses a lot of people. But it's still
not that hard for someone who's got what it takes to
be a wizard."

"Very well then," Moira said. "Can you explain it
to me?"

Karl sighed. The clearest explanation he had ever
seen of the subject started with a quotation from Twee-
dledee and Tweedledum in *Alice In Wonderland*—and
the quotation was very apt.

He thought for a minute.

"Okay, look," he said. "You have a true name, right?
A name that is uniquely yours and must be kept secret
because it identifies you exactly?"

Moira thought for a moment and decided to ignore
the rude and prying nature of the question. "I do," she
admitted.

"But your true name isn't 'Moira,' is it? Moira's just
what people call you?"

"Yes."

"And most people also address you as 'Lady' because
you're a witch. That is, you belong to the class of
witches, right?"

"Yes," said Moira, who was beginning to see where this led.

"All right then," Karl said. "You are named one thing, you are called something else and you're an instantiation of a class called yet another thing." He grinned. "Then you get someone like Wiz, who is Sparrow to most people, Wiz to his friends, is an instantiation of the class of magicians and has a true name. Each of them is different and each of them applies in slightly different circumstances.

"It's the same in programming. A variable is an instantiation of a class, like integers, and it has its own name that uniquely identifies it, like a true name. At any given time it also has a value, which is what it actually *is* just then, but which can change with circumstances. Finally, it can also be known by other names in other circumstances and it can be referred to by a pointer, the way 'Moira' points to you without using your true name. See?"

Moira stood open-mouthed. "You mean *that's* what Wiz was trying to show me?" she asked incredulously. "That's all there is to it?"

Karl shrugged. "Pretty much."

"But that's so *simple*. Why didn't he just say that?"

"Probably because he never thought of it that way. From what everyone says Wiz was a master class hacker and hackers just don't think in those terms." He grinned. "We have a saying about people like your Wiz. Ask them what time it is and they'll tell you how to build a clock." Jerry put the scroll back on the pile.

"Now I'd like to ask you something. What did you mean just now when you said you don't think the way we do?"

"We do not generalize the way your people do."

"Who says so?"

"Why, Wiz."

"I think Wiz is wrong. You don't generalize the way Wiz does, but then most people don't. You're oriented to language, not mathematics. One of the things that confuses it is you're very careful in your speech. You don't use metaphors and similes in the way we do, probably because your language can directly affect the world around you. You can make magic by accident."

Moira thought hard.

"Then you think we can learn this new magic?"

"I'm sure of it. Oh, you'll probably struggle like an English major in a calculus class, but you can get it if you're willing to work at it."

"How is it you are so much more skilled at explaining all this?" Moira asked.

"Oh, that. I was a high school teacher for a while."

"A teacher? Then why did you become—whatever you are?"

Karl grinned ruefully. "Kind of a long story. Seems I started out to be an engineer and in my junior year I decided I'd rather be a teacher. So I switched majors and got my degree in education."

He looked out the window and sighed. "Well, after I had taught math for a couple of years, our high school got an inspection by the accreditation commission. I had more than enough math courses to teach math, but most of them were taken as engineering courses. So the accreditation commission decided they didn't count. I could either go back to college and take twenty-four hours of math courses I'd already had or I wouldn't be certified to teach math and that would count against the school's rating."

"You mean you were not a good teacher?" Moira asked.

"Oh no. I was a very good teacher. The accreditation commission rated my classroom performance 'superior.' But I had taken all my math courses with an ENG prefix instead of a MA prefix."

The hedge witch frowned. "Forgive me, My Lord, but I do not understand."

Karl sighed. "Neither did I. That's why I took a job as a software engineer—for twice as much money."

Moira thought hard for a moment.

"My Lord, would you be willing to take on an additional duty? Would you be willing to teach this to others?"

Karl's mouth quirked. "In my copious spare time?"

"It would do much to ease the suspicion and mistrust."

Karl thought about it for a moment. "I guess I can spare an hour or so a day."

"Thank you, My Lord. In the meantime, you can expect a formal visit from representatives of the Council sometime very soon."

"Ducky," Karl said with a noticeable lack of enthusiasm. "Just what we need. A project review."

Eighteen

PLAYING IN THE BULLPEN

Any sufficiently advanced technology is indistinguishable from magic.

—Clarke's law

Any sufficiently advanced magic is indistinguishable from technology.

—Murphy's reformulation of Clarke's law

Any sufficiently advanced magic is indistinguishable from a rigged demonstration.

—programmers' restatement of Murphy's reformulation of Clarke

"We've got a good team," Jerry told the wizards as they walked toward the converted cow barn, now known universally as the Bullpen.

The late afternoon sun slanted golden across the court and the air smelled of warm flagstones and dust, with just a tinge of manure to remind them of the Bullpen's original purpose.

Jerry kept up a flow of half-defensive small talk, Bal-Simba was soothing and the other two, Malus and Petronus, were distinctly cold.

"Have you had trouble adapting?" Bal-Simba asked.

"Some. It turns out that there's a strong psychological component here. What a piece of code—a spell—does is constrained by its structure, but its manifestation, the demon it creates, is strongly influenced by the outlook and attitude of the programmer." He sighed. "It's tough, but we're making good progress."

"We have confidence in you, of course," the giant black magician told him. "But the Council has a responsibility to oversee any use of magic in the North."

"And to see that magic is used wisely and safely," Malus said pointedly.

"Naturally we're glad to have you, but there probably won't be much to see," Jerry told him. *I hope*, he added to himself.

Bal-Simba nodded amicably. Actually the visit was about as casual as a surprise inspection by a team of Defense Department auditors, but part of the game was to pretend otherwise.

"There have been certain questions about your performance," Bal-Simba said as they approached the door. "I fear you have not made the best possible impression."

"With all due respect, Lord, we didn't choose our programmers to make a good impression. You need a difficult job done on a very tight schedule and we got the best people we could. I'm sorry that we aren't more presentable, but the most talented people are often a little eccentric."

Bal-Simba nodded, thinking of some of the peculiarities of his fellow wizards.

"Some say your people are as flighty as the Little Folk," Petronus said as they reached the door to the barn.

"That's because they don't know them," Jerry said, reaching out to open the small door set in the larger one. "People who do what we do tend to be very concentrated on their work. They may seem a little strange to anyone on the outside, but their main goal is

always to get the job done. We've got a good team here
and they're a pretty serious bunch."

He motioned Bal-Simba and the others ahead of him.
The black giant ducked his head and stepped over the
sill.

They stood together at the threshold to let their eyes
adjust to the dim light. The barn still smelled of hay,
grain and cattle, a dusty odor that tickled the back of
the nose but not unpleasantly.

"Welcome to the . . ." Jerry's head jerked back as
something zoomed past his nose, climbing almost straight
up.

It was a Mirage jet fighter no bigger than his thumb.
As it topped out of its climb it fired two toothpick-sized
missiles toward the ceiling. There above them a half-
dozen tiny airplanes were mixing it up in an aerial
melee. One of the Mirage's missiles caught a miniature
Mig-21 and blew its tail away. A tiny ejection seat
popped out of the plane as it spiraled helplessly toward
the flagstone floor and an equally tiny parachute
blossomed carrying the pilot down to safety.

Jerry and the wizards gaped.

A two-inch-long F-16 peeled off from the dogfight
and dove at Jerry's head.

"Now cut that out!" Jerry roared. The fighters vanished with soft pops and there was a snickering from
one corner of the Bullpen.

Bal-Simba stared off at the wall and carefully avoided
saying anything.

"Ah, yes," Jerry said. "Well, ah, this is where we
work."

The central aisle of the barn was taken up by a
plank-and-sawhorse table piled high with books, scrolls,
blank sheets of parchment, inkpots, quills and wooden
tablets marked and unmarked. At the far end of the
barn the whitewashed wall was streaked and smudged
from being used as an impromptu whiteboard. Next to
the wall sat a waist-high brazier warming an enormous
pot of blackmoss tea.

The stalls were on either side of the aisles and each stall held a littered trestle table and a chair. Most of them also held at least one programmer.

"All these ones are working on one great spell?" the giant magician asked dubiously.

"Yes, Lord. We divide the work so each of us has a specific part. Our first week here was spent doing systems analysis and producing a design document so we'd all know what we were doing."

Jerry gestured at the long table. "This is our central library. We keep the project documentation and specs here where we can all consult them."

Petronus reached out to examine a large book on top of the pile. Just as his fingers touched it, the pile shifted and hissed at him. He yanked his hand back as a scaly head on a long neck rose out of the mass and slitted yellow eyes transfixed him. Sinuously a small dragon flowed out of its lair among the books. It was bigger than the beast which had guarded Wiz's original book, perhaps two feet long. Its scales were the same vivid red, but they were tinged with blue along the edges. It eyed Bal-Simba with suspicious disapproval.

"Another demon?" the wizard asked.

"No, that's a real dragon. Wandered in here one day and decided it liked it."

"Hunts mice real good," Danny volunteered.

Petronus sniffed and the group moved on. The dragon whuffed suspiciously, decided these people bore watching, and trailed after them, eying the hem of Petronus's robe speculatively.

Jerry scanned the cubicles desperately for someone to show off. Cindy Naismith's feminist manner was likely to offend them, Larry Fox hadn't had a bath since they arrived and Danny was too big a risk to even consider. Finally he saw Karl was in his cubicle and steered the group, dragon and all, in there.

"This is Karl Dershowitz, one of our programmers.

Karl, you know Bal-Simba and these are, ah, Malus and
Petronius."

"Petronus," the wizard corrected, stonefaced.

"Ah, yes. Petronus. Anyway, they're here observing today and I wanted to show them what you were
doing."

Bal-Simba pushed into the stall until he stood directly behind Karl. "What have you there?" he asked.

"I'm working on the sequencing module," Karl told
them, slightly awed by Bal-Simba's bulk and pointed
teeth. "This is the part that reports conflicts between
the different processors."

"And this is the—ah—sequencer?" Bal-Simba gestured at what sat on the desk.

"No, this is a debugging tool. Each of these demons
monitors one of the versions of the code and reports
any destructive interactions."

Sitting on Karl's desk were three monkeys. One had
his paws clasped tightly over its ears, another had its
eyes clinched shut and the third was covering its mouth.
"Hear-no-see-no-speak-no-evil," Karl said. "That means
everything's running fine."

"There's something familiar about those three," Jerry
said. "Something in their faces."

Karl looked sheepish. "Well, yeah. That kinda just
happened."

The monkey demon in the middle suddenly opened his
eyes and glared at the one to his left. He reached out
and poked his fingers in the other's eyes. The demon
recoiled and then grabbed his tormentor by the nose,
twisting it sideways and leading him around the desk.
The third monkey broke up laughing at the sight
and the first two turned on him.

"Okay," Karl said, "we've got a conflict here. One of
the processors jumped the queue and grabbed a resource intended for another one. When they got locked
in contention the third processor got more than his
share of resources."

He looked down at the orgy of eye-poking, nose-twisting and noggin-bopping going on on his desk.

"*Now* I recognize them," Jerry said.

"Uh huh," Karl said. "I've got the sound turned off. Otherwise it gets kinda noisy in here."

They watched the byplay between the monkey demons for a while longer.

"I know I'm going to regret asking this," Jerry said at last, "but what's the name of that module?"

"That's the Scheduling Transport Operating-system Object Generator and Editing System."

Jerry's lips moved as he worked out the acronym. Then closed his eyes. "I *knew* I was going to be sorry I asked."

The group backed out of the stall and moved down to the end of the aisle. Several benches had been arranged about the section used as a whiteboard. Jerry gestured for them to sit.

The dragon had decided Jerry and Bal-Simba were all right. He crowded close to Jerry's legs and bumped his head insistently on his calf. Absently, Jerry reached down and scratched him on the scales behind his pointed ears.

"Have some tea?"

Bal-Simba's nose wrinkled. "I thank you, no." The others also shook their heads and the wizards started to sit down.

The dragon sighed luxuriously and pressed harder against Jerry's legs, forcing him to shift his stance or be knocked off balance. Jerry sat down on the bench harder than he intended, causing the other end to jump up and smack Petronus on the bottom as he sat down. The wizard glared, Jerry reddened and the dragon wuffed insistently, demanding more scratching.

"I want to apologize. Things aren't usually this lively."

"I should hope not," Petronus said.

"Quite a display," Malus said. "Attacked by a swarm of miniature demons as soon as we entered."

"Oh, they weren't attacking us," Jerry assured him. "They were playing a game. The idea is to shoot down your opponent's fighter."

"Your *opponent's* fighter?" asked Bal-Simba. "You mean those demons were not self-motivated?"

"Oh no. What would be the fun of that? The idea is to outfly the other guy."

"So each of those—fighters?—was directly controlled by a magician."

"Sure. At least most of them are. A few were probably drones thrown in to improve the dogfight simulation, but . . ."

"Dogs?" asked Malus. "You call those dogs?"

"Well, no, but it's called a dogfight you see, and . . ."

"If the creatures who are fighting are not dogs, why call it a dogfight?" The pudgy wizard waggled his finger at Jerry. "Confusion. That's what this new magic of yours does, it sows confusion everywhere."

"No, you see . . ." But he was interrupted before he could get any further.

"Fox," a female voice proclaimed from the other end of the Bull Pen, "that's disgusting!"

Cindy Naismith came striding down the aisle, eyes blazing, with Larry Fox trailing behind her.

"Jerry, I want you to do something about this right now!"

"Cindy, can't you see we're having a meeting?"

"Now!" Cindy demanded.

Jerry turned to the wizards. "Ah, excuse me, Lords." Then he faced Cindy and Larry. "Let's go talk, shall we?" and he herded them down to the opposite end of the Bull Pen.

"What the hell is this all about?" Jerry hissed as soon as they were safely away from the inspection party.

"It's about the so-called user interface this cretin wrote for the front end."

"The code's in spec," Larry said sullenly.

"Spec my ass!" Cindy blazed. "That routine is pornographic and demeaning to women!"

"Pornographic code?" Jerry asked, totally bewildered.

"Here," Cindy said. "See for yourself!" She turned and gestured to call up the demon. There was a small billow of pinkish smoke above the central table. It writhed and coalesced into solid flesh. Very solid and very pink.

Jerry gaped. "Holy shit!"

The demon was gorgeous, voluptuous and totally nude. A mass of blue-black hair spilled down over her shoulders, her blue eyes were alight with amusement and promise. She smiled at her watchers and ran a pink tongue tip over her blood-red lips in a way that was blatant invitation. Then she stretched and reclined on the table in a way that made her enormous breasts ride even higher on her ribcage and her dark nipples stick out like strawberries.

In the small part of his mind that was not totally occupied by the vision stretched out on the table, Jerry realized that all three wizards could see what was going on. In fact Malus was standing on the bench and craning his neck to get a better view.

"It gets worse," Cindy said. "You should *see* the things she does!"

"Yeah," breathed Jerry. "I mean, no. Of course not!" The demon shifted her shoulders and pointed her delicate toes at him, still smiling.

"Well, it's supposed to be user-friendly," Larry said in an aggrieved tone. "Hey, I offered to do a male version. Tom Selleck or something. But noooo, she wants to spoil everyone's fun."

"If that's your idea of fun . . ."

The demon smiled again and scissored her legs in a way that showed off her dark pubic patch.

"That's enough!" Jerry said sharply, tearing his eyes away from the demon.

"Look," Jerry mumbled, examining his shoelaces, "this module is supposed to help the user, not distract him. Do some work on that interface, all right?"

As Jerry walked away he heard Danny whisper urgently. "Hey Larry, give me that code, will you?"

"Sorry about the interruption," Jerry said as he came back to the wizards. "Now, let me show you what you came to see."

"I think we have seen enough of this—this circus!" Petronus said.

"Quite enough," Bal-Simba agreed amicably. "My Lord, could you create a demon so obedient to your commands as the ones we saw when we first came in?"

Petronus froze. "I would not demean myself . . ."

"But if you wished to, could you?" he shook his head. "I could not, I know. Have you ever seen a demon so instantly responsive?"

"No," Petronus finally admitted. "No, I have not."

Bal-Simba turned to Jerry. "And how long did it take to create that swarm of demons?"

"Hey Danny," Jerry called out, "how long did it take you to write that air combat game?"

Danny stuck his head around the corner of his cubicle. "Jeez, Jerry, you always assume . . ."

"How long, Danny?" Jerry said inexorably.

The young programmer shrugged. "Oh, maybe four hours."

"You see," Bal-Simba said to his fellow wizards. "In less time than it takes us to frame a moderately complex spell, this young one created a dozen demons whose subtlety we cannot match. This shows the worth of the effort, I think."

Petronus snorted. "Trinkets. A handful of magical trinkets."

Bal-Simba shifted his bulk and the bench teetered alarmingly. "You would rather they write their spells large for practice? Or released them outside the confines of this building? No, I think their wisdom in making trinkets is manifest."

"Well," said Malus, looking longingly down the table toward the spot where the "user interface" had been, "they are certainly accomplishing *something*."

"It is obvious they are accomplishing a great deal," Bal-Simba said. "I think their work should continue unhindered."

Petronus looked from Bal-Simba to Malus. "Oh very well," he said at last. "I only hope we do not regret this afternoon's work." He rose and bowed to his colleagues. "My Lords, if you will forgive me, my own work presses." He turned and stalked the length of the Bull Pen without a backward glance.

"I too must be gone," said Malus. "Unless you have another demonstration?" he asked hopefully.

"No," Jerry said firmly. "Thank you for coming, Lord." Malus bowed and followed his colleague out.

"Thanks, Lord," Jerry said to Bal-Simba as the dumpy wizard pulled the door shut behind him.

"Petronus is firm in resolution, but not subtle in debate," Bal-Simba said, smiling to show off his filed teeth. "He gave me an opportunity and I took it." Then he sobered. "Besides, I was afraid of what might happen if we stayed within a moment longer."

"You and me both, Lord," Jerry agreed feverently.

Bal-Simba rose and Jerry rose with him. "I admit I had some misgivings, but it did not go badly, I think."

"I had a few misgivings myself. Uh, we really are making progress. I can show you if you want."

Bal-Simba chuckled. "Oh, I believe you, Lord. And no, it is not necessary to show me. I trust you and I doubt I would understand half of it."

Jerry followed the huge wizard to the door lost in thought.

"You look as if you have something pressing upon your mind," Bal-Simba said as he held the door for him.

"Well, yes Lord," Jerry said as they stepped out into the courtyard. He sighed. "Look, I know this is a new environment and it's a completely different culture and all, and I know that even the laws of nature are different here." He stopped and for an instant looked as if he might cry. "But Lord, this place gets weirder every day!"

Bal-Simba nodded and looked back at the Bull Pen. "My thought precisely," he said in a bemused tone.

Wiz eased his way down the corridor, hugging the wall and keeping a tight grip on his rusty halberd head. Somewhere off in the distance he could hear the faint drip, drip, drip of water. Dripping water meant running water and running water was likely to be cleaner than the foul musty slop he had found so far. So in spite of his misgivings, Wiz pressed on. It was so cold his breath hung in puffs before him. Short, sharp puffs because Wiz was panting from fear.

The corridor was utterly still and completely empty. Save for the soft dripping and the even softer pad of his own feet there was no sound at all. When he stopped the quiet pressed in around him like a smothering cloak.

Most of the lanterns in the stretch still worked, albeit dimly, holding the dark at bay and leaving the shadows as patches in the corners, to writhe threateningly each time the lamps flickered.

At first Wiz thought the patch ahead of him was another shadow. But it did not shift or vanish as he approached. In the dim light he was almost on top of it before he realized what it was.

In the center of the corridor lay a bloody heap of dark robes wrapped about a thing which might have been a wizard. The head had been smashed like a melon and there was a smear of blood and yellowish brains on the wall beside the corpse. The arms and legs stuck out at impossible angles and the torso was bent backwards as if it had been broken like a dry stick over a giant knee.

Wiz gasped and shrank back against the wall. There

were killers aplenty in the ruins, he knew, but nothing he had seen or heard that had the power to take a wizard—or the sheer ferocity to do this.

Then Wiz looked more closely. There was steam rising from the sundered torso, steam from the shattered skull as the corpse gave up its body heat to the surrounding cold. There were even faint wisps of steam coming from the pools of blood surrounding the remains. The wizard had been dead for only minutes. Whatever had done this had to be nearby.

Wiz turned and ran, all thoughts of fresh water forgotten.

Nineteen

HALF-FAST STANDARD TIME

*Putting twice as many programmers on a project
that is late will make it twice as late.*
—Brooks' law of programming projects

"Good morning," Karl said as he walked into his
makeshift classroom.

The faces of his pupils showed they didn't think there
was anything good about it. Their expressions ranged
from grim determination to equally grim disapproval.
He didn't know what methods Moira and Bal-Simba
had used to round up the dozen or so blue-robed wizards who were sitting at the rows of tables in front of
him, but he had heard hints of everything from cajolery
to blackmail.

Well, Karl thought as he turned back to the black-
board. *At least I don't have to worry about this bunch
throwing spitballs*. He turned around to face the grim-
looking men and women in their magician's robes. *Lightning bolts maybe, but no spitballs*.

"Okay," he said. "Let's go back and review some
basics."

"You sent for me, Lord?" Jerry Andrews asked as he
knocked on the door of Bal-Simba's study.

The black wizard looked up. "I did. Please come in and close the door."

Uh-oh, one of those meetings! Jerry thought as he complied.

"I wanted to find out if there was any way you can speed up your project," Bal-Simba said as soon as Jerry sat down.

"Lord, as I told you at our first meeting, this will take time. We have accomplished an amazing amount, largely because you have been willing to let us alone to get on with it. We're way ahead of any reasonable schedule on this project, but we're still only about forty percent done. It just takes time, Lord."

"I know," Bal-Simba said. "But there have been some, ah, changes since our first meeting. You know that we face the possibility of war with the elves and others?"

Jerry nodded.

"What I tell you now is not common knowledge and I would keep it so. In the past three days we have lost two northern villages."

Jerry's eyes widened. "You mean they were invaded?"

Bal-Simba smiled mirthlessly. "I mean we lost them. They are not there any more. Where they stood is virgin forest once again."

"That's scary."

"Perhaps more frightening than you know. Our watchers and other magicians had not the slightest hint that anything was amiss. There was not the least quiver, not a sign that magic was at work."

"That's *real* scary."

"That is also why I wish to keep it quiet for the time being. But you see why we must have your new magic, and have it soon.

"If we had this we could use it as evidence to help us bargain. Or as a weapon should the bargaining fail. In either event, we *must* have it quickly."

Jerry thought hard. Pressure to complete a project early was nothing new and he had been in a few situations where the fate of the company depended on it. But this was the first time being late with a project meant war.

"How fast do you need it?"

"We need it today," Bal-Simba said. "But the need will be critical in a moon or less."

"We'll try," he said finally. "We'll try like hell, but there's no way we can have a working project in that amount of time."

"I understand," Bal-Simba said heavily. "Be assured that if it comes to open war we will return you and the others to your World before matters come to a head."

"Thanks," Jerry said uncomfortably. "Lord, you do understand that we're working as fast as we can? There's just not much more we can do."

"I do understand that and I thank you for your efforts. Meanwhile, is there anything we can do to make your job easier?"

Jerry made a wry face. "I don't suppose you could come up with a forty-eight-hour day, could you?"

"Would that help?" Bal-Simba asked.

Jerry froze. "You mean you *can* come up with a forty-eight-hour day?"

"No," the huge wizard said sadly. "Only a spell makes a night stretch to twice its normal length. The great wizard Oblius created it for his wedding night. It did not help him for he discovered that his reach exceeded his grasp—so to speak." He shrugged. "I do not think it would aid us for you to sleep twice as long.

"Or would it?" he asked as he caught the look on Jerry's face.

"Do you mean," Jerry said carefully, "that you have a spell that makes time pass half as fast?"

"We do," Bal-Simba said, "but it does not mean that time actually slows down. The people inside think so, but to outsiders they seem to speed up. Besides, it only works from sunset to sunrise."

Jerry whooped and pounded Bal-Simba on the back.

"Fire up that spell! We just may be able to beat this sucker yet."

"People do not work at night," Bal-Simba protested.

"You're not dealing with people," Jerry told him. "These are programmers, boy. Programmers!"

Seklos announced his presence to his master by sniffling and wiping his nose on the sleeve of his robe. He had been showing Dzhir Kar progressively less respect as the hunt for the Sparrow dragged on interminably. Besides, his cold had gotten worse.

"We have lost another one," Seklos said without preamble.

Dzhir Kar raised his head. "Where? How?" he demanded.

"In the south tunnels. Isk-Nor. Killed like the others."

Dzhir Kar nodded. So far half a dozen of the Dark League's wizards had disappeared in the City of Night. Two of the bodies had been found, torn to pieces. Privately Dzhir Kar suspected that most or all of the others had deserted.

"I gave instructions that none were to hunt alone."

"He was not hunting. He was returning from a trip to a warehouse when he became separated from his companion."

"You mean he was out looting and found more than he bargained for," Dzhir Kar said sharply. "I warned you all that it is dangerous to go poking about. The City of Night is no longer ours."

Seklos sniffed and wiped his reddened nose on the sleeve of his robe. "And I warned you we must be done with your notion and sport and use magic to find him quickly."

"No! No detection spells. I forbid it."

"This is absurd! If you wish the Sparrow dead, then let us find him and kill him. But this constant chasing about wastes our time and disperses our energies."

"Do you question my authority?" Dzhir Kar said dangerously.

"No master, only your judgment."

Dzhir Kar glared at his second in command. Under Toth-Set-Ra it would have been unthinkable for one of the Dark League, even the second, to use such language to the leader. But Toth-Set-Ra was dead. Dzhir Kar did not have his predecessor's power.

"I will consider what you say," he said at last.

"Consider this also. There are those who grow restive. The deaths and disappearances of their fellows upset them. All are cold and hungry and many wonder if the prize is worth the effort. Today they grumble quietly. But soon they will do more than that. We must either find the Sparrow or call this off and do one or the other quickly."

Dzhir Kar nodded and waved dismissal. The wizard bowed and, still sniffling, backed from the room.

After Seklos left, Dzhir Kar sat for a long time with his head bowed and his hood pulled up around his face. His lieutenant was right, the deaths and disappearances had made the other wizards nervous. If something was not done, he would have a mutiny on his hands—probably led by Seklos.

His position was anything but secure and he and Seklos both knew it. Unlike Toth-Set-Ra, who had a powerful slaying demon at his beck, or the councils which had ruled the Dark League by playing off the shifting factions, Dzhir Kar ruled by the force of his personality alone. As long as he led the Dark League to success, or at least kept it out of major trouble, he would remain in power. But this business had occupied far too many of his wizards far too long in something both boring and dangerous. If that did not change quickly, the Dark League would have a new leader.

He had promised the Dark League that this would be a simple task. Use the turncoat northern wizard to lure out the Sparrow, rely on the homing demon to neutralize the Sparrow's alien magic and then kill him quickly. On the strength of the League's hatred for the Sparrow and the demonstration of his demon, the League wizards had agreed to his plan.

He raised his head and looked over to where his creation sprawled, eyes slitted and tendrils quivering as it sought a trace of the Sparrow's magic. Dzhir Kar frowned. He hadn't told them the whole truth about his demon. A wizard never did, of course, for knowledge was power. But in this case he had concealed a crucial fact and now that concealment was coming back to haunt him.

It was not a desire for sport that kept him from using detection spells, it was necessity. Detection spells would interfere with the demon's senses. If anyone tried to use a detection spell to find the Sparrow, the demon would not be able to sense his magic in time to stop him from casting a spell. The League knew all too well what the Sparrow's magic was like if he were free to employ it.

Dzhir Kar's head dropped back on his chest and his claw hand tightened on the arm of his chair. Close. So very close to success and now time was running out.

"Two no-trump."

Karl, Nancy, Mike and Larry Fox were sitting at the table in the Wizard's Day Room, all hunched over their cards.

"I thought you'd given up on cards," Jerry said as he came over to them.

"We did, but we figured out a way to make it work," Nancy told him.

"Yeah. It turns out that in this universe a shuffled deck of cards is in something like a Schroediger-indeterminate state," Mike explained. "The cards don't have a value until you—ah—'collapse the state vector' by revealing them."

"Which means you can't play a game if no one has seen the order of the cards," Nancy said. "Even Canfield solitaire, you go through the whole pack the first time."

"Anyway, the key to playing is to collapse the state vector after the cards are shuffled and before they're dealt."

"But if you have to look at the cards what's the point of playing?"

"Oh, the players don't have to know the values," Karl said. "It's enough if someone or something else does. So," he gestured at the head of the table, "meet Moe the Dealer."

Sitting there was a small demon wearing a green eyeshade, a violently patterned vest and garters to hold his shirtsleeves up. His skin was a particularly pale and unhealthy shade of green and a large cigar stuck out of the corner of his mouth.

"So youse gonna bid or youse gonna talk?" Moe demanded in a raspy voice.

"He looks at the cards after he shuffles and before he deals," Larry explained.

"Come on, come on, play cards," Moe said.

Jerry shook his head. "Amazing. Well, finish your game. Starting tonight we go on overtime."

Dark purple shadows were already creeping across the landscape when Danny climbed through the trap door and out onto the roof. June was already there, looking out over the World.

"I guess you heard there's a war brewing," he said without preamble as he sat down next to her. June nodded without taking her eyes off the horizon.

"They've got to have the project even faster, so they've worked out something special," he said eagerly. "They're going to use magic to stretch the nights in the Bull Pen so we can get more work done."

June gasped and turned to him, her face chalk white. "*No!*"

"Hey, take it easy, it's not that big a thing."

June grabbed Danny's hand and held it tight in both of hers.

"Do not go! If you go you will never come out again."

"Hey now . . ." Danny said, but June started to cry silently.

He put his arm about her and patted her shoulder. "Look, it will be all right, I promise. It's only for a night."

"A night in such a place lasts an eon," June said. "I will be dead and dust ere you return."

"No you won't," Danny said and reached forward to pat her shoulder.

June released his hand and locked her arms about him fiercely. She pressed her lips to his and her tongue was like a living thing in his mouth.

Wordlessly she drew him down onto the roof slates, fumbling with his shirt as they went.

Half numb and half exhilarated, Danny followed where she led.

The moon peeking over the gabled roof caught the two naked bodies stretched on the slates. Danny rolled over on his side and admired the play of moonlight and shadow on the curve of June's hip.

"You're really something, you know that?" He ran his hand up over her hip and pressed her small breast, feeling her nipple harden in the center of his palm. June smiled contentedly and turned toward him, lifting her mouth up for a kiss.

Danny kissed her long and gently. Then he broke away with a sigh and reached behind him for his clothes.

"You know I'm gonna get in a lot of trouble for this."

June didn't say anything; she just looked at him.

Danny got to his knees and picked up his pants. "I gotta see if I can get in."

June grasped his wrist hard. "You will not go."

Danny fidgeted. "I've got to," he said. "Look, this is

important. For everybody, okay? They need me. I've got to go, okay?"

This time June seemed to accept it. She dropped her hands to her side and nodded dumbly.

He pulled his shirt over his head. "I'm gonna have to apologize all over the place, tell 'em how sorry I am." He stopped talking while he tucked his shirt into his pants. Then he leaned over and kissed her. "But I'm not sorry."

June smiled but her gaze was troubled.

Danny was in a daze as he made his way down the stairs and out into the courtyard. He wasn't sure what, but something had changed up there on that rooftop and somehow he knew the world would never be the same.

He approached the Bull Pen cautiously. It didn't look any different tonight than it had on any other night. The whitewashed sides shone silver in the moonlight and warm yellow light leaked out of the cracks around the door. But as he got closer he felt a tingling on his skin and the hairs on his arms and legs rose.

The feeling got stronger as he got closer. When he reached for the door there was a resistance like moving his hand through water. The latch was hard to work and the door was very hard to open. When he stepped through something pressed against his face and he couldn't breathe. Then he was through the door and everything was normal again.

"Where the hell have you been?" Jerry demanded as Danny came in.

"Just out."

He looked at him suspiciously.

"You were out screwing around, weren't you?"

Danny just grinned.

"Dammit, we're here to do a job, not get laid by the locals. If you can't keep your mind on what you're doing, then you don't belong here. Is that clear?"

Around them the other programmers were bent to their work, studiously ignoring Jerry and Danny.

"Yes, sir," Danny said meekly.

"I don't care what you do between sunrise and sunset or who you do it with. Men, women or underage goats, it doesn't matter. But between sunset and sunrise your ass belongs to me and you'll have it in here working. Do you understand me?"

"Yes, sir."

"Then get the hell over there and get to work."

Danny's ears burned, but somehow the dressing down didn't sting as much. For perhaps the first time in his life, Danny knew that somebody really cared what happened to him.

As Danny took his seat Jerry shook his head and muttered under his breath before turning back to the routine he had been analyzing with Cindy Naismith.

"Are you sure that little punk's nineteen?" she asked. "He acts more like thirteen."

"He has a California driver's license that says he's nineteen." He looked at her. "He been bothering you?"

"No, nothing like that. At least not me any more than everyone else. But what the hell is he doing here?"

"Moira wanted him. Not my idea. Wouldn't be the first time the customer stuck a dud on a project team."

"Yeah, but usually they're the project manager's girlfriend or something."

"His work's not bad."

"No," Cindy admitted. "He likes to hack an easy way out and he hates doing grunt work, but he's bright and he seems to take to this kind of programming."

"Let's just hope his love life lets him get some work done," Jerry grumbled. "We've just doubled our number of programmer hours and we still can't afford to waste any of them."

The sun was just breaking over the distant mountains when the spell quit and the world jerked back to normal for the team. Most of them took it as a signal to stretch, yawn and head for bed. Mike and Larry stayed at their desks, deep in their work even after so many hours. Judith left with the rest, but she wasn't ready for bed yet. Every day at dawn dragon riders left the Capital on patrol. This was the perfect opportunity to see the dragons.

The aeries were in the cliff beneath the castle. Judith was nearly trembling with excitement as she made her way down the long flights of stairs cut into the rock. All her life she had dreamed about dragons, unicorns and other magical creatures and now she could see them close up. Maybe she could even get one of the dragon riders to take her for a ride. A handsome dragon rider.

In her mind's eye she was already soaring over the castle on dragon back when she reached the portal into the aerie. The two guardsmen on duty recognized her as one of the foreign wizards, which meant she was of the Mighty, after a fashion, and thus allowed to go nearly anywhere. It never occurred to them that she did not know what she was doing when she nodded to them and strode out onto the floor of the aerie.

The aerie was clangor, noise and barely organized confusion. Dragons were being harnessed, armed and carefully guided to their places. Swarms of men and women worked around them, grooming them, tending them and carefully moving the ones ready to fly to their assigned places.

The dragons themselves were fit and eager. They pranced and tried to flex their wings in anticipation. It took careful work by their handlers and a lot of attention from their riders to keep them calm.

As Judith watched, another dragon came up to the mark, spread its huge leathery wings and charged straight at the rectangle of sunlight that was the gate to the outside. It plunged through the portal, disappeared from sight for an instant below the sill and then rose into view again, wings beating as it climbed to join its fellows circling above.

Judith was so enchanted she didn't see the dragon

being brought up behind her until she stepped right in front of it.

The dragon snorted explosively, jerked its head back and lashed its tail in surprise. The whipping tail missed another dragon by inches and slammed into a food cart, knocking it over and spilling chunks of beef and cow intestines everywhere.

The second dragon saw the food laid out before it and lunged for the meat in spite of the efforts of its crew. The first smelled the meat and turned, drawing a warning roar from the other dragon. The first one roared back a challenge and both beasts tried to rear and spread their wings in threat.

What had been organized confusion dissolved into chaos, with dragon roars reverberating from one end of the aerie to the other and men running everywhere trying frantically to get the animals under control.

The Master of Dragons, a gray-haired man with the lithe, compact build of a dragon rider and an empty sleeve from the accident that had ended his riding days came charging down from his platform.

"You fornicating moron," he yelled at Judith over the roars of the dragons and the shouts of the men, *"Get the fornicating shit off the floor!"*

While the crews fought to control the dragons, rough hands grabbed Judith and hustled her out the door.

She stumbled through the portal and stood white and shaking under the disapproving eye of the guards for a moment. Then she burst into tears and dashed up the stairs.

With the coming of the programming team Moira had blossomed. The programmers were ignorant of the ways of this World and they had no time to learn. From her association with Wiz, Moira was better equipped to deal with them than anyone else in the Citadel—even if she frequently didn't understand them. So Moira became 'liaison, staff support and den mother' with her own box on the table of organization charcoaled on the wall of Bullpen.

For the first time since she had come to the Capital, Moira had a job that kept her busy and fulfilled. Most of the time it also kept her mind off Wiz.

She did not go into the Bullpen at night, but her days were filled with obtaining materials the team needed, making sure there was sufficient ink and parchment available, and now with the new spell seeing that food would be ready for them when they emerged at dawn. She also served as go-between to smooth matters between the team and the Mighty and the Citadel's people.

Thus she was the one the Master of Dragons cornered later that morning and berated because one of those execrable new wizards had the fornicating stupidity to blunder out into the execrable aerie just as the execrable morning patrols were taking off. This execrable woman nearly caused a dragon fight, disrupted operations and delayed launching half the patrols by nearly a day-tenth. If these execrable aliens couldn't stay in their places he would go to the execrable Council and get an execrable spell to put a fornicating wall of fire across the fornicating door to the fornicating aerie.

"Begging My Lady's pardon, of course," the man said when he paused for breath.

Moira agreed with him, soothed him, promised it would never happen again and sent him away still grumbling but more or less content.

After he left, she sat in the tiny room in the keep she used for an office and scowled at the wall. From the Master's description she recognized that the offender was Judith, but what in the World had she been doing in the aerie? Everyone knew dragons were difficult, chancy creatures whose handling had to be left to experts. Even if someone didn't know that, it was obvious that a fire-breathing monster with an eighty-foot wingspan was not something to be approached as casually as a pony. These people from Wiz's world might be strange and more than a touch fey, but they were intelligent and they did not appear suicidal.

Well, speculation gets me nothing, she thought, rising from her desk. *The thing to do is find Judith and have a talk with her.*

That and give orders to the guardsmen that the team is not to be allowed free run of the castle, she added as she went out the door.

It took Moira the better part of an hour to find the miscreant. She was standing on the parapet looking so utterly miserable that Moira's carefully prepared scolding died in her throat.

"My Lady, are you all right?"

"Oh, hello Moira," Judith sniffed. "No, I'm fine."

"Forgive me, but you seem upset."

Judith smiled wanly. "I was just thinking that you should be very careful what you wish for because you may get it."

"My Lady?"

Judith turned toward her and Moira could see she had been crying.

"You heard what happened this morning? When I went to see the dragons?"

"That was not wise, My Lady. Dragons are dangerous."

"Yeah. Dangerous, nasty-tempered, foul-smelling beasts." She took a sobbing breath. "Up close they're not even pretty."

"I am sorry if they frightened you, My Lady."

"No, they didn't exactly frighten me." She smiled through her tears. "I probably scared the dragons worse than they scared me. I guess I'm really mourning the death of my dreams."

She sniffed again and smiled with one corner of her mouth. "Funny isn't it? I'm thirty-three years old and I've still got dreams. Or I did until I came here. I believe in romance. Not so much the boy-girl kind as, well—romance."

"Romance?" Moira asked, puzzled.

"Yeah. Castles, dragons, knights in shining armor.

All that stuff. And then one day they all come true. And you know what? They're all about as romantic as a Cupertino car wash!"

Moira thought about it for a minute.

"Why should it be otherwise? People are people in your World or mine. As best I can see they all have the same wants and needs."

"Yeah, but it was supposed to be different! Does that make any sense?" Judith asked miserably.

"In a way," Moira said. "I am not what you call a romantic person, but I think I understand somewhat.

"You know they tell the story of Wiz and I throughout the North." A quick smile. "We are heroes, you see. Figures of romance.

"But what we did was not terribly heroic and it wasn't at all romantic. Mostly I was very frightened and cold. Wiz was too angry that I had been stolen to be heroic. We both did the best we could and by fortune it worked out well."

"So what you're saying is there is no romance in the world, in any world?"

"No, but I think there is another element, one that comes between the doing and the hearing. That is what turns something frightening or wearying or utterly miserable into a romance. I think that element is in the mind of the teller."

She paused and looked out over the battlements to the fleecy clouds. "I think you confuse what is outside with what is within you. The dragons, or the freeways, those are the external things. It is not the deeds or the things that make a romance, it is what you do with them inside yourself.

"My Lady, do you remember the day you arrived, when the dragon cavalry swept over the keep? You made us see them in a way we had never seen them before. I think that is the real secret of romance. Not places or people, but the ability to look at the World and see the romance that is there."

Judith quirked one side of her face up into a smile.

"You may be right. I sure don't seem to be having much luck finding that quality outside of me."

"But you have it inside, Lady. That is better than not having it at all."

"I guess you're right," Judith said, fumbling a well-used handkerchief from her gown's sleeve. "Thanks."

"You are more than welcome, My Lady. Just stay out of the aeries, please."

As the days dragged on Wiz came to know his pursuers well enough that they developed distinct personalities. There was the fat one who hated to exercise and who searched perfunctorily and never a place that was hard to reach or might be dangerous. There was the one who was addicted to laying in ambush, but whose fondness for onions and persistent flatulence gave him away. There was the lean one with the long arms who seemed to delight in rooftops and other high places.

And then there was Seklos. Seklos of the keen nose, who never seemed to rest and who searched relentlessly, who poked into every nook and cranny and who checked everything.

This couldn't go on. He would slip sooner or later. So far only more luck than any mortal deserved had kept him alive and free. But that couldn't last.

Meanwhile, the longer this murderous game of hide-and-seek went on, the more likely it was that there would be a war. It wasn't just his life that was on the line here—*although that is a major consideration*, he thought, it was the fate of the entire World.

Well, if he couldn't run forever and he had to survive, there was only one thing to do. He didn't want to fight the Dark League, but they would not rest until he was dead. He had no way out so he had to fight them to the death.

Yeah, but whose death? He shook the thought off and began to consider methods of fighting back.

*   *   *

This place was odd, Wiz thought. It was a tower in the shadow of what had obviously been a major palace. But the tower was squat and ill-proportioned with doorways big enough to drive a truck through.

The peculiar proportions were emphasized by the fact that the top was missing, blasted away during his attack on the city. But it was sound up to the fourth level, which was where Wiz was standing now.

The room was large and roughly circular, with a single large French door that led out onto a tiny balcony overlooking the street below. It gave a wonderful view of the city, but aside from that seemed useless.

So did the contents of the room. It had either been stripped or hadn't had anything in it to begin with. Just a few stone benches around the walls and some miscellaneous trash on the floor.

He was about to leave when he heard voices outside. Someone was coming up the street below and it could only be wizards of the Dark League.

Normally Wiz would have run away, but his new resolve made him step out on the balcony to check out the situation.

The situation could not have been better. Laying on the balcony were several large blocks of stone which must have fallen when the top of the tower went. Coming up the narrow street were two wizards of the Dark League and one of them was Seklos!

Wiz picked up one of the blocks of stone and rested it on the carved stone railing. Then he watched the wizards get closer and closer and smiled.

". . . dragging me all the way up here," the other wizard said as they came closer. Wiz recognized him as the cautious one.

"Because this is where he must be," Seklos said. "Fool, do you not see that the quicker we catch this most troublesome bird, the sooner we can leave this place?"

Wiz put both hands on the block and held his breath.

"But why me?" the other wizard asked.

He never got his answer. At that moment they came under the balcony and Wiz shoved the rock over the edge.

Wiz watched with a sinking heart as the stone smashed into the pavement and shattered a good arm's length behind his intended victim. He scuttled back from the edge dislodging a shower of pebbles in the process.

Seklos' companion gaped at the shattered rock on the pavement behind them. "Dangerous place." He looked up at the tower nervously. "The stones are loose."

Seklos looked up at the parapet. "I do not believe in such accidents." He turned to his companion. "Go, spread the word that this area is to be cordoned off and searched most carefully. I think we may be near our Sparrow."

As he pounded down the stairs, Wiz realized he had made a serious mistake. There was only one door to the tower and that was just around the corner from where the wizards had been standing. If he didn't get out the door before Seklos came looking for him . . .

Too late! He was still nearly a flight from the bottom when Seklos came through the door and into the tower. As quietly as he could, Wiz backed up the stairs.

Seklos came on, staff in hand, ready to strike at the slightest sound or movement. Wiz moved back up the spiraling stairs ahead of him. There was no time to open a door and no room to squeeze past his pursuer. The only place he could go was back into the room where he had thrown the rock.

That'll still work, he thought, fighting down the panic rising inside him. *He can't see me and as soon as he comes into the room I'll be able to slip around him and get down the stairs.* Moving as quietly as he could, he eased through the door and made for the far end, next to the window.

Seklos strode into the room and sniffed the air. His head swung this way and that like a hunting dog tracing a scent. Wiz stood stock still, afraid to breathe. Two more steps and he would be far enough in that he could get behind him and out the door.

Seklos took a single cautious step into the room and scanned from side to side. The wizard stopped short. "What . . ." Then his face split in an evil smile.

"A cloak of invisibility? Clever Sparrow. Oh, very clever indeed. But did they not tell you never to stand in a sunbeam wearing a tarncape?" He raised his hand and flicked his wrist in the direction of the window. Wiz had a glimpse of something silvery flying through the air. Instinctively he dove and rolled.

Behind him the stone wall exploded into flame. Wiz hugged the floor and squinted his eyes shut to block out the heat.

Dust! Wiz thought frantically. *The dust gave me away!* Seklos must have seen his outline in the sunlit dust motes. He raised his head and saw Seklos blocking the doorway, his staff extended out in front of him. Behind him a wall of luminous blue blocked the doorway.

In desperation, Wiz hefted the halberd. He knew he couldn't get in under the staff with the shorter weapon, so he threw it at the wizard, sidearm so it spun horizontally.

As soon as it left Wiz's hands the halberd became visible. Seklos dodged it easily, swaying to one side like a snake. His face lit with unholy glee as it watched it sail past him.

"So you confirm your presence. Thank you, Sparrow. And now you cannot hide. Your cloak cannot save you." The wizard extended his staff and waved it from side to side like a blind man while he fumbled in his sleeve.

On tiptoe Wiz backed away from the questing staff. No good to try to get around him. Frantically he looked for someplace to hide.

The only possible place was under one of the benches. Wiz squeezed beneath the nearest one, face to the wall in a vain attempt to muffle his breathing. He clinched his eyes tight and waited to feel the lethal staff tip in the center of his back.

"Come out, little Sparrow," the hateful, hate-filled voice crooned. "Come out and face your end."

There was a hideous roar followed by a ringing scream cut short in mid-cry. Then there was a thrashing and horrible crunching noise. Wiz forced himself further back into the crevice.

Then all was silence. No sound from Seklos, no sound of anything else. As quietly as he could Wiz twisted around and looked out.

At first he thought it had suddenly turned to night. All he saw from beneath the bench was blackness. And then the blackness moved. The enormous black body hopped ponderously to one side, the huge head turned. Wiz went weak from sheer terror.

The thing looked at Wiz with burning red eyes and then turned away. It lumbered through the last dying vestiges of the blue fire and out the door. Wiz heard it make its way down the corridor.

It took a long time for Wiz to get his heart back under control. The monster had destroyed the wizard and it looked right at him, but it hadn't touched him. The way the thing looked at him Wiz knew it had to have seen him. But it hadn't made a move to harm him. Somehow Wiz did not think it was because the monster was a friend.

Wiz had never seen the huge black creature, but he recognized it from descriptions. It was Bale-Zur, the slaying demon which had brought Toth-Set-Ra to power in the Dark League and then destroyed him when Wiz attacked the City of Night.

There was something about that. Something he had learned. He cudgeled his brains, trying to recall that almost-remembered bit of knowledge. Something he saw? No, something someone told him. Before he used his new magic to travel to the City of Night and rescue Moira. Something someone told him about demons, or dragons, or . . .

Of course! True names. Humans weren't the only creatures with true names. Fully mature dragons had them. And so did some kinds of demons because it was only by knowing their true names that they could be controlled. That was how Bale-Zur found his prey. Unlike other demons, the great slaying demon did not need to know a thing's true name to destroy it. All it needed was for the being's true name to have been spoken somewhere in the World at some time.

And of all mortals in the World, William Irving Zumwalt was the only one safe from Bale-Zur. No one had ever spoken his full name—his true name—anywhere in this World.

Licking his lips, he stepped over the gruesome remains of the wizard. As he did so he kicked something that rolled across the floor.

Wiz was almost afraid to look down for fear his foot had touched some body part. But it was only a silvery sphere about the size of a baseball that had been clutched in what was left of Seklos' hand.

Seklos must have grabbed it when Bale-Zur attacked him, Wiz thought. Overcoming his revulsion, he bent down and picked up the sphere. He couldn't be sure but it looked like the thing that the wizard had thrown at him, the one that spread fire on the stones.

He forced himself to look at what was left of Seklos and realized his left sleeve was lumpy. Swallowing his gorge, Wiz reached into the blood-sodden sleeve and fished out two more of the spheres. He could have done it faster except he kept his eyes closed through the whole process.

The three spheres gave him weapons, his first real weapons that might be effective against the wizards of the Dark League.

The wizards . . . ! Seklos had sent his companion for help. Wiz stuffed the balls into his pouch, grabbed his halberd and dashed down the stairs. There were three wizards not more than a hundred yards up the street when he emerged from the building. Without hesitating, Wiz ran around the corner, leaving the black robes to wonder at the sound of footsteps with no sign of the runner.

Several blocks away, Wiz sank back against the wall of an empty storeroom and listened for any sound of pursuit.

The situation got worse and worse. His cloak of invisibility's spell had some loopholes. Wiz had no doubt at all that there were counter-spells that would render it useless.

Wiz forced himself to calm down and think. Through all the hunger and cold and terror, he had to *think*.

He had to summon help somehow and if he expected to live long enough for that he had to defeat or neutralize the Dark League. Two problems and both of them looked insoluble.

But maybe—just maybe—one problem could solve another again.

He needed magic to get out of here. If not magic to walk the Wizard's Way, then a burst of magic to attract the Watchers who stood guard over the whole of the World.

But it didn't have to be a burst of *his* magic.

Wiz looked at the three spheres in his lap and a plan began to form in his mind.

Dzhir Kar rested his pink scarred forehead in his one good hand and ground his teeth in frustration.

The Sparrow had slipped through his grasp again! They had been within a hairsbreadth of him this time, he knew it. Yet that damnable little bird had fluttered through his clutches once more.

And now Seklos was gone. Seklos the tireless, the indefatigable. Seklos who hated this Sparrow almost as much as he did. Torn apart by something in the upper city while the entire contingent of the Dark League came running to his rescue.

That hadn't been lost on the rest of his band. They

had seen what had happened to Seklos and the sight had done nothing for their ardor in the search. Now most of them wanted to leave the City of Night and abandon the search. Only his overwhelming skill at magic and the loss of the natural leader of any opposition to him kept them here.

Still his demon lay coiled in an alcove of the chamber. Occasionally it would raise its head and the tendrils along its fanged mouth would quiver as the Sparrow considered using magic, but so far there was no magic from this most alien of wizards, nothing the demon could home in on.

It was enough, Dzhir Kar thought, to make a wizard cry.

Twenty

FORCING A FIGHT

Never give a sucker an even break.
                    —W. C. Fields

Especially not if he's a big, mean sucker.
            —the collected sayings of Wiz Zumwalt

Wiz tiptoed down the corridor, convinced that the sound of his heart must be giving him away at every beat. Over and over he repeated to himself the route out of this maze.

It was unfamiliar ground to him. This was the one part of the City of Night he had been striving to avoid ever since he was kidnapped. This was the path to the lair of the Dark League.

There were no guards and no sign of magic protecting this place, which only made Wiz more nervous.

Finally he turned a corner and saw a brightly lighted doorway not thirty feet ahead. There were two black robes standing in front of it talking. Through the open door he could see others moving around.

Wiz stepped back around the corner and for the first time in weeks, removed his cloak of invisibility. Taking one of Seklos's fire globes in his hand he turned the corner again and, before the wizards could react, threw the ball straight at them.

His aim with the ball was no better than his aim with the rock. About two-thirds of the way down the corridor the ball broke against the wall and a sheet of flame erupted between him and the wizards. A lightning bolt lanced through the flames and struck near him. Wiz turned and ran with the shouts of the wizards ringing in his ear.

The tricky part is going to be making sure that everyone arrives when they are supposed to, he thought as he dodged down the corridor. Another bolt of lightning crashed into the stone behind Wiz, knocking off chips and tainting the air with the tang of ozone.

That and staying alive. Wiz ran faster and threw the tarncape around his shoulders.

"*What was that?*" Dzhir Kar roared, rising from his desk. From his place in an alcove off the workroom, Pryddian cringed back.

One of the wizards burst into the room, hair and beard singed and smoking holes in his robe. "Dread Master, the Sparrow has attacked us!"

"Then after him. After him! Everyone!" Dzhir Kar was hopping up and down in fury. "Catch him and bring him to me."

The wizards piled out of the workroom in a rush. Dzhir Kar paused long enough to look over at his demon, still coiled with its eyes closed. He grasped his staff with his good hand and hobbled after his wizards.

"Dread Master?" Pryddian spoke tentatively.

Dzhir Kar gestured and a wall of heatless blue fire sprang into being across the door to Pryddian's alcove. The apprentice cringed back away from the deadly flame.

"Stay there until we return," he croaked and hobbled out.

It turned out to be nearly as hard to keep the hunt going as it had been to avoid it entirely. By alternately

showing and concealing himself, Wiz was able to keep
his pursuers after him. Once or twice he almost had to
shout at them to bring them back on the track. At first
he worried about being too obvious. Then he saw that
the wizards were so eager to catch him that nothing
could make them pause to consider his motives.

He had to wait for several minutes outside the gate
near the strange tower before he was spotted by a
wizard. Then three of them came around the corner at
once and let fly at him with a flurry of lightning bolts as
he dodged through.

"This way, Dread Master, this way," the wizards
chorused a few moments later when Dzhir Kar came
up, using his staff as a crutch.

"He did not go beyond this place," another assured
him. "We came from all points of the compass."

Dzhir Kar peered through the gate at the courtyard
beyond. The square was windowless with walls perhaps
four times the height of a man. A single door gaped on
the opposite side of them from the gateway.

"Trapped!" Dzhir Kar crowed. "There is no way out
of that building. We have him now. Spread out, broth-
ers. Spread out fingertip to fingertip and we will hunt
down our Sparrow." He picked up a handful of wind-
blown dust from the marble paving and threw it into
the air before him.

"Use the dust. It will show his form."

The wizards quickly formed a ragged line. Two paces
apart they advanced across the court, tossing dust into
the air as they went.

Lying on his belly on the roof of the building Wiz
watched them come. It had taken him the better part of
the night to chop and pry a hole in the roof so he would
have this vantage point and escape route. Now all he
could do was watch and wait—and be ready to run if his
plan went awry.

The line of wizards was half-way across the square
when the shadows in the building began to move. As
one man they stopped, forewarned by their magical

senses. The line wavered as some of them stepped back, away from the darkened doorway where something was clearly stirring. Wiz held his breath.

And into the square came the demon Bale-Zur.

Normal mortals would have fled. But wizards need courage beyond ordinary men and women. Besides, they knew it would be futile to run.

A score of wizards threw back their sleeves and raised their staffs almost in unison. Suddenly it was Hell out for the Fourth of July in the square.

Magics flashed and roared across the square. Spells crackled through the air to bounce off the demon like many-hued lightnings. Balls of green and purple and blinding white fire flew this way and that across the square.

None of it mattered. Bale-Zur did not even flinch as he came across the marble flagging with a hopping, toad-like gait. A wizard screamed as the creature reached out with great rending claws.

Crippled as he was, Dzhir Kar could not run. He stood his ground to the end, flinging spells at the demon until the clawed hand reached down and scooped him up to the rending, blood-stained jaws.

The last few wizards tried to run, but it made no difference. In spite of his clumsy gait Bale-Zur was far faster than any human. Their screams mingled with the demon's roars as he crushed the life out of them. Wiz clapped his hands to his ears and turned away from the scene in the court below him.

Then all was silent. There were no more cries, no more roars, no more crash and flash of magic. Suddenly the only sound was the icy wind playing over the stonework and making weird little whistling noises as it stirred the dust below.

Once again the warty head swiveled and again Wiz stared into eyes as red as the fires of Hell. Then the eyes slid over him and the huge toadlike demon turned away. Soundlessly it half-dragged, half-hopped out of the square, heedless of the black-robbed bodies it crushed beneath its great clawed feet.

"Odd," the Watcher said, staring back into her crystal. "What?" the wizard asked.

"There, in the City of Night, a sudden flare of magic."

"Is it the Sparrow?" the other asked eagerly.

"No, it is not the new magic." She shrugged. "Perhaps just a remnant of the Dark League's power."

The other nodded. The Watchers were used to strange things happening in the ruined city. As long as they were not too powerful they were nothing to worry about or to be passed up the chain of command.

Still, the Mighty were frantic to find Wiz and this was an unusual occurrence. The shift commander looked up. "What have we got near the City of Night?"

"No assets in place right now," the patrol commander called back from the other side of the pit. "There is a squadron of dragon cavalry that could swing further south and be there in two day-tenths."

"Then send them south," the shift commander told her. "Have them search over the City of Night carefully." The patrol commander nodded and turned back to her crystal.

"Should we also inform Bal-Simba, Lord?" asked the deputy commander.

"No. No point in that. This may be nothing after all."

With the flash and pulse of repeated magics still ringing in his ears, Wiz made his way to the large open space in the center of the city.

The forces unleashed as the wizards fought for their lives against Bale-Zur would provide a beacon, a magical flare big enough to be seen by the Watchers back at the Capital. Now all he had to do was mark his chosen vantage point and scan the skies for the dragon patrols which were sure to come south to investigate the magical maelstrom he had touched off. There was food and water in his pack for several days, and two more of the fire globes to make a final signal to guide the rescuers in. He had even taken the precaution of gathering up several long pieces of white fabric to use as marker panels. They would stand out vividly against the dark sand.

Carefully he laid down the white cloth taken from the chests in the shape of a large X. He anchored the pieces with handfuls of the fine black volcanic sand that floored the square. That done, he stood up, stretched and leaned over backwards to ease his aching back muscles.

Wiz looked up, squinting into the pale sun. The walls ran straight up and smooth for perhaps thirty feet. Above that they moved out in a series of steps. Like ranks of bleacher seats.

Like ranks of bleacher seats . . . Wiz looked around with a new comprehension. The black sand beneath his feet, the unclimbable walls, the seats above suddenly all made sense. An arena. He was standing in an arena. The central tower must have something to do with the events held here.

Wiz shuddered. Knowing what the Dark League had been he didn't want to think about what those events must have been like.

Well, that's over and done with, he told himself. *Arena or not, it's still the best place in the city to watch for help.*

He looked over the tower speculatively. It was a squat oval with slanting sides perhaps four stories tall. The top was mostly flat with a large square block, man high, in the middle. In use the tower would have been as impossible to scale as the arena walls, but the earthquakes that had accompanied his attack on the City of Night had caused one section of the tower to collapse, leaving a crude stairway of large stone blocks up to the top.

Wiz hefted his pack, picked up his halberd and started across the sands to the tower.

There was a scuffling sound from the far end of the arena. Wiz turned and saw several lean wolf-like shapes almost as dark as the sand emerge from one of the doors.

With a sinking feeling, Wiz realized he wasn't out of the woods yet.

Now what in the World did those sods back at the Capital want? the Dragon Leader thought.

He and his patrol had been on the wing for nearly twelve hours already. Men and dragons alike were tired and even with heating spells they were chilled beyond numbness. The flight would have to stop to rest the dragons on the way back as it was. If they continued south to pass over the City of Night they might have to set down on the Southern Continent itself. The Dragon Leader didn't like that at all. The Dark League might be gone, but there were still things on that continent he did not wish to meet on the ground with half a dozen exhausted men and dragons.

Still, orders were orders. He rose in his saddle against the restraining straps and signaled his men to turn their patrol line south toward the ruined city.

One quick pass, he promised himself. *One quick pass and then it's north and home!*

A weird warbling howl broke the windy stillness of the ruined city.

Dire Beasts!

Wiz had only seen the wolflike creatures once before, by moonlight on the night he and Moira had been chased through the forest by the forces of the Dark League. He had had only a glimpse then and the sight had left him with nightmares for months. Now he counted a half dozen of the great wolflike creatures slinking out into the open space.

Frantically Wiz scrambled up the broken stone on the side of the tower. The blocks were six and seven feet high and sometimes he had to stand on tiptoe or jump to reach the next one. Once his fingers slipped off the smooth surface and he landed painfully on the block he had just left. Another time he jumped back as a block teetered dangerously when he grasped it.

He reached the top panting and gasping. Then he rolled over flat on his belly and peered down into the arena. The Dire Beasts had congregated below, looking up the way Wiz had come. One or two of them broke off from the pack and slunk around the base of the tower, as if looking for another way up.

He half-formed a spell in his mind, but he felt the familiar dread quivering and knew that the demon had survived its creators.

Now the ones that had split off came racing back. The entire pack put their noses together and whined and growled at each other, looking up occasionally toward Wiz. Finally the huddle broke and very tentatively one of the Dire Beasts began to climb.

The things were much better climbers than wolves were, but not as good as a man. Only the one collapsed section of the tower gave access to the platform where Wiz lay.

Wiz put his pack aside and picked up his halberd. He was armed and his enemies had to climb up a steep grade to reach him one at a time. Somehow Wiz doubted that was enough to make it a fair fight.

The dark coastline ahead looked about half as attractive as Hell with the fires out.

Not all the fires on the Southern Continent were out. The volcano that towered above the City of Night was trailing a thin smear of dirty smoke from its top. Rising along its flank, the City of Night was a disordered jumble.

Dragon Leader made his decision. They would come in fast, swooping from altitude to gain speed. One single fast pass over the ruined city and they would be away for an island in the Freshened Sea where they could rest for a few hours. Signalling his men to spread out in a patrol line, Dragon Leader urged his weary mount to climb higher in preparation for the sweep.

*　　　*　　　*

"Got something here," the rider on the far left of the patrol line reported. Dragon Leader pressed his mount's flank with his knees to bring him around to check.

As soon as he glided over the courtyard he saw what had attracted the rider's attention.

Scattered around were several dark-robed bodies, some crushed and dismembered. The walls and paving of the court were streaked and discolored from the aftereffects of powerful spells. One section of the wall had melted and run like candle wax under the magical impact.

Looks like they dueled among themselves, Dragon Leader thought. *That explains the magic the Watchers sensed.* He looked down at the crumpled dark forms and shrugged mentally. *Whatever it was, it doesn't involve us.* He spoke into his communications crystal. "Echelon right and climb for altitude. We need to reach the island before dark."

Now there were four Dire Beasts climbing the broken rock toward him. Wiz bit his lip and watched them come. He fished into his pouch and pulled out one of the fire globes. Animals were supposed to be afraid of fire. Perhaps this would frighten them off.

Lying flat on the stones, Wiz tossed the fire globe over the side. There was a satisfying "whoosh" and leap of flames. After a second, he stuck his head over the edge to see the effect.

He nearly lost his nose for his pains. Not only hadn't the fire daunted the beasts, the first one was almost to the top. Powerful jaws with two sets of fangs snapped shut so close Wiz could smell the stench of the thing's breath. He jerked his head back and rolled away. Then he realized he had to keep the thing off the platform at all costs.

Too late. The wolf thing had gained the platform with all four feet. Hackles up and back fur stiffened into a mane, the Dire Beast advanced on him. Wiz fumbled in his pouch and came up with the second fire ball.

The globe flew straight and true to shatter at the beast's feet. Instantly the animal was engulfed in an inferno. With a howl of agony, it threw itself from the stone platform. It made a blazing fireball all the way to the blackened sand. It struck with a "thump" and lay still.

For a moment the Dire Beasts hung back. Then one of them howled and they charged up the crumbling stone again.

In the back of his mind, Wiz realized he had just thrown away his last hope of signaling should help arrive.

Dragon Leader had just crossed the beach out over the Freshened Sea when his wingman broke in on the communications frequency.

"Smoke behind us."

Dragon Leader twisted in his saddle. A thin black curl of smoke was rising in the distance, back over the city.

He hesitated. Should they turn south again to check it out? It was probably an accidental fire or a new volcanic vent. Their orders had been to search for magic. Certainly it was not magic, he told himself. Therefore it was none of his business.

The welfare of his troop was his business and that demanded he get them to a safe resting place as soon as possible. The other members of the flight craned their necks to see and he could feel them waiting for orders.

"Not our pigeon," Dragon Leader said finally into the communications crystal. "Hold your course." The rest of the troop relaxed. He felt his wingman start to say something and he braced for a challenge to the order, but the challenge never came.

They had flown north for three more wing beats when he sensed a change in the formation. He looked back and saw his wingman sliding in.

The formation had opened out, as it always did on long patrols. Now the wingman was closing into the precise Number Two position, tucked in tight to his leader's right, exactly as he had been taught in riding school. In spite of the long hours they had been in the air, the younger man was sitting bolt upright in his saddle and he was ostentatiously checking his weapons and equipment in exactly the manner prescribed when leaving a combat zone.

Every maneuver, every patrol, you will perform as if it were the real thing! . . . by the checklist, mister!

He felt his subordinate's eyes boring into him and he knew every other man in the flight was watching as well. Dragon Leader had seen nearly thirty winters and suddenly he felt all of them.

"Shit!" he muttered to himself. But he sat up straighter and tightened the straps holding him to the saddle. Then he pressed his knees into his weary mount's side and with a wave of his arm turned his squadron south again over the City of Night.

Wiz thrust desperately at the snarling face just a few inches below him. The creature snaked its head to the side to avoid the thrust and snapped at the halberd head. Claws scrabbled against rough stone as the Dire Beast got first one foot and then another up on the stone ledge. Wiz chopped down at a leg, but the animal yanked it back and the blade struck sparks from the basalt. The head lunged forward and the jaws snapped like a pistol shot. Wiz was forced to give ground as the creature got all four feet on the stone. Behind the first, Wiz could see the head of a second Dire Beast climbing the same path.

Unbidden, Donal's words came back to him. *Put your back to the wall and die like a man.*

Halberd in both hands, Wiz edged away from the snarling monster, back towards the wall. Hackles up, the creature advanced slowly across the rock.

Wiz bumped into the wall and nearly stumbled. He pressed his back against the cold, rough stone and raised the broken halberd. The two Dire Beasts split up and circled to either side of him. Wiz took a deep, rasping breath and squinted into the pale sun, trying to keep track of both creatures at once.

A shadow fell over his face. Above him he heard the sound of wings. Dragon wings.

What in the . . . ?

Dragon Leader scanned the scene below. Down in the arena there were about a half dozen wolves or something attacking what looked like a lone man.

There was even a checklist for cases like this. It called for two dragons to drop low to investigate while the others stayed overhead flying a complex figure eight pattern. Dragon riders knew from bitter experience that there were things beyond the borders of men which were masters of illusion and used that power to lure men and dragons to their deaths.

Dragon Leader watched as the speck on the ground retreated before the two larger, darker specks that split up to come at him from either side. The checklist called for him to spread his formation out while the two scouts descended in broad circles, looking for signs of an ambush. Already the two dragon riders on the rear of the formation were drifting out and getting ready to spiral down on his command.

The tiny figure moved back against the central pylon and raised a weapon of some sort above its head. The attackers were now on either side of him, ready for the final killing lunge.

Bugger the checklist! Dragon Leader winged his mount over and signaled the rest of the squadron to follow. In a compact mass a dozen dragons hurtled down on the arena.

The Dire Beasts were so intent on their prey they had no warning. The first they knew of the dragons overhead was when a fusillade of missiles tore into their pack.

Suddenly two of the beasts were down with iron arrows in them. One of them bit weakly at the bolt that skewered through its flank and the other one was already still. Three more arrows vibrated in the sand where they had missed their targets.

The dragons swept low into the arena, their wingtips almost brushing the dark sand and the wind of their passage, raising clouds of sand behind them as their riders pulled them into steep turns.

The Dire Beasts on the rock hesitated, torn between the nearness of their prey and the threat from the air. Finally a gout of dragon fire decided for them and they broke away, leaping down the crumbled stone and sprinting across the arena pursued by arrows and bursts of fire.

One of the dragons settled onto the ledge behind Wiz. As the animal folded its wings, the rider swung off and walked stiffly to where he stood.

The man was dirty, disheveled and his eyes were rimmed red from fatigue and hours of squinting into the wind. Still he was the loveliest sight Wiz had ever seen.

"Lord, we have been scouring the World for you!"

"Just get me out of here," Wiz said weakly.

PART IV: RUN TIME

Twenty One

BED REST

Sleep? Isn't that a completely inadequate substi-
tute for caffeine?

—programmers' saying

A hospital looks like a hospital anywhere you go. At least this one smelled of sweet herbs and fresh cut hay instead of stinking of disinfectant.

Wiz was in no shape to appreciate it. He was asleep when they carried him in and he was still asleep when Moira and Bal-Simba came to see him.

Moira bit her lip to keep from crying when Bronwyn and Bal-Simba ushered her into his room. They had cleaned him up, but he was thin and drawn with new lines etched about his mouth and eyes. He looked as if he had aged a decade in the weeks he had been gone. He was still and unresponsive and for a terrible moment she thought he was dying.

But Bronwyn touched her arm when she moved toward the bedside. "It would be best if you did not wake him, Lady," the healer said.

"What is wrong with him?"

"Shock, fatigue and starvation mostly. There was some sickness in his lungs but we cleared that up."

"What happened to him?"

"We are not certain," Bal-Simba told her. "He was kidnapped to the City of Night by what is left of the Dark League, but aside from that he has told us very little." He frowned. "He was not in very good shape when we found him."

"Best we leave now," Bronwyn said softly. "He needs to sleep for as long as he can."

"May I stay, Lady?" Moira asked. "I'd like to be here when he awakes."

"It is likely to be a long vigil. He will doubtless sleep the night through and perhaps a good portion of tomorrow."

"Please, Lady?"

Bronwyn sighed. "Very well. But leave him strictly alone."

Moira nodded and settled herself in a chair next to the bed.

Pryddian hunched into the corner to get out of the freezing wind. The stones were like ice against his back and the chill crept closer around him. Overhead the clouds rolled low and slate gray, driven and torn to streamers. He felt a freezing drop on his face and realized it was starting to snow.

He had to find shelter. But there was no shelter to be seen. Behind him was the pitch black mouth of the tunnel he had stumbled from. The buildings on either side of the street had collapsed in heaps and the roadway was full of rubble.

Pryddian was not sure what day it was. At least one had passed since he had been left imprisoned in the workroom, but was it just one or had there been more?

He had been content to wait for the wizards' return—until the lights went out, the wall of fire vanished and the heating spell failed leaving him alone with the demon in icy darkness. It took him a few minutes in the absolute dark to nerve himself to try the door and it took him hours more to blunder out into the wan cold day.

Pryddian shivered as he considered his options. The wizards had not returned from their confrontation with the Sparrow. That meant they were either dead or they had forgotten him in their victory. Remembering the way the light globes had flickered and failed and how the heat cut off suddenly, Pryddian did not think the Dark League had won.

He shivered uncontrollably and his breath puffed white. Now what? He could not walk the Wizard's Way unaided; he did not know how. He could not sail the Freshened Sea back; he was not a sailor and there were no boats left in the City of Night. He did not even have a communications crystal to call the Council and beg for rescue.

Come to that, he could not find his way back to the Dark League's workroom, not through that maze of darkened tunnels. Despair, cold and cruel as the wind, knifed through him as he realized he was probably doomed to dwell alone in the City of Night for the rest of his life. He did not allow himself to think about how long that might be.

He felt more snowflakes on his face, stinging now as the rising wind drove them against his exposed skin. *No point in standing here.* Somewhere in the city there had to be something to eat and a place out of the cold.

Cautious as a mouse, Pryddian, ex-apprentice of both the Council of the North and the Dark League, picked his way down the ruined street in search of food and warmth.

Bronwyn was right. Wiz slept like a log the night through, not even turning. Moira watched and dozed as best she could in the chair, waking every time Wiz so much as sighed.

The middle of the following morning he began to stir. Moira moved to his bedside as his eyes fluttered open.

"Moira?" Wiz said weakly.

"Hush," she said as she caressed his forehead. Instinctively he reached up to clasp her to him.

"Feeling better, are we?" said a brisk voice from the door. Wiz and Moira broke their clinch with a start and turned to see Bronwyn stride into the room with Arianne trailing her.

The healer ran a practiced eye over Wiz, checked his pulse and poked and prodded him a bit and then nodded in satisfaction.

"Will I ever play the piano again, Doc?"

"You mean will you recover? Of course you will. But that is what I need to speak to you about.

"There is nothing wrong with you that time and rest and a little careful nursing will not cure." She looked over at Moira. "Now I could use a healing spell to cure you this afternoon. It would be better if you were left to heal naturally but they tell me the North needs you on your feet as quickly as possible." She frowned her professional disapproval, but Arianne nodded.

"Yeah," Wiz shifted and sat up in bed, "there's a lot I've got to do."

Bronwyn sighed. "Very well, then. I will keep you here overnight just to be sure, though. After that get what rest you can and try to conserve your strength."

She turned to Moira. "Lady, you are bonded to this one. Will you assist me?"

Moira nodded. "Willingly."

Bronwyn took a position on the right side of the bed and Moira stood on the left. Each of them took one of Wiz's hands, and Bronwyn began to chant and gesture with her wand. She tapped Wiz's temples, his throat, his chest and his groin with the wand, then laid it aside and clasped Moira's free hand. Now Moira took up the chant in a minor key.

As they watched, the color flowed back into Wiz's skin and the lines in his face smoothed out. Wiz's mouth formed a little o of surprise as he felt the strength flow back into him.

Bronwyn released her grip, sighed and sagged into a chair.

Wiz shook his head. "Whoooeeee. That is really something."

"Just be careful not to overtax yourself," Bronwyn said from her chair. "Healing spells extract their price."

"I think I know the first one. I'm starved."

"Indeed," Arianne said. "I will see to it. And what will you do afterwards?"

"First I need to talk to Bal-Simba. We're in big trouble.

"And then," he said deliberately, "I'm going to eat a little crow."

Arianne nodded and left. Bronwyn stayed for a few minutes more, resting in the chair and then examining Wiz again before repeating her admonition that he get all the rest he could.

"Bal-Simba or no, I am keeping you one more night," she told him. Then she too left.

Finally Wiz and Moira were alone.

Moira rested her hand on Wiz's shoulder and he clasped it tightly in both of his.

"God, I missed you," he said.

"And I missed you," she told him, putting her other hand on top of his.

"We've got to talk, you know," he said at last.

"I know. I came back from Heart's Ease to talk to you and you were gone."

"Yeah, I thought about you in the City of Night a lot. When I could.

"Moira, I'm sorry," Wiz said. "I let myself get so wrapped up in my own problems that I shut you out."

"And I crowded you too closely because I had nothing of my own here."

He smiled up at her. "We'll just have to try to do better, won't we?"

"We shall both have to try."

"Darling, do me a favor will you? If I start acting like a jerk again, punch me in the ribs. Hard."

Moira took his hand in hers. "I think I can manage that."

He reached up, pulled her down to him and kissed her again.

"In fact I will do better than that," she said with an amused glint in her sea-green eyes. "If you *ever* ignore me again, or treat me like a piece of furniture, I will make you sorry indeed." Moira made a quick little motion with her hand and the air in front of her sparkled with shards of the rainbow. "And believe me, My Lord, I am just the witch who can do it."

Wiz looked at her openmouthed. "You wouldn't do that to me, would you?"

Moira smiled sweetly. "Try me."

There was a discreet knock at the door. They turned and saw a servant carrying a covered tray.

"Your, ah, dinner, Lord," the man said with an odd expression as he laid the tray on the table beside Wiz's bed. He removed the warming cover and withdrew.

Sitting on the plate, neatly trussed and roasted, was a small bird. The odor from the platter had unappetizing overtones.

Wiz looked at it dubiously. Then he poked at it with his knife. Then he looked up at Moira.

"Crow, right?"

Her eyes sparkled. "Well, Lord, you did say . . ."

"I know," Wiz sighed. "I know." Deliberately he cut a slice off the breast, put it into his mouth and chewed a couple of times.

"You know," he said at last. "I think I finally understand that expression."

Wiz was dozing again when he got his next visitor.

"Wiz?" a familiar voice said gently. At first he thought he was dreaming. There was no way he could be hearing . . .

"Wiz?"

"*Jerry!*" Wiz sat bolt upright in bed. "How the hell . . ."

"Relax, I volunteered," his friend told him. "We've got over a dozen people here; programmers, systems analysts, documentation specialists. We've been working on your spell compiler and magic operating system. We call it WIZ-DOS. You're famous, boy."

Wiz shook his head. "I . . . I don't know what to say . . . except God, it's good to see you!"

"I missed you too. ZetaSoft wasn't the same after you left. Look, I know you're supposed to be resting, but there are a couple of things that have been driving us nuts."

Without waiting for an answer he spread four scrolls out on the bed.

"Okay, now here . . ."

"Just what do you think you're doing?"

They both looked up to see Bronwyn standing in the door, hands on hips and fire in her eye.

"This is a friend of mine," Wiz told her. "I was just helping him . . ."

"You are helping nothing!" Bronwyn said, advancing into the room. "You risk relapse My Lord! Especially with the healing spell. You are supposed to be resting and rest you shall." She turned to Jerry. "As for you, you will take your magics and you will go back where you came from." She gestured as if exorcising a demon. "Begone!"

"Look, I need to talk . . ."

"Out," Bronwyn ordered.

"But this will only take . . ."

"Out!" She made shooing motions. "Tomorrow he will be released and he can work himself to death as he pleases. But he will have a good night's sleep before he begins."

"Tomorrow, okay?" Jerry grabbed the scrolls and left.

Later in the afternoon Bal-Simba came to visit him.

"They tell me you are recovered," the huge black wizard said as he entered the room.

"They want me to stay here overnight just in case, but I'm fine."

"Arianne said you wanted to talk to me."

"Yeah. We've got a very serious problem." He outlined his conversation with Duke Aelric and what he had seen on his travels through the Wild Wood.

Bal-Simba nodded gravely at the end of it. "I have talked to Aelric and I already know much of it. Besides, there have been some incidents." He told Wiz about the disappearing villages.

"So it's already started," Wiz said heavily. "Shit! I should have gotten back sooner."

"Little enough you could have done about that, Sparrow. Now, what of Duke Aelric?"

"He thinks we can make some kind of deal. But we're going to have to work fast."

"What would he require?"

Wiz looked uncomfortable. "It's not him, exactly. The way he explained it to me, there are so many factions and kinds of non-mortals that we can't just sit down and bargain. What we've got to do is remove the threat in their eyes so their coalition falls apart. Then maybe we can come to an agreement with the elves."

"And what would this take?"

"Hey, I don't know, I'm just the messenger boy."

"Hardly," rumbled Bal-Simba. "It was obviously your idea. Further, the elves, or at least Duke Aelric, are willing to treat with you."

Yeah, Wiz thought, *only one of them keeps trying to kill me.* "You make it sound like I'm ambassador to the elves or something."

"Very nearly, Sparrow. You have had more success dealing with them than any living mortal."

"Great. Another job I don't want and I'm no good at."

Bal-Simba sighed. "Sparrow, we would be much further along if you would stop prejudging what you are or are not capable of. You can do a great deal more than you suppose if you put your mind to it. Now I ask you again, what will it take to avert a war?"

Wiz thought. "At the very least we're going to have to fix things so they don't feel threatened. That means we're going to have to do something about demon—debug."

"That falls within the purview of you and the team from your world," Bal-Simba said. "What else?"

"Well, we're going to have to stop this mad dash into the Wild Wood. We may be able to work out some kind of homesteading arrangement later, but for right now we need to keep people from going further."

Bal-Simba stroked his chin and the little bones of his necklace clicked against each other. "As easy to sweep back the sea, I fear."

"Can't you order them to stop?"

The giant wizard smiled wryly. "Sparrow, even at the height of our power the Council never had that kind of hold over the people. Were we to issue such an order it would be ignored and there are not enough guardsmen to post at every forest road and trail."

"You've got to do something."

"We can only try."

"I understand you've got a whole team of programmers here," Wiz said to change the subject.

"Almost a score of them, recruited from the Valley of Quartz."

"You mean Silicon Valley."

"That is what I said, is it not? In any event they have been working on your system of magic and making excellent progress—or so they tell me." He chuckled. "Meanwhile they have been, ah, enlivening things here to no end."

"I dunno," Wiz said. "You make me feel superfluous. I've been gone and you and Moira have been doing all the work. All I managed to do was get myself kidnapped and chased all over the City of Night."

"Hardly. Aside from wiping out the remnants of the Dark League, you were the one who approached Duke Aelric with the notion of a treaty."

"You could have done that."

Bal-Simba shook his head. "No, Sparrow, I could not. In the first place he never would have talked to me. In the second place I would not have had the courage to do something so insanely dangerous."

"Oh," said Wiz in a very small voice.

"Well, I do not wish to tire you, so we will leave these matters for the morrow."

"Fine. I'm pretty bushed. I'm going to get a snack and go back to sleep."

Bal-Simba made no move to leave.

"Is there something else?"

"There are questions we must answer and soon," he said at last. "Some things yet unclear about what happened to you."

"For instance?"

"Was your kidnapping connected with the attempts on your life?"

"No. That was someone else. I think I can take care of that."

"Ahh, I see," he said and then hesitated again. "I understand Ebrion is dead."

"Yeah. I was there when it happened."

The wizard looked closely at him. "Was he involved in your kidnapping?"

Wiz opened his mouth and then stopped. Telling Bal-Simba what had happened would definitely discredit Ebrion's faction—the people who had been trouble ever since he arrived at the Capital. But discrediting them wouldn't make them go away. They'd still be here and they'd be even angrier and more frustrated.

Always leave your opponent a line of retreat—unless you want a fight to the death.

Wiz realized Bal-Simba was watching him intently.

"Would it do any good if I said Ebrion was involved?" he said at last. "I mean in the long run?"

The giant black wizard considered. "In the long run? No, not really."

"Then let's say he died trying to save me and leave it at that."

"Sparrow, you never cease to amaze me," Bal-Simba rumbled. "You grow constantly in wisdom."

Wiz snorted. "To schoon ve get old und too late schmart." Then he sobered. "I just hope it really isn't too late. I made a royal mess of things this time."

"Things are in an, ah, 'interesting' state," Bal-Simba agreed. "But certainly not beyond hope."

Twenty Two

MENDING FENCES

Good client relations are the key to a successful project.
—consultants' saying

The Mighty in the Capital gathered in the chantry the next morning in no very good mood. They knew that Wiz had been kidnapped by magic and they knew Ebrion was dead. Some of them, guiltily remembering old conversations and half-dropped hints, suspected very strongly the two events were not unconnected. Most of them didn't know enough to suspect, but they had an uneasy feeling that someone's head was on the block.

As the blue-robed men and women took their seats in the carved throne-like chairs around the room they murmured and muttered among themselves. Bal-Simba had commanded this meeting, but obviously the Sparrow was the one who would do the talking.

Wiz stood up as soon as Bal-Simba called them to order.

"This isn't easy for me to say," Wiz looked out over the assembled group. "But you were right and I was wrong. I am sorry. No matter how my magic compiler turns out, humans are still going to need your wisdom and your sense of restraint. I was so wrapped up in the technical details I couldn't see that.

280

"My blindness has had very serious consequences. Now I can only hope to undo the damage I have done."

He took a deep breath and went on. "I can't change the past, none of us can. But we can put it aside and go on from there. I'm asking you to work with me, both with the problems we have right now and in the long run.

"I hope that we can work together in spite of what happened in the past. We need each other." He paused. "At least, I need you. Thank you for listening." With that he stepped away from the podium to a smattering of applause.

"What of Ebrion?" someone called from the back of the room. Suddenly there was dead silence. The Mighty froze where they were and everyone looked at Wiz.

Wiz licked his lips. "I am sorry to say Ebrion is dead. He was a good man and he always acted in the way he believed was right. He was killed trying to protect me."

There was an almost audible sigh from the assembled wizards.

Several of the Mighty crowded around afterwards. The first to reach him was Malus. "Well, my boy," Malus said. "Well, well." Then the fat little wizard hugged Wiz to him.

"The fault was hardly yours alone, Lord," Juvian said, stepping up to him. "We have had our blindnesses." Several of the others pressed forward to offer their support as well, and for several minutes Wiz, Moira and the wizards stood making strained small talk.

"If you will excuse me, My Lords," Wiz said at last, "I have to meet with the programming team this afternoon and I want to get something to eat before then."

Malus followed them out. "I wanted you to see something," he said once they were alone in the corridor. "Your friend Karl has been teaching us while you were gone." He shook his head. "It is hard, very hard, this new magic of yours, but I have been practicing and, well . . . **greeting exe.**"

Suddenly, written between them in glowing green letters six inches high was:

HELLO WORLD

"It is my first spell with the new magic," Malus said shyly. "How do you like it?"

Wiz grinned, Moira hugged the tubby little wizard and kissed him on the cheek.

"I think that's wonderful, My Lord," she said, "and I'm sure Wiz does too."

"It's great," Wiz agreed. "It's one of the best presents I could have had. Thank you, Malus."

"That speech has to be the hardest thing I ever did," Wiz said as they made their way back to their chamber.

Moira squeezed his hand more tightly. "Perhaps it was also the bravest."

He put his arm around her waist and kissed her. Then he opened the door and ushered her back into their apartment.

"The place looks bare with all my notes and stuff gone," he said, looking over at the table beneath the window.

"They went to a good home," Moira told him. Personally she thought it was a great improvement, but she wasn't going to say so now.

"What have we got to eat? I'm starved and it smells wonderful."

Moira brought the dishes out of the cupboard where they had been magically kept warm. "I had luncheon sent up from the kitchens. Beef barley soup, roast beef, potatoes and bread and cheese."

"Heaven."

Wiz ate ravenously, enough for three normal men. Moira contented herself with a cup of soup and watched him pack the food away.

"Well," he said pushing away from the table at last, "that was wonderful, but I need to go meet the programmers."

Moira shook out her mane of copper-colored hair. "I

was hoping you could spend some time with me this afternoon," she said softly.

"I'd like to darling, but I've got to get up to speed on this."

Moira put her arms around his neck. "Won't it keep for a while?"

"Look, I really do need to get to the team meeting." Moira melted against him and pressed her lips to his for a long, slow kiss.

"Of course," he said as the kiss ended, "I could always tell them I was held captive by a wicked witch."

Moira opened her green eyes wide. "Wicked, My Lord?"

Wiz pulled her to him. "Darling, when you get going you're the wickedest witch that ever was."

As always the Council of the North met in the morning. However this time Wiz was sitting in the center of the long wooden table, next to Bal-Simba and he was anything but bored with the proceedings.

". . . so that's it," he concluded. "Unless we can curb the invasion of the Wild Wood and stop people from using **demon_debug** we are going to have a war."

For once there were no objections from Honorious, no sniping from Juvian and no clarifications from Agricolus. Every man and woman at the table looked grave.

Juvian, who oversaw the Council's dealings with the hedge witches, pursed his lips. "All easier said than done, I fear. The villagers prefer **demon_debug** because it is so effective against magic."

"**ddt** is just as effective and a lot less harmful to the environment. We've got to get them to use it instead of **demon_debug**."

The sorcerer rubbed a pudgy hand over a jowl. "That will not be easy, Lord. We do not have the authority we once had."

"They'll listen to you if they ever want another bit of magic out of me," Wiz said firmly. "Look, this has got to stop. Unless magic is actively dangerous it is not to be destroyed."

Juvian shook his head. "I do not know, Lord."

"Just tell them that if they don't stop, I'll come there and start throwing lightning bolts."

"If you wish it we will, of course, but I do not know if they will listen to us."

"We have got to *make* them listen."

"We will do our best Lord, but it will be difficult."

"Okay," Wiz sighed, "what about limiting migration then?"

"That is not merely difficult, that is impossible," Honorious said. "The farms are too small and the soil is too poor. On that the peasants will not listen at all."

"We don't have to freeze our boundaries exactly where we are. The part of the Wild Wood closest to the Fringe was human territory once anyway. But we can't have uncontrolled expansion."

"Then tell us how to prevent such expansion, Lord."

"If we don't prevent it we'll be at war."

The old wizard sighed heavily. "Then, Lord, my advice is to prepare for war. For the people will not obey us on this."

All up and down the table the wizards looked even grimmer. But none of them disagreed with Honorious or offered an alternative.

Twenty Three

BRAINSTORM TIME

*At some point in the project you're going to have to
break down and finally define the problem.*
                                        —programmers' saying

"Okay," Larry Fox said, "what about **corned__beef**?"

Wiz had spent most of the previous afternoon and a
good part of the morning meeting the team and reviewing what they had done. Now he was beginning to
tackle the problems Jerry had dumped in his lap—
literally—two days before. All the stalls in the Bull Pen
were taken so they had wedged a table in down by the
whiteboard and tea urn. He and Larry had spent hours
going over obscure bits of code and untangling particularly strange demons.

"**corned__beef** is a hashing routine, obviously," Wiz
told him between bites of his third sandwich of the
afternoon. "It's a fast way to search for a demon—a
routine—by name."

"But where's the rest of it? We figured out that it was
doing a hashed look up, but we couldn't see how you
searched the entries."

"Mmmf," said Wiz around his mouthful of sandwich.
He shook his head and swallowed hard. "It's a perfect
hash. One item per entry, always." He took another big

285

bite of his sandwich. "You take the first characters of the demon's name, multiply that by a magic number, add to it and then divide by another magic number. That gives you the number that serves as a subscript to the array. If you pick your numbers right you always get a unique entry for each item."

"That's weird!"

Wiz shrugged. "It works."

"One more question. Why do you divide by 65,353?"

"Because you've got to divide by a prime number, preferably one at least twice as large as the number of entries you want in the hash table. 65,353 is a Mersinne Prime and it was the largest prime I could remember."

Larry frowned. "Are you sure 65,353 is prime? I don't think it is."

Wiz shrugged and took another bite. "It worked."

"Okay," Larry said, "I'll clear the rest of these changes with Jerry or Karl and get right to work on them."

"No need for that. I intended to fix those other points anyway and it's in the language specification."

Larry hesitated. "I'd still better clear them."

Wiz started to object and then stopped. It really wasn't his project any more, he realized. The original specification might be his, but even that had been modified in the process of development. Now it was a team project and Jerry Andrews was the team leader. It hurt to recognize that, but fighting it would only damage the project.

"Fine," he sighed. "Let me know what Jerry wants to do about it."

The next afternoon the entire team gathered in the Bull Pen. One of the long trestle tables had been cleared and stools and benches were pulled up around it. Wiz sat at one end of the table with Moira and Jerry by his side. In the center was the new version of the Dragon Book, with the small red dragon curled peacefully asleep atop it.

"The news from the Council isn't good," Wiz told

them. "I was hoping they could solve their immediate problems by traditional methods once they understood what the problem was. They've been pushing for us to wave a magic wand," he smiled wryly at the phrase, "and make them go away. Well, as of this morning, it is definite. There is simply no way they can do it. We've got to come up with a magical means to head off a war."

"Not much to ask, is it?" Nancy said.

"Okay," Wiz said. "We've got two problems here. One of them is the hacked version of that protection spell. The second one is we've got to keep people from penetrating further into the Wild Wood until we get things straightened out."

"What's the main problem?" Judith asked.

"The spell, I think. That's what seems to be doing the most damage right now. We've got to either neutralize it or keep people from using it."

"Can you not neutralize their magic as you did at the City of Night?" Moira asked.

"The worms? That's too non-specific." He shook his head. "No, we can't afford to soak up all the available magic. That would leave the humans right back where they were before we started. We need something more subtle."

"But we have to have it quickly," the redheaded witch said. "We cannot afford to waste time in pursuit of this 'elegance' you keep talking about."

"So we're gonna need something quick and dirty." He held up a hand. "But not *too* dirty. Does anyone have any ideas?"

"Sounds like a job for a virus," Nancy said.

"Naw, as soon as they see the program is infected, they'll switch back to the old one."

"A birthday virus!" Danny shouted suddenly.

"A what?" Wiz asked.

"A virus that doesn't trigger until a specific event occurs. We set the magic event far enough in the future that the program will have had time to spread everywhere. Then it triggers," he waved his hands, "poof! The spell doesn't work anymore."

"You know," Jerry said suspiciously, "you talk like you've had a lot of experience at this."

The other shrugged. "It's, you know, been a special interest of mine."

Jerry snorted. "When we get back, remind me never to use any software you had anything to do with."

Wiz ignored the byplay. "Okay, what keeps them from going back to the old spell?"

There was silence down the table.

"We can't just wipe it out of their memories, can we?" Jerry sighed.

"Even if we could, there are sure to be written copies around. When the new program self-destructs, they'll just go back to the old one."

"Can we come up with a spell to attach itself to **demon__debug** and destroy it?"

Wiz thought hard. "I did something like that against the Dark League. The problem is, when it destroyed the spell it took out everything for about thirty yards around in a humongous blast. We don't want to kill them and it would be a big job to weaken the effect."

"Aw, they'd get the message after the first couple of explosions," Danny said.

"No," Wiz said firmly.

"Well . . ." The young programmer's face lit up. "Hey wait a minute! Suppose they get the idea the spell's no good?"

"The problem is that it *is* good against magic. Too good."

Danny smiled an evil smile. "Not if we're the ones making the magic."

Wiz looked at Danny and then at Jerry. "Now that's got possibilities. Suppose we cook up something **demon__debug** *doesn't* work against?"

"Yeah," Jerry said slowly. "Something that will convince them they don't ever want to mess with **demon__debug** again. Danny, stick around after the meeting, will you? I think I know how we can put that arcade-game mind of yours to work."

Wiz made a check mark on the slate in front of him. "Okay, that gives us a handle on one problem. Now for the other one, keeping humans out of the Wild Wood."

"I don't suppose we can just make a law?" Jerry asked hopefully.

Moira snorted and shook her head so violently her copper curls flew in front of her face.

"That is what the Council has been trying. The hunger for land is deep in our farmers and the soil within the Fringe is thin and poor." She reached up and brushed a strand of hair off her upper lip. "Besides, I think you misread the relation between the Mighty and the people. The Mighty are guardians and protectors, not governors."

"And right now the Council's influence with the people is at an all-time low," Wiz said grimly. *Thanks in part to my meddling.*

"So we're going to need a barrier," Judith said. "A wall."

"They would climb a simple wall," Moira told her. "Or else batter breaches in it."

"What about your basic wall of fire?" Karl asked.

"How do you keep from burning down the Wild Wood?"

"We could do a line of death," someone else suggested.

"We don't want to kill them, just keep them in," Wiz said.

"An electrified fence?"

"That's a thought."

"Yeah," Danny said, "with mine fields and guard towers!"

"That is *not* a thought," Wiz said firmly.

Again everyone at the table fell silent. The little red dragon whuffed in his sleep and scuffled the papers beneath him with tiny running motions as he chased a dream mouse.

"Okay," Cindy said slowly. "What about making them not *want* to go beyond a certain point?"

"A geas?" Moira shook her head. "You cannot lay geas on an entire people, including ones you have never seen."

"But **ddt** does essentially that for magical creatures," Cindy said.

"That isn't a geas," Wiz told her. "That's a repulsion spell. Different animal."

"Well, how about a repulsion spell then?"

"Repulsion spells attach to specific objects," Moira explained. "You would have to put the spell on every rock, every tree and every finger-length of soil along the line."

"That's not a problem—in theory," Jerry said. "We can write a program that will do it. It would take a lot of demons . . . No, wait a minute! We could use the principle of similarity. Mark the line on a map."

"Yeah, fine," said Nancy. "Where we are going to get a map accurate enough to make a spell like that stick? Have you seen what these people call a map?"

"Okay, so we make our own map," Wiz said.

"How are we going to do that?" asked Karl. "You can't just sketch it from dragon back."

"If we have to mark everything individually, it will take years to get the barrier up," Jerry said. "I don't think we've got years."

"We will be fortunate if we have weeks," Moira told him.

"Wait a minute!" Wiz put in. "We can use a modified version of my searching spell. Generate thousands of mapping units. We'll have our data in a couple of days."

"Searching spell? You mean that R-squared D-squared thing?"

"No, the three-layer search system. You've used it, haven't you?"

"That is the spell I was telling you about, Lord," Moira said to Jerry. "The one we could not find."

Wiz frowned. "There was a copy in my notes. Well,

it doesn't matter. It won't take long to rewrite it and I'd want to translate it to run under the latest version of the compiler anyway."

Wiz made another mark on his slate.

"That's it then. Okay people, split into your teams and let's get cracking. We've got a lot of work to do here."

"Are you sure this will work?" Bal-Simba asked dubiously as Wiz, Jerry and Moira showed him the team's latest creation.

"It will if they try to use **demon_debug** on it," Wiz assured him. "The basic spell is a modification of the one I used to create the watchers against the Dark League."

"And it will harm no one?" the giant black sorcerer pressed.

"It can't do physical damage to anyone, Lord," Jerry said confidently. *Of course, what it can do to their mental state* . . .

"Amazing," Bal-Simba said as he studied the creature on the table before him. "Where did you get the idea for these things?"

"Where I get all my best ideas," Wiz said jauntily. "I stole it."

Twenty Four

DEMONS GO HOME

Customer support is an art, not a science.
—marketing saying

So are most other forms of torture.
—programmers' response

"Lady, Lady come quickly!" Mayor Andrew pounded
frantically on the door and looked fearfully over his
shoulder toward the village square. "We are beset!"

"Unnugh?" Alaina rolled over in her bed and tried to
shake the mead fumes from her head. She threw the
dirty bedclothes aside and stumbled to the door, cursing as she banged into an overturned stool.

"Not so loud," she grumbled, fumbling with the bar.
"Not so bleeding loud." She threw open the door and
glared at Andrew. "Now what is it?"

In answer he pointed back into the village. Pale
translucent shapes floated here and there over the houses,
flitting down the streets and hovering before windows.
Now and again a bone-chilling shriek broke the night's
silence.

Alaina gathered herself. "Magic, eh? Well we'll see
about that." She snatched a grubby cloak from the hook
beside the door and threw it over her night dress.

Barefoot and with her hair in disarray she marched toward the square with the mayor trailing close behind.

One of the ghostly shapes floated down out of the night sky at her, gibbering as it came. Alaina stopped short and flung her arm up to it.

"demon__debug BEGONE," she commanded in a cracked voice. "exe!"

The pale form stopped in mid-flight, shuddered and dropped to the earth, coalescing and changing form as it did so. By the time it reached the ground it was a small green man-like thing with a bald head, pointed ears and a wide mouth. In the flickering light of the mayor's torch, Alaina could see that the little creature was bright green.

It blinked once, extended a foot-long tongue and licked one of its eyebrows, like a cat grooming itself. Then it smiled up at her nastily.

"Ya know, Lady," the little green man said with a distinct Brooklyn accent, "ya really shouldnna have done that."

"I tell you we are overrun with these things!" Alaina screamed into the communications crystal. "They are everywhere."

One of the little green men sat on top of the image formed above the crystal, his legs dangling down in front, as if he were sitting on top of a television instead of in mid-air. She brushed at him like shooing a fly, but her hand passed through the little man's legs. He stuck out a foot-long pink tongue and gave the hedge witch an especially juicy raspberry.

From where he sat in the Council's great hall, Wiz couldn't see the little green man. But Alaina's gestures told him clearly what must be happening.

"How long have you had this problem?" he asked sympathetically.

"Since last night. These things are driving us mad and when I call for help, you make me wait for near a

day-tenth before anyone will speak to me. Nothing but
that terrible music in the background while I wait."

Alaina put her head in her hands. The day had been
the worst of her life. In laying the banshees she had
created dozens of the little green men. Now they were
all over the village, getting into everything, making
rude and obnoxious comments to everyone and not
giving anyone a moment's peace.

Worse, there was nothing you could do to them.
Magic didn't seem to work and physical objects passed
completely through them. Mayor Andrew was nursing a
broken hand after trying to hit one of the little creatures that happened to be standing in front of a post.
He was so angry at Alaina he wouldn't even come to
her for healing.

"I am sorry about the wait," Wiz told her. "We are
very busy here and none of our service representatives,
ah wizards, were immediately available." Out of the
corner of his eye, Wiz could see all the communications
positions in the great hall filled with wizards talking to
people just as he was. But this one was special. Part of
the reason Alaina had to wait was he wanted to handle
this village himself. "Now, about these little green men.
How did they appear?"

"First there was a plague of banshees and when I
tried to exorcise them, we got—this." She waved her
hand helplessly. "Oh, I would rather the banshees,"
she moaned.

"We have not been able to re-create your problem
here," Wiz told her. "There is nothing in **ddt** that could
produce an effect like that."

"I didn't use **ddt**, I used **demon_debug**," Alaina
said.

Wiz frowned and pursed his lips. "Well, as you know,
demon_debug was not our spell. We cannot be responsible for the consequences if users attempt to apply
spells with unauthorized modifications."

Alaina moaned again.

"However," Wiz went on, "we have encountered this

problem before. The spell you used was not thoroughly tested before release and contained some serious bugs that interact destructively with certain kinds of magic. In fact, we find it actually attracts those kinds of magic. You were quite fortunate, you know."

"Fortunate?" Alaina asked miserably. Now three of the little green menaces were dancing a jig between her and Wiz's image. They were accompanying themselves with their own singing and none of them had the slightest sense of pitch or rhythm.

"Fortunate," Wiz said solemnly. "It might have been dragons."

"Eh?" said Alaina, straining to hear over the caterwauling.

"*I said it might have been dragons,*" Wiz shouted.

Now the green creatures had split up. Two of them were playing nose flutes which droned together like out-of-tune bagpipes while the third took center stage to perform a solo—and extremely rude—version of the Highland Fling.

"*Help us, Lord,*" Alaina shouted hoarsely over the racket of the demons. Wiz winced and muted the sound from his crystal.

"As it happens we do have a beta version of **ddt** Release 2.0. It should be very effective against these secondary demons." He pursed his lips severely. "However I would strongly suggest that you do not use any unauthorized spells from now on. The incompatibility problems are likely to become much more severe."

"Anything," Alaina said feverently. "Anything at all. I'll burn every copy of **demon__debug** I can get my hands on. Just rid us of these monsters!"

"I'll get a messenger off with **ddt** Release 2.0 right away," Wiz told the hedge witch. "And remember, no unauthorized spells."

He left Alaina blubbering thanks as the image faded.

"That'll hold her," he said as he turned away from

the now-dead crystal to Moira. "What's the matter?" he asked as he caught her look.

"Wiz, this is cruel."

"What they did to that rock creature was ten times worse," Wiz said. "At least these demons won't hurt them and they'll vanish at a touch of Release 2.0. Besides, I want to make sure that new spell gets spread to every part of the human inhabited world—and that no one tries to use **demon__debug** again."

"Still, you make them suffer needlessly."

Wiz rose and held her close. "Not needlessly. If we don't stop them there won't be any magical beings at all left anywhere inside the Fringe."

"And would that be such a bad thing?"

He took her arms. "You don't mean that. Magic is just as much a part of this World as humans are. You don't handle something by destroying it. You come to terms with it and learn to use it."

Moira sighed and Wiz felt her relax in his grip. "Oh, you are right, of course. But I wish there were some other way."

"So do I," Wiz said. "I don't like this either." *Except in certain selected cases.*

"Well, what do you think?" Jerry asked the group gathered around the long table in the Bull Pen.

Moira gave a little gasp. "It is beautiful."

"It should be accurate enough to do the job," Wiz said judiciously as he looked over the map.

The little red dragon wandered over, sniffed at the map, decided it wasn't good enough to eat or interesting enough to play with, and returned to his nap on top of the nearby books.

He was the only one in the room who was not impressed. It was a very special map. The parchment it was drawn on was made from the skin of a wild ox from the Wild Wood. The inks used in the drawing were made of pigments taken from the wood itself. Black from the oak galls, browns and dull reds from the earth of the Wild Wood and the blues and the greens from minerals taken from its rocks. The pens and brushes used to draw the map were also made from Wild Wood products. Hairs from the tails of forest martens and squirrels, pens from the quills of forest birds and elder bushes. Even the water to mix the inks and the pumice to pounce the skin had come from the Wild Wood.

Unlike any other map ever seen in the World it was also accurate and to scale, thanks to modified versions of Wiz's searching demons and an Emac Jerry had hacked to do the cartography.

The effect was breathtaking. The mountains seemed to rise up out of the parchment and the brooks and rivers appeared to flow in their beds. Even the forests seemed to be alive.

They all admired the map silently for a moment. Then Jerry picked up the wand that lay beside the map. It was made of ebony and ivory and was about the size and shape of a conductor's baton.

"I still feel silly waving a magic wand around," he said to no one in particular.

"Just think of it as a funny looking mouse," Wiz advised.

"Okay, phase two." Jerry took the wand and drew it along the line on the map. Where the wand passed a trail of glowing green remained.

There was a stirring in the air, but nothing else changed.

"That's it?" Judith asked.

"That's it," Jerry said. "You wanted lightning bolts maybe?"

"Is it permanent?" Moira asked.

"Until it's reversed," Jerry said. "But we can reverse it any time."

"This will work until the Council can come up with some kind of policy they can enforce," Wiz said. "It also establishes our good intentions with the elves and the other non-mortals. As long as the barrier's in place I don't think we will have a war."

*　　*　　*

Einrich topped the rise and stopped. The path ahead of him lay clear, but he could not go that way. His ox whuffed and stamped nervously, catching his master's indecision.

The peasant scanned the forest. The trees here were no different than the ones in the valley behind them. The same huge old giants sheltering an undergrowth of ferns. But it was different and he could not go that way.

The trail ran on ahead as it ran behind, winding between the big trees, skirting logs and avoiding the thickly grown patches where a tree had fallen and saplings and bushy new growth competed for the light. But he could not follow the trail on.

Einrich frowned and without knowing quite why, turned back. The valley behind was far enough.

Twenty Five

PROJECT'S END

Programming is like pinball. The reward for doing it well is the opportunity to do it again.
                                    —programmer's saying

". . . and a fifty percent bonus for successful completion of contract," the clerk said, adding a second, smaller stack of golden cartwheels to the stack already on the table. "Sign here please." Karl bent down and marked the leather-bound ledger next to his name. Behind him the other programmers were lined up to receive their pay.

"Hey, I like this," one of them said. "No invoicing, no hassles with the bookkeeping department and nobody trying to hang onto the money a few days more to improve their cash flow. Why can't all assignments be like this?"

"Speak for yourself. When I get home I'm going to hit the hot tub for about two days solid."

"I'm for a Big Mac first," someone else said. "No, make that six Big Macs."

At the side of the room Bal-Simba smiled. "I am almost sorry to see them go. They have certainly enlivened this place."

"Um, yes," said Malus, who was standing between

299

Bal-Simba and Wiz. He didn't say it with a lot of conviction. "Uh, they are *all* going back, aren't they?"

Wiz shook his head. "No. I learned my lesson. Jerry's going to stay behind on a long-term contract to help with the programming. He isn't the teacher that Karl is, but he's a lot better than I am. In another year or so he can leave and we'll be able to use our own people."

"Oh," said Malus. "But just one, you say?"

"Just one."

Moira, who was standing behind them, grinned at the byplay and turned her attention back to the programmers. They were all glad to be going, she saw. The work had been interesting, but the job was done. Now it was time to move on to other things.

Moira felt a pang. She would miss them, with their strange jokes and their casual insanities and their odd, warped way of looking at the universe. She would miss the camaraderie she had shared with them and even their cheerful way of working themselves into blind exhaustion to meet their goals.

But much as she liked them, they were not of her World. Malus was right. They did not belong here and it would be hard on everyone if they stayed.

Still, it hurt to say goodbye.

"Lady?" a voice said softly. Moira turned and saw it was Judith. She had changed from the long dress and girdle she had worn around the Keep and back into her slacks and unicorn T-shirt, the first time she had worn that outfit since arrival.

"I wanted to thank you before we left."

"Thank me?" Moira said blankly.

"For your advice. You know, up on the battlements that day. About romance and where you can find it."

Moira bobbed a curtsey. "I am glad it pleased you, My Lady."

Judith made a little face. "I don't know that it pleased me, but it helped. You were right. If I want to see the romance in the world I am going to have to stop looking for someone else to create it for me." She smiled wryly. "If I can't count on anyone else to make my dreams real I'll have to do it myself."

"How will you do that?"

"I'm going to write a fantasy trilogy," said Judith. "It's going to be full of romance and color and heroics."

"And dragons?"

Judith grinned. "Oh yes. Lots of dragons."

"Well, you'll have the money to do it," Nancy said as she and Mike joined them. "If you're not extravagant you can live for a while on what this job paid, even at Bay Area prices."

"Are you planning to live at ease on your new wealth?" Moira asked.

"Nope," Mike said. "We're going to open a shop specializing in real-time programming and process control," Mike said.

"Yeah," Nancy added. "After this gig *anything* is gonna be easy." She looked over at Judith. "We were hoping to get you to join us, but I guess not."

"Oh, all this talking about leaving reminds me," Moira said. "Will you excuse me, My Ladies, My Lord?"

"You will be here to see us off, won't you?"

"Oh yes," Moira said. "But there is one other detail that must be attended to. Please excuse me." She grasped Judith's hands in hers. "And good luck."

"My Lords, Ladies, may I have your attention for a moment?"

Heads turned toward the dais where Moira was standing alone. "While you are all gathered here, and before you depart, there is one other denizen of our World we wish you to meet."

She gestured toward the side of the stage and a demon lurched out from behind the curtains. Nearly everyone in the room, programmers and wizards alike, gasped.

It was twelve feet tall, horned and fanged, with a barbed tail sticking out from underneath the jacket of his pin-striped suit. Its forest green skin contrasted vividly with its dark purple shirt and its stark white tie. Under one arm it carried a violin case big enough to hold a bull fiddle.

Moira smiled sweetly. "I am certain you all remember the non-disclosure agreement you signed when you took this job?"

The programmers gulped and nodded.

"This is Guido," Moira said. "He is our contract enforcer."

Guido favored the group with a smile that showed all three rows of dagger-like teeth.

Nobody said anything.

"Naturally we will insist on strict observance of the non-disclosure clause," Moira said and smiled sweetly again.

"Can that thing reach us when we get home?" Karl whispered to Jerry.

"You want to find out?"

Karl thought a minute. "No, not really."

Neither of them said anything as the demon clumped back behind the curtain.

"Boy, that's one way to get everyone's attention," Karl said.

Jerry scanned the room, counting people with his forefinger. "Not everyone. Danny's missing."

"The little twerp's probably late as usual."

"Hey, Fox," Jerry called across the room. "Where's Danny?"

Larry shrugged. "I dunno. He collected his money and split."

"Well, if he doesn't get back here soon he's going to miss the bus. Damn! I'd better go find him."

Moira had come up to Jerry at the end of the exchange. "No, My Lord, you stay here. I will go find him."

Danny turned out to be in the first place Moira checked, which was his room. He was wearing an open-throated collarless shirt, light leather jerkin and trousers tucked into high soft boots. He was stuffing his belongings into a leather traveler's pack. June stood next to him, so close he nearly bumped into her every time he turned to take more things from the cupboard.

"That is hardly appropriate for your world," Moira said, eying his clothing.

"I'm not going back," Danny said defiantly. "I'm going to stay here." June stood close and squeezed his hand hard.

Moira looked hard at June. She had a definite glow about her that meant only one thing to the hedge witch's trained eye.

"You are pregnant!" she said accusingly.

June smiled shyly and nodded.

"You see," Danny said triumphantly. "I can't go back."

Fortuna! Moira thought, *didn't the little ninny have enough sense to take precautions?*

"You cannot stay, either. How do you plan to support yourself—and your family?"

"I'm staying," he said gruffly. "Here at the keep or someplace else, but there's nothing back there for me. And I can work. It's not like I'm lazy or anything.

"Look," he went on, almost pleading, "Wiz is going to need help, right? I mean like there's still a shitload of stuff to do. Well, I can help him."

Moira realized she was completely out of her depth.

"I think we had better talk to Wiz about this," she said finally. "I don't think he is going to like it."

Wiz didn't like it. He scowled through the whole recitation, or as much as you can scowl while you're eating an apple. When Danny finally ran down he continued to scowl and kept on eating. Then he tossed the core of that apple away, selected another one from the bowl and took a hefty bite out of it while he tried to think. Danny stood silent and held one of June's hands in both of his, as if he were afraid she would vanish if he let go.

"Won't there be trouble if you don't go back?" Wiz asked at last.

Danny shook his head vigorously. "Nah. My dad

doesn't want anything to do with me since I dropped out of school and my mom's remarried. I'm over eighteen, so what could they do anyway?"

"You realize that if you don't go back now it may be a long time before you get another chance?"

"I don't want to go back. I want to stay here with June."

Wiz thought for about as long as it took him to finish the apple.

"Leave us alone for a few minutes, will you?"

The couple left the room, still joined at the fingers.

"What do you think?" Wiz asked as soon as the door closed behind them.

Jerry shrugged. "I don't know how much help he'd be, but I don't think it would be a problem to have him around. He's got more sense than most hackers his age." He caught the look in Moira's eye. "Programming sense," he amended.

"Moira?"

"I doubt it will last. Both are children in more than just years and neither has a strong family upbringing. Still, they deserve the chance to try and I am not sure what June would do if they were parted forcibly." She looked at Wiz. "It has to be your decision, Lord. Ultimately you would be the one responsible for him."

Wiz grabbed another apple from the bowl and took two bites. "I'd just as soon he went back. He's got potential, but sometimes he's so obnoxious I want to kick his ass from one end of the castle to the other." He sighed. "On the other hand, I don't like playing the ogre by separating them and he sure can't take her back to Cupertino." He stood silent for a moment, chewing reflectively.

"Okay, if we can paper this over so he's not missed, I guess he can stay." He looked sharply at Moira. "What's wrong?"

"Wrong?"

"You've got that look in your eye."

"Oh, nothing," Moira said. "It is just that I got an

odd feeling . . ." She shook herself. "No, nothing at all."

Wiz knew better than to pursue that. "All right, bring them back in here."

"Okay," Wiz said as he faced the pair. "You can stay. If," he waggled a finger at Danny. "*If* we can arrange this so you won't be missed. You can't just drop out of sight."

"That's easy," Danny said. "I'll write my mom a letter telling her I've taken a long-term contract overseas." He grinned. "That's even true. Then I'll throw in a couple of more letters to be mailed on her birthday and stuff. That way she won't worry and we'll just gradually lose touch."

Wiz wondered what Danny's mother would make of getting letters on parchment, but he decided not to ask.

"All right. Get those letters written and get them back here before it is time to leave. We'll see they get sent."

"I hope I'm not going to regret this," Wiz said after the pair raced out of the room.

"I wouldn't lay you odds," Jerry told him.

Again the programmers—less two—gathered in a tight knot inside the circle inscribed on the chantry floor. As the sundial's shadow shortened, they chattered among themselves and called goodbyes to the friends who had come to see them off. Wiz, Moira and Jerry stood on the dais next to Bal-Simba and waved back until the shadow reached its mark and the wizard motioned them to silence.

Once again the six-part chant welled up and the air shimmered and twisted about the group in the center of the room. The voices grew stronger and the people grew fainter until at last there was nothing but emptiness where they had been. Then the chant itself died away and nothing was left but the echoes.

In unison the wizards dropped their arms and at Bal-Simba's dismissal stepped away from their places.

As the others filed out of the chantry the huge black wizard stepped down from the dais and ritually defaced the circle with his staff.

Wiz, Moira and Jerry remained for a couple of minutes more, looking at the place where their friends had been.

"Well, come on," Wiz said finally. "We've got a full day ahead of us tomorrow."

"How do you feel?" Moira asked Wiz as they walked hand in hand back to their apartment.

"Tired, hungry and very glad it's over." He frowned and sighed. "Only it isn't over. We're going to have to arrange some sort of meeting with the non-mortals to work out a treaty, and we've got a pile of work to do on the software."

They came to the door and paused. "But at least it's over for today and yes, I'm very glad of that." He bent his head down to kiss her and she responded enthusiastically.

"But first, food," he said as he pushed open the door to their rooms with his foot. "What's for dinner?"

Moira smiled mysteriously. "Something very special."

"Special or not, I hope there's a lot of it. I'm starved again."

"Sit down and I will bring it to you."

Wiz plopped himself down at the table and poured out a large glass of fruit juice from the pitcher sitting on it. He tasted it and then added several dollops of honey.

"Here it is," Moira said as she came through the door with a large flat box in her hands.

"Pizza!" Wiz said lovingly, caressing the cardboard as she set it on the table. "A real pizza from Little Italy!"

"I got it when I visited your world," Moira told him. "I have kept it hot and fresh by magic since we returned."

Wiz opened the box and breathed deeply. "Pepperoni, sausage and mushrooms. With extra cheese! This is wonderful."

"Best of all, the cooks say that now that they know what a pizza is supposed to be, they can make them."

"Wonderful," Wiz said, concentrating on separating a slice of pizza without losing the toppings.

"I thought you would be pleased."

"Oh, you have your compensations, wench," he said mock-loftily as he lifted the steaming slice to his mouth.

Moira smiled sweetly, waited until just the right moment and jabbed her elbow into his ribs—hard.

And Wiz Zumwalt—mightiest sorcerer in all the World, conqueror of demons, twice victor over the Dark League and keeper of the World's balance—tried to breathe tomato sauce through his nose.

ANNE McCAFFREY
ELIZABETH MOON

Sassinak was twelve when the raiders came. That made her just the right age: old enough to be used, young enough to be broken. Or so the slavers thought. But Sassy turned out to be a little different from your typical slave girl. Maybe it was her unusual physical strength. Maybe it was her friendship with the captured Fleet crewman. Maybe it was her spirit. Whatever it was, it wouldn't let her resign herself to the life of a slave. She bided her time, watched for her moment. Finally it came, and she escaped. But that was only the beginning for Sassinak. Now she's a Fleet captain with a pirate-chasing ship of her own, and only one regret in her life: not enough pirates.

SASSINAK
You're going to love her!

Coming in March, from
BAEN BOOKS

MAGIC AND *COMPUTERS* DON'T MIX!

RICK COOK

Or . . . do they? That's what Walter "Wiz" Zumwalt is wondering. Just a short time ago, he was a master hacker in a Silicon Valley office, a very ordinary fellow in a very mundane world. But magic spells, it seems, are a lot like computer programs: they're both formulas, recipes for getting things done. Unfortunately, just like those computer programs, they can be full of bugs. Now, thanks to a *particularly* buggy spell, Wiz has been transported to a world of magic—and incredible peril. The wizard who summoned him is dead, Wiz has fallen for a red-headed witch who despises him, and no one—not the elves, not the dwarves, not even the dragons—can figure out why he's here, or what to do with him. Worse: the sorcerers of the deadly Black League, rulers of an entire continent, want Wiz dead—and he doesn't even know why! Wiz had better figure out the rules of this strange new world—and fast—or he's not going to live to see Silicon Valley again.

Here's a refreshing tale from an exciting new writer. It's also a rarity: a well drawn fantasy told with all the rigorous logic of hard science fiction.

February 1989 • 69803-6 • 320 pages • $3.50

FRED SABERHAGEN

Fred Saberhagen needs very little introduction these days. His most famous creations—the awesome Berserkers—are known to SF readers around the world. He's reached the bestseller lists several times, most recently with his "Book of Swords" series, and his novels span the territory from hard science fiction to high fantasy. Quite understandably, Saberhagen's been labeled one of the best writers in the business.

These fine novels by Saberhagen are available from Baen Books:

PYRAMIDS

A fascinating new twist on the time-travel novel, introducing a great new series hero: Pilgrim, the Flying Dutchman of Time, whose only hope for returning home lies in subtly altering the history of our own timeline to more closely reflect his own. Fortunately for us, Pilgrim's timeline is a rather more pleasant one than ours, and so the changes are—or at least are supposed to be—for the better. Learn why the curse of the Pharaoh Khufu (builder of the Great Pyramid) had a special reality, in *Pyramids*. "Saberhagen's light, imaginative and enjoyable adventures speed along twisting paths to a climax that is even more surprising than the rest of the book."
—*Publishers Weekly*

AFTER THE FACT

This is the second novel featuring the great new series hero, Pilgrim—the Lost Traveller adrift in time and dimensionality. His current project: to rescue Abraham Lincoln from assassination, AFTER THE FACT!

THE FRANKENSTEIN PAPERS
At last—the truth about the sinister Dr. Frankenstein and his monster with a heart of gold, based on a history written by the monster himself! Find out what happened when the mad Doctor brought his creation to life, and why the monster has no scars.

THE "EMPIRE OF THE EAST" SERIES
THE BROKEN LANDS, Book I
A masterful blend of high technology and high sorcery; a unique adventure in a world on the brink of ultimate change; a world were magic rules—and science struggles to live again! *"Empire of the East* is one of the best science fiction fantasy epics—Saberhagen can be justly proud. Highly recommended."—*Science Fiction Review.* "A fine mix of fantasy and science fiction, action and speculation."—Roger Zelazny

THE BLACK MOUNTAINS, Book II
East meets West in bloody conflict on a world where magic rules, but technology is revolting! *"Empire of the East* is the work of a master!"—*Magazine of Fantasy and Science Fiction*

ARDNEH'S WORLD, Book III
The gripping climax of the "Empire of the East" series. "Ranks favorably with Tolkien. Exceptional in sheer unbridled zest and imaginative sweep."
—*School Library Journal*

* * *

THE GOLDEN PEOPLE
Genetically perfect, super-human children are created by a dedicated scientist for the betterment of Mankind. As the children mature, however, they begin to wonder if Man *should* survive . . .

LOVE CONQUERS ALL
In a future where childbirth is outlawed and promiscuity required, one woman dares fight the system for the right to bear children.

MY BEST

Saberhagen presents his personal best, in *My Best*. One sure to please lovers of "hard" science fiction as well as high fantasy.

OCTAGON

Players scattered across the continent are engaged in a game called "Starweb." Each player has certain attributes, and can ally with or attack any of the others. But one player seems to have confused the reality of the world: a player with the attributes of machinelike precision and mechanical ruthlessness. His name is Octagon, and he's out for blood.

You can order all of Fred Saberhagen's books with this order form. Check your choices and send the combined cover price/s to: Baen Books, Dept. BA, 260 Fifth Avenue, New York, New York 10001.

ENTER A NEW WORLD
OF FANTASY . . .

Sometimes an author grows in stature so steadily that it seems as if he has always been a master. Such a one is David Drake, whose rise to fame has been driven equally by his archetypal creation, Colonel Alois Hammer's armored brigade of future mercenaries, and his non-series science fiction novels such as **Ranks of Bronze**, and **Fortress**.

Now Drake commences a new literary Quest, this time in the universe of fantasy. Just as he has become the acknowledged peer of such authors as Jerry Pournelle and Gordon R. Dickson in military and historically oriented science fiction, he will now take his place as a leading proponent of fantasy adventure. So enter now . . .

AUGUST 1988 65424-1 352 PP. $3.95

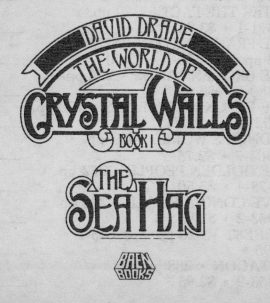

DAVID DRAKE
THE WORLD OF
CRYSTAL WALLS
BOOK 1

THE SEA HAG

BAEN BOOKS